THE ROAD THROUGH THE WOODS

Janet Doolaege

Published by New Generation Publishing in 2019

Copyright © Janet Doolaege 2019

Cover image: © Martin Dolan
Cover design: Alain Perry

First Edition

The author asserts the moral right under the Copyright, Designs and Patents Act 1988 to be identified as the author of the work.

All Rights reserved. No part of this publication may be reproduced, stored in a retrieval system or transmitted, in any form or by any means without the prior consent of the author, nor be otherwise circulated in any form of binding or cover other than that which it is published and without a similar condition being imposed on the subsequent purchaser.

www.newgeneration-publishing.com

New Generation Publishing

FOREWORD

This story can stand alone.

However, if you wondered what happened after the end of *Candlepower,* read on.

"Nel mezzo del cammin di nostra vita mi ritrovai per una selva oscura, ché la diritta via era smarrita."

LA DIVINA COMMEDIA

Dante Alighieri

CHAPTER ONE

At dusk, your imagination may play tricks on you. But I know what I saw.

It must have been around six o'clock on a raw January evening, and the sky still held the faint glow of sunset above the dark mass of tree branches, their tips splayed in witch-like fingers. I stood with one foot on the bike pedal and the other on the ground, looking up. I'd been taking the long way round from the factory back to my parents' house as I was sick of being splashed and dazzled by traffic on the dual carriageway. This was a narrow, winding road flanked by a long, high stone wall. I'd been cycling along beside the wall, wondering vaguely what Mum might have prepared for supper, when a movement high up caught my eye. It was only a moment's glimpse.

I saw the outstretched wings of what was, apparently, an enormous dark bird, and then the silhouette of a person, way up in the treetops. The next instant, both had gone, merged into the wavy, humped outline of the tree nearest to me on the far side of the wall. It was a cedar.

I stood, gazing upwards, hoping to see more, but nothing happened and I couldn't hear any noise until a car came along behind me and I quickly moved the bike to the side of the road. Then I cycled on, past a wide gateway in the stone wall. I glanced in through the tall gates, but all was shadowy, an avenue of trees leading into darkness. I had an idea that there was a house somewhere inside those grounds, but I knew nothing about it, and I put on some speed, feeling chilled, tired and hungry. It had been a long, dull day. The light from my bicycle lamp wobbled to and fro on the damp road surface as I pedalled.

***

"No phones at the dinner table," said Mum, as mine began its ringtone.

"That will be lover-boy," smirked Maya.

I switched it off. Although I was now a graduate, the fact that I was still living with my parents meant that they made the rules, just as they'd always done in the holidays when I came home from boarding school. My sister, Maya, was still attending the local grammar school and had no choice, but she rebelled in subtle ways, as I very well knew. Mum would have had a fit if she had seen the tiger tattoo at the top of Maya's right thigh.

We were sitting in our usual places at the table, as Mum liked us to have what she called a "proper family meal" in the evenings. A draught blew in from the hall, making the curtains shift, followed by the sound of the front door closing. My father had just come home from work and we had been waiting for him.

"The damn train was late again," he grumbled, flinging his newspaper and coat on to the sofa. "Signal failure as usual. Ah, food! I'll change later." He loosened his tie.

My father used to have pale blond hair, but now it's grey and receding and he wears glasses. He looks, I suppose, quite distinguished, as befits an editor on a current affairs programme at the BBC. He has always been a bit of a charmer, my Dad. My mother has kept her pretty, feminine looks, although she has grown quite plump in recent years. She used to work as a nursery nurse, but gave that up as soon as Dad was earning a good enough salary – soon after Maya was born, in fact, and shortly before we all moved down here from Surrey to a more countrified place. I could remember the house in Surrey quite well. It had felt like home. Here was still unfamiliar because I had scarcely been living with the family until very recently. First I'd been at boarding school, then at uni, and in the long vacations I had always done temporary work. Even in the school holidays I had sometimes gone to France to stay with my aunt, and then I'd done a stint at the Sorbonne in Paris. So living in the family home felt quite strange and sometimes a bit confining and irksome.

"Just a small helping for me," said Maya. She is always worrying about her weight, although I know she occasionally binges secretly on chocolate.

"You have to keep your strength up," Mum told her. "Jaki was quite late, as well," she observed to Dad. "Did they keep you late in the office?" she asked me.

"Not really. I had to finish something. Then I took a long way round, because of the traffic."

"Which way was that?" asked Dad. He is always interested in itineraries.

I told him. I wondered whether to mention what I had seen. No, perhaps not. He would immediately have an explanation, and I wanted to hold on to the mysterious feeling. "There's a long wall that must belong to some big estate. Do you know it?"

"Oh, that place. I know where you mean. What's it called, now? Oldwood Court, I think."

I helped myself to cauliflower cheese. "And what is it? I mean, who owns it? Some kind of institution?"

He shrugged. "I couldn't tell you. It's privately owned, I think, but I don't know any more than that."

"There's a big house in it called the Rajah's house," said Maya. Attending the local school, she knew the area better than I did.

"Oh. Rajah's? Why's that?"

"Dunno." Maya glanced at her phone, then saw Mum's face and put it down.

"I don't like to think of you cycling along roads on these dark evenings. It can't be very safe," said Mum.

"I always wear my helmet. But I don't have much choice, do I? Not until I can find a proper job, or get a car, at least."

My father let pass the remark about the car. He had paid for driving lessons while I was still a student, and I had passed my test at the second try, but he had drawn the line at buying me a car. In any case, how could I have afforded the petrol? I hadn't got a permanent job, and the need to repay my student loans felt like a crushing weight on my shoulders. There was no reason why he should buy me a car. I was lucky to have a roof over my head.

When would I ever be independent?

"No more job interviews?" he asked.

"Nope. Nothing," I said gloomily. I had sent off my CV nearly a hundred times, but usually I didn't even receive a reply. Twice I had been called for interview, but nothing had come of it. I was part of the great wave of unemployed new graduates, surplus to requirements in the job market. All I had been able to find was my present three-days-a-week internship in the handbag factory, and I'd only got that because Hugh's father had pulled some strings.

"It's such a pity you didn't study one of the difficult subjects, like medicine or engineering," sighed Mum.

It was my turn to sigh. We had been through all that so many times. Obviously I had had to choose the subjects I was good at, and my course was quite difficult enough: English and French. In fact, I'd had an advantage over some of my fellow students, since Dad is half French, and French had been spoken a lot in our household while I was growing up – spoken fluently by Dad (Granny was French), haltingly by Mum, but regularly spoken.

"Anyhow," said Maya, "we all know you won't need a job once you're married. You'll be, like, totally a lady of leisure, while darling Hugh brings home the bacon."

"I will not. I want a proper job. I want a career. I want to do something worthwhile, I keep telling you." Maya couldn't resist winding me up.

"Of course you do," soothed Mum. "Still," she added brightly, "It's nice to know that Hugh is doing so well, isn't it? And his family will always be there to help. You don't really need to worry."

There was little point in arguing. I looked down at my engagement ring: an emerald, "to match my eyes", flanked by two diamonds. At the end of June, immediately after my twenty-first birthday, I would be marrying Hugh. Everything was mapped out.

Hugh and I had met at boarding school. You might almost say that we had been childhood sweethearts, although he was two years ahead of me. He was the bold, clever mathematician, who shone at athletics, adored by nearly all the girls. I was the studious, painstaking, nerdy type, but for some reason he had fancied me. Probably it was my blond hair and green eyes that attracted him, more than my personality. At any rate, on a school outing to the coast he gave me my first kiss, and after that we became an item. Hugh and Jaki. It seemed like fate, and I felt I'd won the jackpot. We had attended different universities – he had gone to the London School of Economics – but had kept in constant touch and met up whenever possible, even after he had graduated and found his first job. Moreover, his family lived only a few miles from my own, down here in the south. What could be more convenient?

"We'll soon have to start making proper plans for the wedding," said Mum contentedly, "and for your dress. We need to know who is going to make it. At least I have that beautiful white shantung already. I think a princess line would suit you."

"There's loads of time for that," I said.

"I am not wearing pink at your wedding," said Maya.

"We'll talk about bridesmaids later." Mum began to clear away the plates.

My father had already picked up his newspaper again.

After supper, I retrieved my phone and called Hugh as I walked through the hallway. He answered on the second ring.

"Hello, babe. Sorry I couldn't make it tonight. I was in an endless meeting."

"I did wait for you, but then I thought you must be tied up, so I came home. What about tomorrow?"

"Sorry. I have to go in again tomorrow. Small crisis. That's why the meeting was so long."

"You have to work on Saturday again? That's tough."

"It goes with the territory, I'm afraid. I'll only get to the top if I show willing, keep myself available at all times. You know what it's like."

I didn't, actually. Nobody ever asked me to work on a Saturday. Nobody seemed to notice whether I worked or not, to tell the truth.

"What about Sunday?"

"Sunday should be OK. In the afternoon. I'll bring the car round and pick you up. I've got a surprise for you."

"Oh? Oh – lovely."

I went into my bedroom and closed the door. My room was on the ground floor and had not been intended as a bedroom. It even had French windows leading on to a small patio, and although I liked it, it didn't feel like familiar territory. The whole house, in fact, didn't feel exactly like home, as I had not grown up in it.

The table in front of the windows was strewn with unfinished sketches of the view of the garden. My sketches were all in black and white, mostly in Indian ink. At this time of year, tree branches stood out in all their elaborate, naked glory, dividing and dividing again, criss-crossing, interlacing, becoming thinner and thinner against the sky until they looked like fine lace, or even grey mist. I never grew tired of the shapes they made.

Now, however, there was nothing but darkness beyond the window, and I switched on the light and opened my laptop to see whether there were any more emails from prospective employers. Nothing. I searched for more ads. Graduate Trainee Selection Consultant. Technical Manager. Production Shift Supervisor. No job offers seemed to match my qualifications, but I sent off my CV anyway.

Did nobody, anywhere, want me?

Hugh wants me, I reminded myself.

Faintly at the other end of the hall I heard the landline ring, and my father's voice answering it. From overhead, sounds of Maya playing a video game came through the ceiling. I continued to scroll through job advertisements, but with half an ear I could hear Dad talking quite loudly. Then he rang off and Mum said something.

I opened the door, peered out and saw them standing together. "Has something happened?"

They both looked towards me.

"It's your Grandad," said my father. "He's had a fall."

***

On Saturday morning, I cycled into Oakfield. Both Maya and I had offered to go with Dad on the fifty-mile drive to see Grandad, who was in hospital under observation, but he had said that it wasn't necessary. There were no bones broken, and he would report back that evening. On the other hand, if I could pick up the shoes that he'd taken to be repaired, that would be useful. So, as there were still no urgent letters or emails for me to answer, that's what I did.

Oakfield used to be a quiet market town, but with the rapid expansion of the handbag factory it had become quite a lot busier, with delicatessens opening in side-streets and old, traditional pubs turning into gastropubs. Charity shops and estate agents abounded, and a new housing development was spreading relentlessly across adjacent farmland. The town contained a Women's Institute, a Rotary Club and a Freemasons' meeting hall, but there was no artistic activity that I knew of. Even the library had been a victim of government closures.

I attached my bicycle to some railings, thinking that if I had come in by car, I would have been unable to find anywhere to park. Only the ancient stone church, of Saint Michael and All Angels, stood with its unusually high, square tower like a rock in a whirlpool among the Saturday morning noise and bustle.

Having collected Dad's shoes from All Soles and bought the self-raising flour that Mum needed, I strolled through the lych-gate into the churchyard.

The wide path to the south door was lined with tall yew trees, their foliage almost black. I wondered how many years they had stood there, like guardians. Along the church roof and on the tower, stone gargoyles leaned out with folded wings and fiercely gaping mouths designed to drain the winter rainwater away from the walls. I looked up at them, but my head began to swim a little, as if the tower were tilting forwards above me, so I looked down towards the door.

We're not a religious family, even though Maya and I had both been christened to please Granny. Consequently I had never been inside. Hugh had said he wanted a church wedding. I tried the heavy wooden door.

It was locked.

I turned and left the porch. To the right, the churchyard was bordered by a line of pollarded lime trees., Their branches had clearly been pruned severely, year after year, and now ended in gnarled stumps: no graceful shapes there for me to draw. Nothing at all for me, in fact.

Wandering back through the town, I wondered about poor Grandad, hoping he would be all right. He used to be a lecturer and he has published collections of poetry. I hadn't seen him since Granny's funeral, more than three years previously. I wished I had seen more of him, but he lived too far away, and I had been busy with school and university.

That busy time had now come to an abrupt end.

I paused in front of the newsagent's, then went in. I could buy a local paper, and – who knew? – there just might be something suitable in the Jobs Vacant columns.

While I was waiting to be served, I glanced at the small advertisement pinned to a noticeboard. Good homes sought for three kittens. Painter and decorator, excellent references. Professional dressmaking: original designs. Dressmaking? It was worth checking. I took out my phone and noted the landline number. The lettering on the card was attractive: very black, handwritten, italic script. I supposed I would have to start thinking about my wedding dress.

The sky threatened rain. I perched on the edge of a bench by the bus stop to look at the paper, the wind rattling it as I perused the columns. Nothing at all. So many jobs, but nothing for an arts graduate with a gift for writing prose in English and French.

Where did I fit into the world of work?

Carrying shoes, flour and a useless newspaper, I went disconsolately to collect my bike.

***

Hugh lay flat on his back, as he always did after sex, and I lay on my side, nestling against him.

"I'd say that was a seven," he said. "You?"

"Oh, yes. Seven," I said into his shoulder. He liked to give marks out of ten to our love-making, a habit that had seemed odd and unromantic to me at first, but I had grown used to it. If I were truthful, the experience had been more like a five, but I didn't want to tell him so because I knew he would start to analyse and speculate on what could be done differently, but I felt that analysis was pointless. There was no need for acrobatics. Sex just wasn't always full of sparks and ecstasy. Why should it be? We had been together so long that we were almost like an old married couple.

"So did they really need you in the office yesterday?" I asked.

"Need me? What do you mean? Of course they needed me."

"I mean, did you manage to solve the crisis, whatever it was?"

"Oh, that. Well, we're getting there. There's going to be some reorganization, but I can handle that."

He raised himself and sat on the edge of the bed. I contemplated his bare back, strong shoulders, neatly clipped, curly fair hair.

"Want something to drink?" he asked.

"Just a glass of water."

I watched him dressing. When he put on his trousers, he always put his left leg in first. He disappeared briefly into the bathroom and then into the kitchen, where I heard the fridge and a cupboard being opened.

I sat propped on the pillows. He had been renting this two-roomed flat ever since he had started work at the factory. It was pale, modern, functional – and characterless, I thought, but didn't say so. His parents lived within easy driving distance, in a sumptuous three-storey house, and he could have commuted to work from there. But he had wanted a private place of his own, and, of course, "a place where we can be together," as he had said.

He returned with my glass of water and sat on the end of the bed, sipping a soda and looking at me with a contented expression.

"You know, I never thought I'd find so much satisfaction in this kind of work. Developing a product, seeing how all the different parts of the company work together, planning for expansion. It's exciting, frankly. I've had a hint that I may be in line for an assistant directorship eventually– maybe as soon as next year."

"That's great." I tried to sound enthusiastic. "I can't say I'm really enjoying being an intern. Just this stop-gap, until I can find a proper job."

"Still nothing promising?"

"Zilch."

"I suppose you might have more luck if you tried for jobs all over the country, or even abroad. But it's got to be somewhere fairly local, if I'm going to have the career I want here. I wouldn't want you to be in Scotland, or somewhere."

I sipped some more water. There was absolutely nothing local, and certainly nothing that suited my qualifications.

He leaned over and kissed me on the cheek. "If everything goes as well as I'm hoping, you won't actually need a job, you know. When we're married, you can be a lady of leisure. You can spend more time doing your drawing. I know Mum and Dad will give us a down payment on a house, and then – "

That was exactly what Maya had said at home.

"But I've told you, I want a job! I want to be independent."

"OK, OK, of course you do, babe. But just in case you don't find one that suits you, well – it's good to know that we won't be paupers, isn't it? When you're the young Mrs Markham-Hunt?" He kissed me again.

That title belonged to his mother, I felt, but I forced myself to nod. "You're right. Sorry. It's just that I feel as if I'm … floating on the surface of life at the moment."

"Then I'll be your anchor."

I looked at him, warm brown eyes, strong features, and thought that I was an ungrateful cow. How many girls would give anything to be in my place, preparing for marriage with a handsome guy who had a wealthy, generous family and brilliant career prospects? I was lucky. I was very lucky.

"Do you want to go out to eat – ? Oh, wait. I said I had a surprise for you."

He went into the other room and returned carrying a large, stiff paper bag embossed with the firm's logo.

I removed several sheets of purple tissue paper and pulled out the hidden item.

"It's the very latest model. It's not even in the shops yet. It'll be launched in London Fashion Week and then the big London stores will get it first, because they're on the waiting list. So you're one of the very first."

It was a handbag. The factory produced designer handbags that had suddenly become all the rage only a few years ago, since which time the business had expanded at surprising speed, recruiting staff, adding new buildings, buying adjacent land for staff car parks. These handbags were made of semi-transparent plastic with spiral designs of various colours incorporated in the plastic by a secret process. They looked almost like holograms. This one was a mass of interlocking purple and silver spirals, with silver reinforced corners and a silver clasp. It was certainly very striking, although the pattern made my eyes go funny.

"It's gorgeous," I said, and clambered out of bed to fling my arms round him. "Thank you, darling."

Help, I thought. I'll have to use it, but it will make all my clothes look dowdy.

Hugh was happy, and chatted on about work and prospects and the need for products with a unique selling point, while we got ready to go out. His kitchen was always bare and spotless, and he certainly never did any cooking. When we were married, would he expect me to cook for him? I wondered. Perhaps I ought to practise a few recipes. When we were students, he had seemed quite content with my spaghetti bolognese or cheap burgers, but as a rising young star of the firm he might expect more, and there would be business contacts to cater for.

In the pub, his mood gradually began to change. I had noticed this before, a couple of hours after sex, particularly if he had had a glass of wine. He began to criticize certain members of the team and wrong-headed decisions.

I tried to remain bright and cheerful, but then he announced that he wanted us both to go skiing for a week. A friend of his had offered to lend us his flat in a chalet in St. Moritz. It would be a good break, something to look forward to.

I hesitated, and he saw that I wasn't keen. We had been skiing last year, or rather, he had skied and I had tried to learn, but basically I had been terrified. When standing at the top of even a nursery slope, I couldn't launch myself and enjoy the downward rush as you are meant to do. I have never been a daredevil and I felt as if I was teetering on the edge of a precipice. Then I would force myself to start, but tried to go slowly, and ended up veering wildly, losing my balance and falling. I felt so stupid. Hugh couldn't understand why I couldn't just let myself go.

But it was the height. Even looking up at the mountain peaks gave me a strange feeling.

"OK," he sighed in the end. "If you really don't want to go, I don't want to force you. Maybe I'll go on my own. But it won't be the same, will it?"

I felt like a spoilsport. "I'm sorry, darling. You know it's not my scene."

"Don't worry about it." He looked at his watch." I'd better take you home. You're working tomorrow, aren't you? Must get your beauty sleep."

In his car, we glided smoothly along the main road, less busy now than it always was in the rush hour on weekdays. He switched on the radio for the news headlines, then switched it off again without asking me whether I was still listening.

"By the way," he said. "Don't forget Tuesday night, will you? Wear something a bit fancy."

On Tuesday, there was to be a farewell buffet in the largest meeting room for one of the senior directors who was retiring. I would not normally have been invited, as a mere intern, but I was included as Hugh's fiancée.

"Oh, Hugh – could you turn left there, just ahead? There's a place I'd like to drive past. I think it's some kind of old estate, or … "

"What? Where? No, sorry, some bastard is driving right on my tail. I can't turn off now. Why do you want to make a detour, anyway? I thought you wanted to get home."

I sank back in my seat and said nothing. Oh, well. It was just a thought.

CHAPTER TWO

The hum of conversation was louder than the background music under the brilliant LED ceiling lights. Smartly dressed people, none of whom I recognized from the Accounts Department where I had been working for the past week, stood about in enthusiastically chatting groups, while waiters in white jackets circulated with glasses of champagne and waitresses presented trays of exquisite snacks. Beyond the plate-glass windows, rain and wind raged in the failing light.

I kept close to Hugh at first, smiling, smiling, being introduced to people whose names I promptly forgot. I was wearing a sparkly white top, black trousers and a jacket that did not quite match the trousers, but I hoped that nobody would notice. Many of the women wore tailored suits and skirts with sheer tights and high heels.

They were business people. Many of them had been recently head-hunted. It was no good: I didn't belong with them. I felt like a shabby academic, despite my sparkly top, and I wondered whether any of them had ever heard of John Donne or Baudelaire. How many of them were capable of holding their own in the sort of tutorials we had had at uni? Conversely, I knew I couldn't engage with them in discussions of sales figures and shareholder value and market trends. We were different kinds of people, speaking different languages.

Hugh seemed to be in his element. Was it because he had read economics? When we were both students, he had been different and more casual, surely. But then, I had only been able to see him on the occasional weekend or in the vacations, and mostly we had talked on the phone. Somehow, almost without my noticing it, he had developed into this smooth and confident executive.

Two men had approached our group with noisy bonhomie, and I shuffled backwards a little to give them room. Hugh now had his back to me, in his sleekly fitting suit. He looked flawless, but had anyone else ever noticed that his right ear stuck out slightly more than his left? I wondered.

I grinned to myself and drank some more champagne.

The conversation seemed very animated, and two women had also joined the group. I took a canapé from a passing tray, ate it and wandered over to the window. Rain was collecting in pools on the stretch of concrete, beyond which a row of six forlorn-looking palm trees in large concrete troughs thrashed their leaves in the wind.

"Crazy to put palm trees there," said a voice next to me, and I turned to see a young man with a narrow, pointed face, reddish brown hair and a green and grey tie that was slightly askew. Like all the men, he was wearing a suit, but he didn't look as if he had been poured into it.

"Hi," he said. "I think I've seen you before. By the coffee machine?"

I admitted that it was very likely. I tended to escape to the coffee machine. We introduced ourselves, and I learnt that his name was Gavin.

Just then, somebody started tapping on a glass with a spoon for quiet, and the speeches began. We had to applaud as every speaker finished, and I looked around for somewhere to put my glass. Gavin took it from me and placed it beside his own on the low windowsill. We stood side by side, listening politely and applauding as the departing director was wished a long and happy retirement and a wonderful new life.

"Do you think he will start a new life? Sounds good, doesn't it?" said Gavin in my ear.

"I expect he'll spend his time playing golf. I wish I could start a new life," I muttered back.

"You do?"

But then the director made his final joke, urged everyone to have another drink, and was engulfed in a huge wave of applause, during which I became aware that my phone was ringing in my bag.

I fished it out hastily and answered it, turning aside and pressing my fingers against my other ear. I could scarcely hear the woman's voice on the line.

"You left me a message," it said, very faintly. "You need a dressmaker?"

"Thank you, yes," I said. "Do you – can you – In fact, I need a wedding dress."

"A wedding dress?" said the faint voice. "Oh, yes. I can certainly make a wedding dress for you." Did the person have a faint foreign accent? It was hard to tell.

She asked when I could come for an appointment, and we agreed on Thursday morning, and then I repeated her instructions for finding her. With a faint shock, I realized that she was talking about the road where I had stopped the other night. She was giving me directions to the very gateway in the long wall.

"Oh, yes, I know where it is," I assured her.

When I ended the call, Gavin had already moved to a polite distance, although he was still looking in my direction.

Picking his way through the crowd, Hugh was making his way purposefully towards me.

"All right, babe?" He gave me a peck on the cheek. "Look, would you mind awfully if I didn't drive you home? Giles and Julian have just asked me to go for dinner with them because they want to discuss something – well, something quite important. Normally I'd have said no, and I don't like leaving you like this, but – "

"Don't worry," I said quickly. "I'll be perfectly OK on the bike."

"Well, if you're sure …" I could see Giles and Julian and their wives or girlfriends hovering in the distance.

"Off you go. Tell me tomorrow how it went."

"I will. Take care, now." He went.

Outside, I could see that it was dark and windy. I couldn't tell whether it was raining or not. Perhaps I ought to change out of my finery and collect my bike right away, without waiting for the weather to get any worse. After all, there was nobody here that I wanted to continue talking to – except possibly that guy Gavin, but he seemed to have vanished.

Sure enough, it was spitting with rain when I left the

building. I had packed my trousers and sparkly top in the bike's paniers, and was pretty well covered by my cape and helmet, but it wasn't a pleasant night for a cycle ride. Cars were still parked in the recently enlarged car park.

I struggled along against the wind, cursing the traffic that spattered me with mud and dazzled me with oncoming headlights. Normally Hugh would have put the bike in the boot of his car on a night like this and driven me to my parents' door. But I knew it wouldn't do for me to stand in the way of any crucial networking.

A van overtook me slowly and drew up ahead, its indicator flashing. What was this? Somebody wanting to ask the way? Some psychopath intending to kidnap me?

The driver got out and shouted, "Jaki?" through the rain.

It was Gavin again.

I pedalled forwards and dismounted.

"I thought it must be you. Not too many Sacs de Luxe staff cycle to work. Want a lift?"

I hesitated only fractionally. He flung the bike into the back of the van and I climbed into the blessed warmth of the cab. We immediately started talking easily, as if we already knew each other, laughing and joking about my predicament. I grumbled about the lack of a bus service to the factory and he admitted that he spent a lot on petrol. It turned out that he lived in a village six or seven miles beyond my parents' house, so at least I wasn't taking him out of his way.

"Oh," I said, "Unless you wouldn't mind making a detour along here."

"Turn left? No problem." He turned.

"You see, I'd just like to take another look … I have an appointment at this place behind the high wall with loads of trees, and I'd like to take another look at it."

"No problem," he said again. I looked at his profile. Pointed nose, sharp jaw-line, hair a little longer than was currently fashionable. He sensed me looking, and glanced at me briefly.

"You mean what they call the Rajah's house?" he said.

"Oh! You know it, then?"

"I go there sometimes, to do some work in the grounds. Keep the brambles under control. So you're going to meet – ?"

"The dressmaker. That's right."

"I'm glad," he said. I thought it an odd thing to say, but didn't ask any questions.

We had reached the long wall and he was slowing down. We came to a halt more or less where I had stopped the other night, the windscreen wipers keeping up their steady rhythm.

I wound down the window and peered upwards. Raindrops fell on my face, but nothing out of the ordinary was happening in the topmost branches, tossed by the wind.

***

Thursday dawned gleaming and cold. The wet and stormy weather had blown itself out, and I set off on the bike after breakfast with the length of white shantung in a panier. Mum had fussed around with tissue paper and plastic bags, but the sky was clear with no sign of rain. I breathed in the clean air. Maya had already gone to school, and Dad had left even earlier to catch his train to London. Mum was going to a coffee morning to discuss a jumble sale. I alone was free and without any obligations or work commitments, and that should have been pleasant, but somehow it wasn't.

In the daylight I had a clearer view of the long stone wall and the trees that soared above it, a mixture of deciduous trees, now leafless, and conifers. The gateway was flanked by pillars topped by stone urns, and the iron gates were shut. As instructed, I rang a bell at the side, and slowly the gates swung open inwards. I pushed the bike through and began to walk along the curving drive, an avenue of lime trees.

With a slight start, I heard the gates clang shut behind me.

I walked on, glancing to right and left at the sunlight slanting between the trunks of trees and illuminating the tangle of dry bracken and carpet of fallen brown leaves below. Some tree trunks were thickly clad in ivy, and tendrils of ivy had begun to crawl out across the gravel track ahead of me. How big was this place? The trees seemed to stretch far away on all sides. I couldn't see through them to the wall which I knew must be there, surrounding and separating this wood from the world of traffic and workaday activities outside. It was very quiet. The treetops shifted with a faint hushing sound in a gust of wind. I paused to look at the patterns they made, bold and graceful, criss-crossing against the sky. I wanted to draw them. But I had promises to keep … The lines of Robert Frost's poem repeated themselves in my head. Whose woods these were, I didn't actually know. I had forgotten to ask the dressmaker's name.

Almost before I was expecting it, the drive curved round and I came face to face with the house. I stood still. My eyes moved wonderingly over arched mullioned windows, towers and turrets, finials and pilasters, tall square chimneys. How old must it be? Victorian? Older? A carriage sweep surrounded a circular rough lawn and led to the wide steps and the front door. The heavy door now opened, and the dressmaker herself stood in the doorway waiting for me.

I have tried to remember my first impressions of her, but they are overlaid with so many later memories that it's hard to say exactly what struck me about her: she was tall, certainly, and she was not young, although I couldn't guess at her age. She held out her hand to me as I approached, and her handshake was firm for someone elderly. Her eyes were very blue in a pale, lined face, high cheek-boned, free of makeup, and her snow-white hair was drawn back. She wore black trousers, a black top and a heavy amber necklace.

"So you are to be the bride?" Her voice was soft and musical.

I suddenly felt uncertain. "I … well, yes, I …"

She showed me where I could prop the bike, and when I had taken the silk from the panier, I followed her into the house. As I walked behind her, I saw that her beautiful white hair was gathered in a black velvet bow at the nape of her neck.

We had entered a great hall, lofty and wood-panelled, with a vast empty fireplace and a huge, faded, rather threadbare carpet, patterned in pale gold and soft pinks and blues. A grandfather clock, a carved cabinet, but otherwise very little furniture. A faint scent of woodsmoke filled the air, with a hint of something floral – rose or jasmine.

"This was my great-grandfather's house," she said, and again I thought I detected a slight foreign accent. "I'm glad you have come. I am Lily Green. Please call me Lily."

What an elegant, old-fashioned name. "I'm Jaki – " I told her, and stopped. I had never been keen on my surname, Hayward, which to me had always conjured up a picture of an uneducated yokel leaning on a five-barred gate. A horrible girl at school used to call me Haywards Heath, or Heathie, which I hated. "Jaki Saunders," I added, using my mother's maiden name.

"I thought …" she said, with a faint frown. "But it doesn't matter. Come into the morning room. There will be more light."

The morning room was bathed in light, but it, too, contained very little furniture. Three leather armchairs and a sofa were grouped around the empty fireplace with its ornate overmantel. Another threadbare carpet covered the expanse of floor, and to our left was a shining black grand piano. On the right, beyond the fireplace, stood a tall cheval mirror, shaped like a portal, the tops of its two supporting wooden posts carved in the shape of pineapples. The atmosphere was warm, although no fires were burning. I noticed a couple of heavy cast-iron radiators, but it must cost a fortune to heat such a large house, I thought, unless perhaps she lived in only a couple of rooms. Some elderly people did that when their houses were too large for their budgets.

"What a wonderful place," I said. "Do you live here alone?"

"Alone, yes. That is … I have some help. And visitors."

Perhaps somebody came from the village to do the housework.

Lily asked when the wedding was to be, and whether I had any particular ideas about the style of wedding dress I wanted. I hadn't actually given it much thought. I handed over the silk, and Lily shook it out in a wave, looking at the threads and feeling the quality.

"A white wedding," she said. "Will you wear a veil? Do you want to look virginal?"

I gave a snort, in spite of myself. I explained that Hugh and I had been sexual partners for several years already.

"So now you want to move the relationship on to another level?"

I looked at her, open-mouthed. Well, of course … I fiddled with my engagement ring. I had a sudden vision of myself, billowing in white, being led down the aisle on my father's arm. Like a lamb to the slaughter, said a voice inside my head. Where had that come from?

"My mother thought a princess style might suit me," I said.

"Come," said Lily, and led me over to the cheval mirror. She swathed me in the silk, tugging it here and there, stepping to and fro behind me thoughtfully.

I gazed at my reflection. I would have to wear plenty of makeup, or I would look much too pale and washed out in white. The glass of the mirror was a little dim, and there seemed to be slight ripples in it. Suddenly I thought I saw a quick movement in the reflected room, a kind of wisp of something dark, moving quickly. I turned, but there was nothing there.

"You have beautiful golden hair," said Lily. "You remind me of someone I once knew."

Golden hair! That was a flattering description, and I wasn't going to argue.

Lily said that she would think about styles, and design a pattern. Then I would have to come back and we could discuss details and fittings.

"Meanwhile, would you like a cup of tea?" she asked.

I'm more of a coffee person, but I was curious to see more of the house, and I followed her into the panelled hall, through a green baize door, along a stone passage and into a large kitchen with tall dressers and cupboards, an old-fashioned cooker and a big table in the centre. I could imagine servants sitting around it for meals.

Lily boiled the kettle and I sat on an upright chair. We

looked at each other. She smiled, her blue eyes lighting up. I felt emboldened to ask questions.

"Please tell me: why is this house called the Rajah's house?"

She laughed. "It isn't. My great-grandfather had this house rebuilt and extended when he came home from the Indian Civil Service. He wasn't a Rajah. He was English, and so was his son, my grandfather, who inherited it. But he – my grandfather – married an Indian woman, and that was considered a degrading thing to do. His family would have nothing more to do with him after that, and her family disowned her. They were Brahmins, you see."

She poured boiling water on tealeaves and took two thin china cups and saucers from a cupboard.

"How sad."

"Yes, particularly as his wife didn't live long. She died giving birth to my father, and after that my grandfather became something of a recluse, seeing nobody local, spending much of his time travelling to and from India and the Far East, buying antiques and filling the house with them. And so it came to be known as the Rajah's house"

Where were all those antiques now? I wondered. And was she herself a recluse? I could have asked her, I suppose, but sometimes I feel my French granny over my shoulder, saying, "Don't keep asking personal questions! It's not polite."

"But tell me about you," she said.

I was looking for a real job, I told her. I explained about the part-time temporary contract at the factory, and I got some of my frustration off my chest by describing how many posts I had applied for and how few opportunities there seemed to be for new graduates, particularly in this part of the country. I moaned, too, about all the debts that I would have to repay when I did eventually find a job.

"What did you read at university?"

"English and French."

"Vous parlez donc français?"

Oh! Of course, I answered her, and we had a conversation in French. She spoke the language like a native. So that accounted for the faint accent that I had detected!

"Are you actually French?" I asked.

"My mother was French, and I lived in Paris once, a long time ago." She gave a small sigh.

"I had such a great time in Paris when I studied there as part of my degree. I must go back some time soon."

"Perhaps for your honeymoon?"

"Um … " I thought Hugh had other ideas, such as the Canaries. I traced the grain of the wooden table with my finger. Of course, we would have to discuss the matter before too long, but it all seemed a bit unreal.

Just then, a tapping at the window distracted my attention. I could see across a cobbled courtyard to a long outbuilding with wide, closed doors, which had probably been the stables at one time, but I couldn't see anybody out there. The tapping came again.

Lily rose and went to the window. She opened it and, quick as a flash, a robin flew in and perched on her outstretched hand, poised on thin legs, bobbing and flicking its wings. Its eyes were black dewdrops and its breast a splash of orange in the subdued colours of the room.

Lily went to a cupboard and fetched a packet of pellets. The robin took them from her hand, one after the other, bobbing down and then up. He seemed perfectly tame.

Fascinated, I stood and moved towards Lily, wondering if I could feed him too.

But in that instant the robin had flitted out of the window, so silently that I didn't see him go.

***

"How much does she charge?" asked Dad. "I hope this dress won't cost me an arm and a leg."

"I forgot to ask," I said. "Sorry. I should have thought. I was just so interested in seeing that place and talking to her."

Maya and I were washing up the saucepans after supper, while the dishwasher hummed with the plates and cutlery.

"Oh, Pascal, you wouldn't begrudge Jaki a nice wedding

dress, now, would you?" said Mum.

"Only kidding." Dad folded his newspaper. "My eldest daughter must have a beautiful wedding dress. I hope this woman does a good job."

"That shantung is very – well, very white," I said. "Maybe I ought to have some black embroidery on it, to make a contrast."

"You can't wear black on your wedding day!" Mum was horrified. "It would be unlucky."

"Only kidding," it was my turn to say. Privately, I thought it would be rather eye-catching.

"A lot of kidding going on around here," said Maya loftily. "Though it's cool that you actually saw the Rajah's house. And this old lady, she, like, lives all alone in this big, spooky mansion?"

"I didn't think it was spooky. Perhaps you could come with me another time."

"Yesss! You're on. I wonder whether she lets out any big rooms. We really, really need somewhere bigger for our dance class."

"I don't know what rooms she has. I only saw one room and the kitchen. Anyhow, don't start getting ideas. But the grounds – the grounds are fantastic. So many huge, beautiful old trees. There's an avenue that leads up to the house, but otherwise it must be like living in the middle of a forest."

"You and your old trees! What are you like?"

"If she's a good dressmaker, perhaps she could make the bridesmaids' dresses, too," put in Mum. Maya was to be a bridesmaid, of course, and a couple of old friends from school had also agreed in principle, although what sort of dresses they should have was another question that remained undecided.

"Not pink," said Maya.

"All right. Don't keep saying that! Actually green might be nice."

"What! Green! Absolutely out of the question," said Mum.

"We are talking about Oldwood Court, aren't we?" said Dad suddenly. "Have you seen today's paper?"

"No. Why?"

"Well, you know the new road scheme? Wait, there's a map here somewhere." He turned over the sheets of newsprint, turned them back again. "Ah, here. It looks as if the new road will go straight slap-bang through your forest."

I grabbed the newspaper and stared at it.

The map was rather blurred, but the outline of the house was there with the avenue leading up to it, and the grounds stretched out around it. Only the part of the wall with the gates was visible, and the rest of the wall continued off the map. Superimposed on the whole, running diagonally from the lower right to the top left-hand corner, was the heavy dotted line, in red, of the new road.

My eyes skated over the article below it. " … to ease the traffic flow … heavy congestion at peak times … district council … Local Enterprise Partnership … "

"But they can't do this!" I was appalled.

Dad shrugged. "They've been talking about it since last year. It looks as if they've finally got the go-ahead. A pity about your trees, but the main road is getting impossible in the rush hour. Several times I've nearly missed my train in the morning."

"I've heard it's because of all the heavy lorries going to and from the factory. I suppose they do need a faster road to the coast," said Mum.

"The factory? Stuff the factory! Surely they don't need to bulldoze everything just to suit the factory!"

Mum frowned. "You'd better not talk like that to Hugh, had you?"

"Why not? I'm going to talk to him right now. I can't believe this."

"It's called the march of progress," said Dad.

***

I had to wait until Saturday to discuss the problem with Hugh. I tried several times on Friday to reach him on the phone, but each time we were interrupted by another incoming call and we agreed that I would meet him at his place. On Saturday morning, when I pressed the buzzer at his flat, he came to the door in his Japanese kimono, tousle-haired and unshaven. He gave me a bristly kiss.

"I've only just woken up. I'm whacked. It's been all go, this week."

"I'll make some coffee," I offered, and he disappeared into the bathroom.

When he re-emerged, in jeans and cashmere sweater, smelling of aftershave, we chatted about this and that, the wrong-headed ideas of his line manager, his parents' plans for a trip to Hawaii, and so on. I brought the conversation round to my visit to the dressmaker.

"Oh, right, and I must get a better suit made," he said. He didn't comment on my description of the Rajah's house.

Then I told him about the road scheme. "Isn't it absolutely terrible?" My voice brimmed with indignation.

He looked puzzled. "I'm surprised you didn't know about it. It's been on the cards for ages. I've heard my father talking about it." Hugh's father was on the town council and he also owned the golf club. "He says it's necessary, and I believe the firm is co-sponsoring it, so it won't cost the taxpayers much."

The firm! I said nothing for a moment. So I was working for a factory that was going to help fund such destruction. "Do we really need another road?"

"I'd say we do. You've seen how bad the traffic is. Everyone complains."

"But they'll have to cut down all those beautiful old trees, and I suppose they'll bash down the wall. And then there will be horrible noisy trucks roaring right past the Rajah's house – unless they demolish that as well. Could they? Could it be a compulsory purchase?"

"I don't know, but you can't keep all these oldie worldie places forever. This is the twenty-first century. We need the transport infrastructure." He came over to where I stood, leaning back against the kitchen table, and put his arms around me. "Why are you so worked up about this, anyway?"

"I don't know." I thought about Lily, and the spacious, quiet old rooms of the house. I visualized myself walking slowly up the lime avenue.

"Let's get out of here, shall we?" he said. "I need to go to the bank and order some Swiss francs."

"OK." I washed up our coffee mugs and put them away. I knew he didn't like to leave unwashed crockery standing around, and all cupboards and drawers must be properly closed.

"Who was that guy you were talking to on Tuesday evening?" he asked as we strolled towards his car. "He looked like a gatecrasher."

"Did he? I only know his name is Gavin and he's an IT technician. He told me he's on a zero-hours contract. I don't think that's fair."

"Not fair? Come on. Nobody can expect a job for life any more. We only take people on when we need them, otherwise we'd never be competitive."

We take people on. He identified so closely with the firm. "I still don't agree with that. And if someone offered me a real job for life, something that I could commit to, I'd take it like a flash."

"Well," he said, grabbing my hand and swinging it to and fro, "I'm offering you a job for life. You're going to be my wife, aren't you?"

I thought of his mother and her lifestyle, and his parents' large, stockbroker type of house with its triple garage. They played bridge and did a lot of entertaining. Hugh was an only child, but he had told me that he himself would like to have three children, and of course we would buy a house big enough for a family. It sounded very comfortable. The children would attend good schools and friends and business associates would come to dinner parties. My life seemed to be laid out before me. … like a map with a road running through it, I thought, and then decided that I wouldn't think about that now.

I didn't bother to tell Hugh that Gavin had given me a lift home. I didn't want him to feel guilty for not chauffeuring me to my parents' door on that wet night. His job must come first, of course.

***

When, a week later, the phone call came from Lily, I felt a thrill. She had sketched a pattern, she told me, her voice faint and remote as always on the line. Could I come round again and look at it?

The morning sun streamed through the trees as I set out once again along the gravelled drive towards the house. The rays lit up clumps of brilliant green moss here and there, and between the grey trunks of the lime avenue I could see what seemed to be little pathways leading deeper into the woods. Somewhere out of sight a robin sang, a thin, sweet, liquid stream of sound, and I wondered if it could be the same robin that had flown into the kitchen. The woods must be full of birds and animals, not to mention plants of all kinds. I wanted to go exploring, but I knew Lily would be waiting for me.

As before, she stood on the threshold dressed in black, her hair snowy white and her necklace amber. Her smile was like the winter sunlight in her pale face, and her eyes were intensely blue.

This time she took me into the library, another vast room with a big empty fireplace and a long oak table in the centre. Floor to ceiling shelves held a number of books with gilt bindings, but half the shelves were empty. Heavy curtains hung at the tall windows giving on to a grey stone terrace, and beyond the terrace, once again there were the trees.

"Here are a few sketches," said Lily, when we had seated ourselves at the table.

She had drawn the front view, side view and back view of the proposed dress, long and sweeping, according to the princess line that Mum had suggested, and she pointed out a few details, talking about darts and tucks; but I was overwhelmed with the general impression. I had never owned such an elegant piece of clothing before.

"I ought to feel really special in this," I said.

"Bien," she said. "The silk is perhaps a little plain, though. I wondered whether you might like some kind of embroidery on the bodice."

"Can you do that?"

"Of course."

We talked some more about the dress, but I was itching to ask her how much she knew about the road scheme, and finally I burst out with a question.

"Yes," she said quietly, "but I will fight it."

"Oh, you must! This is such an amazing place. The house, the trees ... I love the trees. I'd like to draw them. It must be saved. Is there anything I can do to help?"

She looked at me for a long moment. "I wonder," she said.

"Could I come here some time and do some sketching in the woods? I wouldn't disturb you."

"Of course," she said. "Come whenever you like. While the trees are there..." She rose and went to stand beside the central tall window. I went to join her. There they were, tall and still, trees beyond trees, some bare, others evergreen, reaching out and pointing upwards to the blue of the winter morning sky.

She turned towards me. "This house could still be important. Its spirit is not yet dead. But it would be nothing without the trees, nothing at all."

"They mustn't destroy them," I said. "Who needs more roads? Some of your trees must be hundreds of years old."

"Hundreds," she agreed.

"And could you go on living in this house if they – if they – "

"No. I could not. There has been some talk of turning it into a hotel. But I hope it will not come to that."

"A hotel!" I imagined a reception desk in the entrance hall and rich, vulgar guests talking loudly. "It mustn't happen. Is there anyone who can help?"

"Help?" she said wistfully. "I have help, but not perhaps the kind of help ... Of course, there is Gavin," she said in a stronger voice. "He is a good young man. He has done some maintenance work, clearing brushwood, that sort of thing. I know I can rely on him."

"Yes," I said. "I think I know him."

A sudden gust of wind made the branches sway, and we watched a swirl of dead leaves rise in a whirligig in the corner of the terrace.

***

I wanted to talk to Gavin, but I didn't know his surname and I didn't know where to find him in the warren of the company's interconnected buildings, floors, work spaces and offices. I had a feeling he was peripatetic, moving around and sorting out people's computer problems as and when they needed him.

Meanwhile, I was suddenly transferred out of the Accounts Department and into the Export Unit, on the grounds that my French would be useful for liaison with the Paris office. I felt that I was being shifted around to fill a gap. In fact, Mr. Clarke's assistant had just gone on maternity leave, and I would be standing in for her.

I tried to familiarize myself swiftly with the ongoing files, and it was on the second afternoon that Mr. Clarke, balding and arrogant in a pinstripe suit, ordered me to check through a long and contentious statement.

I didn't care for Clarke. I had only been there five minutes when he began to compare me unfavourably with his absent assistant, and he seemed to dislike me personally for some reason. Everything I did seemed to exasperate him.

The statement in French was full of errors, and I went through it carefully, underlining everything that was wrong and inserting the corrections in red characters.

"Well, well, what's this?" he said when he saw it. "Quite the school-marm, aren't we?"

"There are quite a lot of errors," I said stiffly. That was probably not the wisest thing to say, because I learned later that he had drafted it himself and that he prided himself on the excellence of his French.

He pretended to look at it more closely. "No, no, Miss

Jaki, I'm afraid you're wrong there: es on the end of envoyé is wrong." He gave a false chuckle.

I stared at him. "No, it isn't. Les factures que vous nous avez envoyées – the participle must agree with the noun when it precedes – "

"Come on, come on. Don't talk to me about participles. I know what I'm doing, and I'd appreciate it if you would just follow my instructions while you're working for me." His voice was chilly now.

"But I – "

"And another thing. Just because you're engaged to our young rising star, the wondrous Markham-Hunt, you needn't think you can throw your weight about."

"Throw my ... ?" I was astonished.

"Exactly. Quite frankly, I don't care for your attitude, young lady."

"Oh!" I was so outraged I couldn't speak. I pushed back my chair and headed for the door.

"Where are you going?"

"To the loo. Is that permitted?" I marched out.

I didn't actually need the loo. Seething, I strode along the corridor and ran down the stairs to the next floor. I could have written that statement myself without any errors, and much more cogently. Hell, I knew how to write. I'd been complimented on my writing. I'd won a competition at school, and at uni I had always handed in my essays on time. Pompous fool.

At the foot of the stairs there was a space with a couple of uncomfortable modern chairs and green houseplants in pots.

There, feeding coins into the coffee machine, was Gavin.

"What's up?" he said. "Need a coffee? Here, let me."

We stood facing each other, sipping what passed for cappuccinos. He kept glancing at me, waiting for me to speak.

I told him what had just happened, and he listened, nodding.

"I don't think I can go on working here much longer," I said at last.

He laughed, and transferred his plastic cup from his right

hand to his left. He held out his right hand. "Join the club. I've a strong feeling I won't be here much longer, either."

We shook hands.

"Are you handing in your notice?" I asked.

"Being laid off, more like. They're downsizing anyway. No point in paying superfluous people when shareholders want a bigger slice of the pie."

"Oh, I'm sorry," I said. "I mean – will you be all right?"

"I'll find something else. I already do some odd jobs."

"Such as working for Lily Green?" I asked eagerly. I told him about our meeting and launched into a rant about the road scheme. He seemed to know a lot about it already, including the name of the developers who were in on the deal.

"But can anything be done?" I demanded.

"I hope so. Hey … " He looked straight at me, then away, then back again at me. "I don't suppose … "

"What?"

"Would you like to try and help? First of all we need to make a good case for preserving the woods. You say you're used to writing stuff. Could you write something persuasive, maybe?"

"No problem. Count me in," I said fervently. Great. Here was somebody who wanted to do something useful, not merely work to boost shareholder value. What had Lily said? A good young man.

"I'll have to introduce you to Martha," he said.

"Martha? Does she work here?"

"No, but we're both members of the same movement: Trees First. Do you know it?"

"I've heard of it. I'm not really an expert on trees, although I really, really like them. I draw them, you see."

"You do? An illustrated pamphlet would be even better."

We grinned at each other, possibilities opening up around us.

He asked whether I could meet him at Oldwood Court on Friday, when he would be able to teach me more about the trees and we could discuss ideas. Friday? That was a non-working day for me, and since Hugh would be at the office, he wouldn't expect me to be available. Then the following week he would be going skiing. I'd be free.

"Fine. Why not?" I said.

CHAPTER THREE

We were sitting at the supper table, and Maya was chattering on about jazz dance, modern dance, break dance and I don't know what, when a phone call came through on the landline, and Dad went to answer it in the hall.

"I don't know why it's OK to answer the landline but we can't use our mobiles," grumbled Maya.

"Because you don't use them like proper phones. You're always poking at the screen, texting and so on," said Mum. She is so twentieth-century.

Dad came back, his face worried.

"That was Grandad's neighbour. He's had another fall, and he could have been lying there for hours if she hadn't dropped in."

"Oh dear," said Mum. "Well, it does look as if we'll have to … "

Their eyes met.

"Have to do what?" I asked.

They both looked from me to Maya.

"We think he ought not to go on living in that house on his own," said Dad.

I thought about my grandparents' house. The last time I had seen it, it had been rather dusty and run down, with piles of books and papers everywhere. Our French Granny had kept it spick and span, but in the three years before she died she had been very frail, in and out of hospital several times, and Grandad, as a rather absent-minded academic, had in any case never been one for tidiness and housework.

"So where could he go?" Surely not to some awful retirement home, I thought. He would hate that.

"We've been discussing this," said Mum, "and we think

that really there's only one solution. He'll have to come and live here."

"Here? But there isn't enough space."

"There could be," said Dad.

"There will be if you and Maya double up," said Mum brightly. "Maya's room is bigger, so you'll have to share it with her, and then we can put Grandad in your room. On the ground floor, so he doesn't have to cope with the stairs."

I was struck dumb. I gazed at Maya and saw the same dismay in her face.

"But we can't – " began Maya.

"Now, don't start raising objections. You love Grandad, don't you? You want us to do what's best for him."

"Of course we do," I said. "But – "

"And it won't be for very long, will it? Only a few months, because in June you'll be getting married, Jaki. I'm sure you can put up with each other for such a short time."

I was not at all sure that we could. Maya was not too bad a sister in her way, but her room was a mass of dance-related clutter, clothes, shoes, posters on the walls, video games. What about the noise she made? Where could I put my stuff? There wouldn't even be a free table for drawing, and sharing a computer was obviously out of the question.

"I know what," I announced. "I've got a better idea. I'll move in with Hugh."

Mum's mouth turned down at the corners. "Oh, Jaki, I don't think that would be advisable. I know we're liberal-minded these days. But actually living together before such a big, fancy wedding? I don't think that would look quite right. What do you think, Pascal?"

Dad shrugged. "Space will have to be made somehow."

"It's no big deal, nowadays" I said. "I'm sure Hugh will be OK about it."

"Yes, it's totally the right solution," said Maya emphatically, and I hid a grin.

"Well, I don't know." Mum sounded very doubtful.

"It could be a good test. See if he can put up with you," said Dad. "No, I don't mean that. Don't glare at me! If Hugh is all right with it, I'm sure everything will be fine. Your Grandad is my main worry right now."

***

It was all systems go. Hugh was leaving for his skiing trip on Saturday morning, Dad would drive me to Hugh's flat with all my stuff on Saturday afternoon, and on Sunday he would drive up to fetch Grandad.

When I had revealed the plan to Hugh on the phone, there had been just a fractional pause, and then he had said, "Of course, sweet babe. No problem at all. You know I want to have you with me all the time. What? Yes, of course I'm sure."

So that was settled. On Friday I hadn't been able to get away until early afternoon, what with packing up my clothes and drawing materials and books that I would really want to have with me, and helping Mum to sort out bedding and clean towels for Grandad. All my university books and papers went into cardboard boxes in the roof. I couldn't quite bring myself to get rid of them, having spent such a long time working for my degree.

The upshot was that it was after two when I walked through the gates into Oldwood. Lily had said, faintly over the phone, that I would be able to find Gavin easily, and that we could both come to the house for a cup of tea later if we wished.

The weather had held. The tips of the lime twigs glowed crimson, while the tops of the silver birches were dazzling white and delicate as flowering grasses against the blue of the sky. No leaves had yet appeared, but I felt that they were there, pushing upwards through the bark. The earth smelt of leaf mould. Something rustled in the undergrowth. It sounded like an animal. A fox, perhaps? Could there be deer living in these woods? I stood still and peered through brittle stems. Then I saw the source of the noise: a male blackbird, sleek, with a beak as yellow as a crocus, vigorously turning over the dead leaves for hidden grubs. Soon the birds would be nesting.

I walked on.

How was I to find Gavin? He had given me his phone number, and I pulled out my phone, but saw that there was no signal. How strange. Perhaps I could call "Coo-ee," but I didn't like to make a noise in the hush of these woods.

I thought I could smell smoke. I paused, leaning my bike against a tree. I sniffed and left the path, striking off into the heart of the woodland, the leaves making swishing sounds as I walked and my feet sinking into the rich leaf mould with every step. It was impossible to walk in a straight line, and I made detours around bushes and fallen branches. Twigs snapped and I caught my clothes on brambles. After a time, I was not sure how far behind me the path lay. Pale cushions of primroses gleamed here and there beside tree roots. I could no longer hear any traffic noise, and I could still smell smoke, a little nearer now.

Then I heard distant piping. Someone was playing a tune that I didn't recognize.

I walked on, my footsteps noisy, in the directions of the smoke, and the piping stopped before I emerged into a clearing where a small bonfire was smouldering. Beyond the bonfire, half hidden by the plume of smoke, someone was sitting on a log. I made a detour around the fire and called hello to Gavin. He rose to meet me. His clothes were brown and green, almost like camouflage, and he was holding a penny whistle.

"I heard you playing."

"I was just taking a break. I wondered whether you were really coming, actually."

I explained the situation with Grandad, and he told me that he had been clearing brambles and brushwood since the morning. A garden fork and a hefty pair of secateurs lay on the ground. He came regularly with tools to help Lily, he told me. "Man with a van, that's me," he said.

"So have you left the factory?"

"Out on my ear."

"You mean they sacked you?"

"They 'let me go', as they say nowadays. But let's not

talk about that place while we're here. Do you realize that this may be one of the few remaining pockets of ancient English woodland? There's hardly anything left. It's all been felled. But in here, I could show you some beautiful old oaks, hundreds of years old, not to mention all the other trees – some of them introduced later, like the horse chestnuts. They're from India."

"Are they? There's an Indian connection with the house, too. Lily was telling me about her grandfather."

"Right. The whole place is full of history, and this woodland is absolutely crucial for birds and other wildlife. Shall we walk?"

He pocketed his penny whistle, carefully forked damp leaf mould over the fire and raked aside any smouldering twigs, and we set off through the trees. As we walked, he told me about the different species of tree, identifying them as we came to them and giving me snippets of information. Some of them I recognized already, but he was far better informed than I was. I didn't know the names of all the different conifers. When I did recognize a tree, it was usually by the shape of its branches, reaching up, dividing and fanning against the sky, or swooping down and rising at the tips like a wave. What were those tangled balls, high up? Birds' nests?

No, he told me. They were bunches of mistletoe. I glanced at him as he talked, his narrow face alive with the importance of what he was telling me.

"I love sketching trees," I told him, "especially in winter. The bare outlines. But soon these will all have leaves."

"Not yet. Leaves depend on the light. We're not past the equinox yet. Look at this beautiful beech! Look at the roots, and the spaces between them like little caves. They might make a good drawing, don't you think?"

We walked on.

"There's a big cedar near the wall," I said. I hesitated. What should I tell him? "The other week I thought I saw … someone on the top of it."

"Oh, that will have been Lily. Come – I'll show you."

He seemed perfectly confident of his direction, although I

wasn't very sure which way the gates lay. After a few minutes, I caught a glimpse between the tree trunks of the long stone wall, much of it covered with ivy on this side, and he led me parallel with it until we came to the great cedar. It was vast, its branches spreading over a wide area, and on the near side I could see a wooden spiral staircase that had been built close to the trunk, curving upward through the branches.

"There's a platform at the top," said Gavin. "Want to come up?"

"No!" I shuddered. "I don't like heights." That was an understatement. I hated them.

"That's a pity. There's a good view. I love climbing trees – always have done. You feel you're part of this great living being, especially when the wind moves the branches. After all, trees are the biggest living creatures that we see every day, and yet most people take them for granted."

I could picture him as a wiry boy, scaling trunks, scrabbling for footholds and handholds.

All right, so there was a staircase leading up the tree, and presumably Lily sometimes went up it. But in the dark? And what about ... ? I decided that I would say nothing about what I thought I had seen. No doubt it was just a branch or something.

Over to our left, we heard the sound of an engine and the creaking clang of the gates opening. As we approached, we saw an old, battered Skoda just entering. Lily was at the wheel, and she opened the car door and called that she could give us a lift back to the house.

I sat next to her and thought that it seemed somehow odd that someone like her should be driving a car. But after all, why not? Presumably she had to go and do shopping like everyone else. We passed my bike, still propped against a lime tree, and she drove us up to the house and through an archway into the cobbled yard where Gavin's van was parked. She opened the door to the kitchen and we followed her in.

It was warm inside, and there was a smell of freshly baked bread. Lily told us that she had gone into town to buy "a few odds and ends", but could offer us bread and butter and honey and tea, and we all sat around the scrubbed table. It felt cosy. I wondered how many meals had been prepared here in the days of cooks, housekeepers, maids and kitchen boys.

Now there was only Lily, but for some reason the place didn't feel empty. I wondered whether she was lonely, living alone among so many big rooms and shadowy corners.

"I'm afraid your wedding dress isn't quite ready for a fitting yet," she told me.

I reassured her that I was in no hurry. I saw Gavin looking at me thoughtfully over his tea-cup.

"You're engaged to that – to Mr. Markham-Hunt, aren't you?" he said.

"To Hugh. That's right."

His eyes rested on my engagement ring.

"Tell me," I hurried on, "What are you planning – I mean, to fight this road scheme? What can we do?"

"Jaki wants to join us," he told Lily. "Another recruit! We'll get there. We must organize a campaign."

Lily looked from him to me and back with a tired smile. "I appreciate it. Resistance uses up so much energy. Sometimes I feel ... quite exhausted. But with help, anything is possible. I keep summoning help."

"What are you doing tomorrow night?" Gavin asked me. I nearly said that I would be with Hugh, but then remembered that he would already have left for Switzerland.

"Right. Do you know that pub the Three Lions, in town? We could meet there, and I'll introduce you to Martha."

***

That evening I sat in front of the computer in my nearly empty bedroom, reading up about forest destruction. I was appalled by the figures. Trees were so important, absorbing carbon dioxide, producing oxygen, providing shelter for wildlife, stabilizing the soil – and yet humanity was destroying forests on a vast scale, mainly in order to produce palm oil and grazing for livestock, but also just to make room for more and more buildings and roads and traffic. Illegal logging was also rife. I had known about this trend, of course, but the sheer scale of the destruction was shocking. The more I read, the angrier I felt.

Humanity was such a thoughtless, greedy species, proliferating all over the planet. Soon there would be ten billion of us. Ten billion! Yet people went on having children. How would they manage when resources got too scarce? How would they find jobs, come to that? I was sure my parents hadn't thought about jobs when they went ahead and had two daughters. Hugh's words swam into my mind: "I'd like to have at least three children … " Of course, if we were well-off and well connected, perhaps our children would not have to worry. The wealthy were an elite apart, and after June I would be one of them, enjoying all their privileges, presumably. How lucky was that?

Something Lily had said while we were drinking tea came back to me. "Of course I want this place to be saved. But for its own sake, not for me. I don't think it's fair that I should be enjoying it alone, in solitary splendour. You know you are both welcome to come here whenever you like, and you can bring other people – friends."

I hugged myself. There was some beautiful sketching to be done, maybe in charcoal as well as Indian ink. When could I go again?

But I also needed to think about writing. What could I write that would make people see the value of Oldwood Court and realize what a stupid and unforgivable idea it was to bulldoze a road through it?

I opened a blank page on the computer and began to type a few notes.

***

"You must come back to see Grandad. Come to lunch tomorrow," urged Mum, as Dad and I were loading my stuff into the car on Saturday.

I felt I was setting off to start a new term at uni instead of going only a few miles away. Maya was to follow us on my bike, as there was no way it would fit in Dad's boot. Then she would drive back with Dad before he went to fetch Grandad. I think Dad is quite happy to have any small problem of logistics to solve.

"He's being a bit difficult about it," Dad said, as the car purred along." He values his independence, but he just has to face the fact that he's getting old and frail. Luckily he hasn't lost his marbles, so I've managed to convince him that this really is the best solution. He insists it's only temporary, though."

"Poor Grandad," I said. Dad could be quite overbearing sometimes. I wondered whether I would ever put down roots anywhere and be reluctant to leave a place.

Hugh had left his flat as neat as a hotel suite: no pictures on the walls, no piles of books and papers, no sentimental knick-knacks. They were not his style. His books were lined up in order of size on two shelves.

"Not untidy, is he?" said Dad appreciatively. "Where will you put all this stuff?"

"I'll have to think about that," I said.

Maya rang the bell, having left the bicycle in the sheltered area downstairs.

"Is this the love-nest?" She walked in and gazed around. "Hmm. Very neat. Doesn't look much like your sort of place, sis. I'm dying of thirst. Is there any Coke in the fridge?"

She opened it and grimaced. Hugh didn't go in for Coke.

I felt slightly annoyed. Did my family think that I was utterly slovenly and untidy? What did they really know about me? Anyway, I could surely adjust to my surroundings.

When they had gone, I had some difficulty in stowing away my belongings. All the cupboards and drawers were already full of Hugh's things. I had to push his clothes to one side so that I could hang mine in the wardrobe, and I stuffed socks and underpants into a single drawer to make room for my own underwear. My books I arranged in piles according to subject on the various fitted cabinets, and my laptop had to go on the small kitchen table, as there was nowhere else to put it. The place was beginning to look a bit cluttered, but of course it was designed for a single occupant.

This was only temporary, I reminded myself. When Hugh returned from his mountain jaunt, it would be nice to wake up with him in the same bed every day. What did he usually have for breakfast on a working day? Probably he just grabbed a cup of coffee and dashed out. I would prepare a proper breakfast, with orange juice and yoghurt, I thought. Just like in a hotel.

He had probably arrived in Switzerland already. No doubt he would text me later. Meanwhile I would go out and buy some groceries. Then I would do some more research on forests, and then – I glanced at my watch – then I would go to the Three Lions pub and meet Gavin and Martha. Gavin hadn't told me anything about her, but she must be either his wife or his girlfriend.

***

"Over here!" I saw Gavin waving to me from a corner table, and next to him sat a dark girl with a square bob haircut and a fringe.

The Three Lions was the kind of pub that had dark beams and horse brasses, an artificial log fire and a carpet with swirling patterns. From the public bar came the sound of darts. The place was already quite full, with a small crowd around the bar.

When Gavin had introduced us and gone to fetch drinks, Martha and I smiled at each other tentatively.

"Gavin didn't expect to meet anyone in that factory who cared about trees," she said, after we had exchanged a few pleasantries.

"Nor did I. The factory is just a temporary job and I need to move on. Trees are so much more important than handbags!"

Gavin laughed as he put our glasses on the table. He was drinking beer and Martha and I had asked for cider. "Not all women would agree with that, I'm afraid."

"Well, we're not 'all women', are we?" said Martha. She had very dark brown eyes that gleamed when she looked at me. She was attractive, and I wondered how long she and

Gavin had known each other, but it was too early to ask that kind of question. I warmed to her immediately.

"So tell me about this organization. Trees First, I think you said?"

Martha took some pamphlets out of a floppy satchel that was definitely not a bag from the factory, and told me that I could take them home to look at. Apparently the organization had a branch in the county, but not in Oakfield itself.

"What we need to do is work out some kind of plan," said Gavin. "Pool our resources. Get organized. Jaki, you told me that you like drawing trees, and you say you can write."

"We were thinking of producing a pamphlet ourselves," said Martha. "Something eye-catching."

"Or putting an ad in the local paper – if we can afford it," said Gavin. "We need local support, besides getting Trees First behind us."

"I can do a colour design," said Martha.

"And I know all the technical stuff, and I can put in the info about the trees themselves, but we mustn't be boring," said Gavin.

We began to toss ideas around. I had brought a few sketches to show them. They both nodded approvingly, and Martha showed me a lovely little note-card that she had designed, with a red, blue and gold pattern around the edge. After I had bought a second round of drinks, we were soon talking animatedly, interrupting one another and laughing. Gavin made copious notes on a large pad. Martha used her phone to take snaps of my drawings, Indian ink outlines of trees seen from my bedroom window.

"I think we're getting somewhere," said Gavin.

I felt energized. This wasn't a job, but it was definitely something worth doing, and the weight of uncertainty seemed temporarily lighter.

"When shall we talk to Lily about all this?" asked Martha.

"Oh," I said "So you're a friend of Lily's, too?"

Martha said, "It's at least partly for her sake that we want to do this. She's wonderful. Weird, maybe. But I think she's great, and so does Gavin."

I scarcely know her, I thought. Is she weird?

Gavin tapped his chin with his pen. "If we're to drum up local support, it would be good to have the ear of somebody influential in the town." He looked straight at me, then down at my engagement ring. "Jaki is marrying into the Markham-Hunt family," he told Martha.

There was a pause. "Congratulations. So when's the wedding?" asked Martha.

I told her.

"So ... Markham-Hunt is a town councillor, isn't he? And some kind of businessman? Is there any chance he might be able to swing opinion in our favour?"

I looked down at the table. "I don't know." But I felt I did know. I was almost certain that nobody in that family would be interested.

"How about an online petition?" I suggested.

"Mmm ... yes. But how can we get people to really care about these trees? I don't mean just trees in general."

Gavin launched into a speech. "These trees? They're special. They're ancient. They're part of our disappearing heritage. They're — "

I sat back and listened to him as he held forth eloquently about ancient woodland, biodiversity, carbon capture. He can really talk, this man, I thought, as I looked at his narrow, animated face and emphatic gestures. A born orator, apparently. I would never have thought it of him when we first spoke at that cocktail party.

"OK, OK," laughed Martha. "You're preaching to the converted here."

He broke off in mid-sentence and seemed to become aware of who we were. "Sorry."

"No," I said, "That's brilliant. I need to mug up on all this stuff. And you must definitely be the spokesperson."

Just then, my phone pinged with a text from Hugh, saying that he had arrived safely in the Swiss Alps. Love and kisses, it said.

***

The next day was Sunday, and I biked over to my family's house to see Grandad and have lunch with them all. Of course I wanted to see Grandad, although partly I would have preferred to spend the day alone, quietly drawing and making notes before I had to go back to work on Monday.

They were all in the sitting room when I walked in. Straight away my eyes went to Grandad, sitting in an armchair with a stick leaning against his thin legs. His white hair stood out in two little clouds on either side of his bald, faintly freckled head, and he peered at me over his glasses for a second. Then his lined face creased into a smile.

"Don't get up, Grandad." He looked smaller than the last time I had seen him, I thought, as I walked over to him to say hello.

The grasp of his veined hand on my arm was warm. "Jacqueline, dear – I mean Jaki – you look more and more like your aunt every time I see you."

I caught a faint frown on Mum's face. She prefers to believe that her daughters both take after her, although as far as I was concerned, comparisons with Aunt Stella in her heyday were complimentary. After all, thousands of fans had thought that she was beautiful and sexy.

"We haven't heard from Stella for a long time, have we, darling?" said Mum to Dad.

"We speak on the phone sometimes," said Grandad, "but – hrrrm - I haven't seen her since your mother's funeral, Pascal." He sounded sad.

"She'll be over soon. She'll be over for Jaki's wedding," said Dad heartily. He held up the sherry bottle and raised a questioning eyebrow at me. I nodded and moved to take a glass.

Grandad put down his own glass, barely tasted. "So you will soon be marrying that golden lad," he said, gazing up at me and rocking his head to and fro.

Golden lads and girls all must,

As chimney-sweepers, come to dust.

Shakespeare's words rose unbidden in my mind as I was sure they had done in Grandad's. Grandad was a published poet, after all. Hugh was a golden lad, true enough. Handsome, charming, fair-haired and rich, and he had always been deferential towards Grandad on the few occasions when they had met. But I didn't want to talk about him now, or about wedding preparations.

I sat down on a low stool near Grandad.

"Jaki, my dear, I'm distressed to be pushing you out of your room like this. And such a lovely room, too, opening straight on to the garden."

I told him that it didn't matter in the least, and so did Dad, saying that in any case it was the best all-round solution until some possible better arrangement could be found.

"It must be only temporary," said Grandad fretfully. "It's extremely kind of you and Lisa, as I've said before, but I must go back. I'm going to miss all my books, and I couldn't think of going into a retirement home. What? – a care home, with a crowd of elderly people? It's unthinkable."

"Well, well, it's too early to think about all that," said Mum. "I'll just go and see to the lunch. It's nearly ready." A waft of Sunday roast came through the door as she left.

"I'm glad you like the view from Jaki's room," said Maya, looking up from her phone. She stood up and half-twirled on one foot. "She's forever sketching it. Trees, mainly. She's got a thing about trees, these days."

"Why not? They're beautiful and important," I protested.

"They are indeed." Grandad reminded me of a poem that he had written about an aspen. I had only a vague memory of it and promised to look it up. All his volumes of poetry were in the bookcase, regularly dusted but seldom opened.

I told him a little about Oldwood Court and the threat hanging over it, and he listened attentively, asking a few questions. That was what I liked about Grandad. He really paid attention to what you said to him, even if at other times he seemed vague. I was just telling him about Trees First and about Gavin and Martha's plans, when Maya, who had been fidgeting more and more, chipped in about her dancing, and Grandad politely turned the conversation to his other granddaughter.

Dad had gone to see how Mum was getting on, and now he put his head round the door to announce that lunch was ready. Maya and I both helped Grandad out of his chair, and he moved forward, stooping, leaning on his stick.

I resolved never to grow old.

"I didn't expect you to marry quite so young," said Grandad as I passed him the roast potatoes. "Straight out of university. Hmm. I thought young people nowadays wanted to see more of the world before they settled down."

"I'd like to see more of the world, but I can't even get a job."

"There seems to be very little available locally," said Dad.

"Locally? Have you tried to find a job abroad, in that case?" Grandad looked at me over his glasses.

"Hugh wouldn't like that, would he?" said Maya. "He's all set to be a hotshot in the firm here, and I bet he wouldn't want to move abroad."

I was quite sure he wouldn't. I wriggled my shoulders uncomfortably. He probably wouldn't want to move too far away from his parents, either. We would no doubt be seeing a lot of them.

"You'll soon be starting house-hunting, won't you?" said Mum. "Didn't you say he already had enough for a deposit?"

"Yes, but there hasn't been time. He's too busy at work, and anyway, there's the flat. We'll be all right there for a bit."

"Huh, it's tiny," said Maya. "Hardly big enough for one person. I'd find it claustrophobic, living right on top of each other like that."

"Well, you're not going to live in it, are you? You're not the one who's marrying Hugh," I said crossly.

"Thank God!"

"Maya," reproved Mum.

"Sor-ry," she drawled.

***

Over the next ten days, I worked hard on sketches of trees, and wrote and re-wrote paragraphs about the importance of preserving ancient landscape and preventing deforestation. In the office, my mind was not on Clarke's reports and figures on the handbag trade. Consequently, relations became increasingly strained. He was particularly nasty when he found me doing a moment's research on the internet about the number of hectares of woodland still remaining in England, and I bit back the urge to tell him that at least that information wasn't dull and soul-destroying, like his files.

To tell the truth, the office work I was hired to do was beginning to seem unbearable, and even at the coffee machine there was nobody interesting to talk to, now that Gavin had gone. What was I doing there? Even the air smelt of plastic, and my eyes itched.

This was not the future I had dreamed about when I was a student. Of course, my dreams of the future had always included Hugh, and very soon we would be bound together officially. He texted me every day, enthusing about the quality of the snow, and soon he would be back. That was something to look forward to, wasn't it? Perhaps it would be better not to look too far into the future.

I had been meeting Gavin and Martha nearly every evening to discuss plans, and it occurred to me that when Hugh returned he might want me to be more available in the evenings. But then, he was often kept late in meetings, so perhaps he wouldn't mind. We could be together at weekends, couldn't we? – although he had been talking recently about trying to improve his golf game, probably under pressure from his father. I didn't mind. Let him play golf. It wasn't my scene, but I could occupy myself independently. There were important things to do.

An online petition was another idea that we had tossed around.

"Do you think petitions are really effective?" Gavin had asked. We were walking along Oakfield High Street towards the church, where the van was parked.

"They can be if somebody famous endorses them," said Martha.

"Know anybody famous?"

We shook our heads.

Martha said, "Never mind. We can still try. If people actually see the oldest trees, and how special they are, surely they'll realize that they have to be saved."

"It's an idea," said Gavin. "Tomorrow, if it doesn't rain, I'll go to Oldwood with my camera and try to take some artistic shots."

I wished I were going with him.

He usually dropped me back at the flat before driving home with Martha. She insisted that I sit in the passenger seat while she crouched on the floor in the back, which was probably against the law, but neither of them seemed particularly bothered and the distance wasn't that great. If we drove past Oldwood Court, I always glanced up into the topmost branches of the cedar, but I never saw anything out of the ordinary: just branches outlined against the clouds or the stars.

***

When Hugh returned from Switzerland on the Thursday evening, he arrived an hour early. I wasn't ready for him. The kitchen table was littered with paper, drafts of what I was writing, reference material that I had printed out from the internet, my laptop and two half-empty coffee mugs. I had thought of making spaghetti bolognese for supper and had got out a packet of spaghetti and a tin of tomatoes, but had then been sidetracked by a text message from Martha. My parka was slung over the back of a chair and my boots stood at angles by the door, just as I had taken them off.

Hugh stumbled over them as he came in with his bulky travelling bag and backpack. His smile turned briefly to a frown, but then he dropped his luggage on the floor as I went to him and wrapped my arms around him. We kissed briefly.

"Missed me?"

"Of course." That wasn't quite true, I thought. I had been too busy to miss him desperately.

"I see you've made yourself at home. What is all this

stuff, anyway? Work?"

"Sorry, sorry. I'll make some space." I hurried about, stacking papers, shutting down the laptop, hanging my parka neatly in the cupboard while he dragged his luggage into the bedroom and began to unpack. We shouted to each other through the open door.

"So what have you been doing with yourself?" I heard hangers being shunted along a rail.

I started to tell him about Trees First, and how important trees were for the environment generally, absorbing carbon and releasing oxygen, but then I realized that he wasn't really listening. I heard him mutter, "Not much room with all these clothes in here."

After while he came back with a huge box of Swiss chocolates that he presented to me, and then he sat down and suggested we have a drink.

While we sipped Martinis, he told me a great deal about the ski slopes, the maintenance of the ski lifts, the quality of the snow, the ambience of the après-ski. His face was suntanned.

"Were there lots of glamorous people?"

"Oh, the usual crowd. A few celebrities. A lot of top models, too."

"Really? Did you talk to them?"

"Oh, I talked to everyone. But I don't really want to spend time with top models, babe. It's nice to come home to someone plain and natural like you."

Plain and natural? Is that what I was? I had been going to change my clothes and do something to my hair before he arrived, but I had been too engrossed in what I was researching and writing. No doubt I looked very plain and natural compared to the St. Moritz crowd.

"Are you hungry? I was going to make some spaghetti."

He pulled a face. "This time yesterday I was having fabulous cheese fondue with Glüwein. Let's go out."

I didn't really want to go out again in the cold, but I went into the bathroom to put on some makeup. When I emerged, he said, "What was all that you were saying about trees?"

57

I began to tell him again: about Oldwood Court, ancient woodland, Trees First, and Gavin and Martha.

"Oh, that guy," he said vaguely. "You did mention him." He was looking around the kitchen at all my things, books piled on work surfaces, pens and pencils stuffed into a jar. "You know," he said, "I'm glad you've found something to do that really interests you. But you do realize, don't you, that that Oldwood Court place is a lost cause? That road will definitely be built."

"It's only a project. If enough people oppose it – "

"Oppose it?" He raised his eyebrows. "Come on. I don't think my father would like to hear you saying that."

"Why? Does he care much about it?"

"I'd say he does. He has shares in the construction company. And then there's that old house, stuck in the middle of a wood at the moment. I know that a friend of his has his eye on it, as a future hotel."

"But – " I was speechless. He hadn't mentioned this before. Did he share all his father's views?

"Come on," he said. "Let's go. I'm hungry."

***

Maya was waiting for me outside the gates of Oldwood, tapping her foot, her hands in her pockets and her short fair hair tousled by the wind.

Mum had phoned me to say that Maya had been talking non-stop about how much she wanted to see the Rajah's house, and would I mind asking Lily if my younger sister could accompany me to my next fitting? Lily's voice, echoing and distant as usual on the phone line, said that of course, any sister of mine would be welcome. So Mum dropped Maya off when I was due to cycle over there – not necessarily for a fitting, but because Gavin and Martha would also be there, discussing plans with Lily.

The gates creaked open when I pressed the bell, and we stepped through them together into the lime avenue. It was one of those afternoons of wind and gleams of sun that sometimes occur in early February and remind you that spring really is coming, not today, not tomorrow, but soon.

"Wow," said Maya. "This is cool."

"Wait till you see some of the really old trees. Look, let's go into the wood a little way and I'll show you."

"But I want to see the house. And this strange lady. I mean, isn't she, like, kind of weird? I've heard things at school."

"Weird? No. What have you heard?"

"Oh – just … things."

She followed me off the main track and along one of the little twisting paths between the trees that I was beginning to know from my sketching sessions. Our feet sank into leaf mould and the occasional bramble clutched at our clothes, although Gavin kept them cut back to some extent. Ivy climbed up some of the silvery boles of beeches, and in the distance a crow was cawing. Overhead, the crowns of the trees shifted in the wind, and splashes of sunlight illuminated the different shades of brown and grey and the brilliant green moss on the trunks and roots.

"So do you know the names of all these trees?"

"Some of them. I'm learning." I pointed out oak and ash and hazel, juniper and holly.

"Oh, I know holly," said Maya impatiently. "If there are lots of berries, doesn't that mean that there will be a hard winter?"

"Gavin says not. He says that the trees are responding to past conditions, not foretelling the future."

"You often say, 'Gavin says'."

"Do I? Look, come along this way. I want to show you something else."

We picked our way forward and emerged in a small clearing where the ground sloped gently downward. At the foot of the slope shone dark, rippling water. It was a small lake, and at the farther end stood a semi-circular, turreted structure like a little temple, and a bare weeping willow beside it hung over the water. Its branches glinted gold, drooping to meet gold and shimmering reflections in the surface of the lake. I had already sketched this place, one of my favourites, and remembered my excitement when I had looked into the grey stone temple and found the source of the water, a bubbling spring. It was the first time I had ever seen a spring.

Maya walked forward and peered into the water. Then she looked beyond, to where the water joined a meandering stream leading into the undergrowth.

"So is this the water supply for the house?"

"Perhaps it was, in Lily grandfather's time. Come this way a minute. I want to show you another tree." I jerked my head to the left and led the way along another path.

"Don't you ever get lost in here?" asked Maya.

"I thought I might, at first, but somehow the path always seems to take me back to the house or the drive."

We had come to a larger clearing, in the centre of which rose the most magnificent oak I had ever known. My arms would not have met around its sturdy trunk, and the strong branches spread symmetrically, higher and higher, to the feathery fans of its crown. No circular scars or bosses defaced its rough bark; apparently no one had ever chopped off its branches. I had already sketched it, looking upwards from the base (which tended to make my head swim), but it was difficult to capture its full glory as I couldn't stand far enough away, the view being blocked by other trees. It was a solitary giant. I didn't tell Maya that I had tried to span its trunk. She might have laughed at me for being a tree-hugger.

"Wow!" said Maya. "Awesome. It's like, you know, Tolkien? The Ents and stuff? I can see why you're hooked."

I was gratified. Perhaps she was beginning to appreciate the trees, although she had never shown any interest before. She continued to gaze upwards for a few moments. Then she turned to me again.

"But can we go to the house now?"

All right, it was the house that really intrigued her. When Maya has an idea in her head, she can't be distracted for long. We set off towards Oldwood Court, whose roof and chimneys were just visible through the farthest treetops.

***

When I pushed open the heavy front door, Maya was all eyes, taking in the lofty entrance hall, the wide, dark staircase leading upwards, the soft colours of the carpet. I breathed in the scent of rose and jasmine.

From the morning room came the sound of a piano, accompanied by piping. There Lily, with her back to us, was playing the grand piano, and Gavin was standing beside it, playing his penny whistle. He broke off when he saw us and waved cheerfully, whereupon Lily turned and rose, and so did Martha, who had been busy writing in a notepad near the fireplace.

Introductions over, Lily said to Maya: "I'm so glad you have come to support us. We need younger people. Perhaps you could talk to your friends at school about – about the threats to the trees and the house?"

"Talk to … ? Uh, yeah … Yes. Right," said Maya.

She and her friends had already been talking about Lily, I thought. I hoped they weren't spreading silly rumours.

"That's right," said Martha. "The more young people who join our campaign, the better."

"I have to show you my photos," said Gavin to me.

Lily was still looking encouragingly at Maya. "So you are the dancer?"

"Dancing is my life," said Maya solemnly.

"Would you dance for me? Just something spontaneous?"

Lily never wasted time on small talk. If she was interested, she came straight to the point, although what she said was often enigmatic. Maya hesitated and said that she didn't have the right shoes, but I knew that it wouldn't take long to persuade her to show off.

Lily sat down again at the piano and began to play a piece that I learned later was called *Woodland Sketches* by Edward MacDowell. It began gently and then gathered speed, and soon Maya had flung off her jacket, boots and socks and was dancing barefoot, rising and falling, swaying and twirling. She is a changed person when she dances, so graceful, I have to admit, and her expression is one of bliss.

Lily brought the piece to a close, and Gavin and Martha applauded.

Maya stood flushed and triumphant. "I do need to practise more," she said.

Lily suggested that she continue to practise in the morning room while we adjourned to the library to discuss our latest plans, so we left her bowing and curtseying in front of the cheval mirror.

Gavin spread out on the library table some fine prints of photos he had taken of sunset through bare trees, and a particularly stunning one of the lime avenue curving away into the distance. Lily admired them, but said to me, "I think your sketches capture the spirit of the individual trees." So I felt useful, too. I hadn't yet shown her what I had been writing.

"The people at Trees First say that we must have several angles of approach," said Gavin. "We know why we want to save this place, but how can we persuade other people? That's the question. We need to get the media on our side."

"And we must point out that it's a waste of public money, and it's being done mainly to swell Sacs de Luxe's profits, not for the community," said Martha.

"I don't know how you can go on working for that firm," said Gavin. "One brief taste of it was enough for me."

I looked down. I didn't know, either. "It wasn't really my choice," I mumbled.

"Ah, but I was forgetting. Your fiancé is a rising star there, isn't he? Future assistant director, probably."

There was an awkward silence. Martha broke it, kindly. "Then of course there's the environmental angle. What about the wildlife?"

"The birds," said Lily.

"I saw a red squirrel the other day," I put in eagerly.

They were impressed. Really, a red squirrel? They had thought there were only greys around Oakfield. Perhaps Oldwood was one of the few remaining havens for red squirrels in the whole of the country. We got on to the subject of wildlife in general, and possibly rare species of tree, and Sites of Special Scientific Interest, and how the online petition was doing, and how Gavin's next move would be to contact the local paper.

Apart from Lily, we were all talking at once, and were busy making lists, when Maya burst into the library.

She was very pale.

"Maya, dear, are you all right?" asked Lily.

"I ... yes ... I promised Mum I wouldn't be late," said Maya in a small voice. She glanced at me. "I said I would phone her, but ... I couldn't."

"Mobile phones won't work here," said Lily, standing up. "Come with me, and you can use the landline."

"Is your sister usually nervous?" asked Martha "She looked as if she'd seen a ghost."

I said that I had better accompany her to the gates, if Mum was coming to fetch her, and I went to collect my things.

Maya, having made her phone call, was taking leave of Lily. She looked more like her confident self.

"You would be very welcome to come again," said Lily.

"Thank you. What I would really like – " She looked down, then up again at Lily. "What I would really like would be to explore this house," she said in a bolder voice.

"Why not? If you're interested. You must arrange something with Jaki."

We set off down the drive in the gathering dusk. The days were slowly growing longer, but spring was still far off. A high, white moon could be glimpsed through the topmost branches that were still shifted and tangled by the wind.

"So what happened there?" I challenged her.

She didn't answer immediately. "Don't you think the whole place is kind of spooky?"

"Spooky? No, it's just old. Why?"

Maya stopped walking and confronted me. "You know I was dancing on my own? In front of that tall mirror?"

"Yes?"

"Well, I – I saw something."

"What sort of thing? Where?"

"I don't know. In the mirror. It came and went so quickly. But it was – a dark thing. But I'm not going to be scared," she added determinedly, and marched on towards the gates.

A very light finger of fear touched the back of my neck. Hadn't I caught a glimpse of something in that mirror?

"Well," I said, "It was pretty dark in the morning room. And Lily is a lovely person, isn't she?"

"Mmm," said Maya, striding ahead. I couldn't tell what she meant.

Mum's headlights swept up to the end of the gates, and as Maya opened the passenger door I could hear Mum complaining about all the traffic on the dual carriageway. She shouted to me from the driving seat, asking if I would like to come home with them, but I said that I had my bike and would cycle home later.

Home, I had said. Where was home? Our house in Surrey had been sold. Somebody else was occupying my old college room. There was no longer any room for me in my parents' house. I meant the flat, of course. That had to be home for the present.

CHAPTER FOUR

"Shit," said Hugh. "Why is there never any paper in this printer when I need it? You seem to have used up reams of the stuff. I've only printed three pages, and look how pale the print is."

"Sorry." I had been going to change the cartridge. I began to look for a fresh one in the bottom of the cupboard, but the cupboard door knocked over a pile of my papers which spread out fanwise on the parquet.

Hugh sighed. "Leave it. I'll get it."

I started to sort things into tidier piles, but there really was not enough room. I had bought cardboard folders, but they didn't solve the problem of the sheer bulk of documentation I had, and when Hugh was using his computer, there was not enough space for me to work on the table. Laptops aren't designed to be used on laps.

When he had printed out his documents, made corrections, backed them up and reprinted, he said, "By the way, Mum and Dad want us to go over there for drinks on Saturday. And then I thought we could go and see that film."

He had mentioned a new blockbuster, just released, which I was not desperately keen to see as the critics had said that it was very violent. I also needed to check some details with Gavin and Martha, but I supposed we could do that over the phone. And if it made Hugh happy …

He had been in a foul mood the previous night. He seemed to think that starting to make love was like turning on the ignition of a high-performance car, and when it didn't start first time, he got angry. I hadn't had much experience, but I knew that this happened to all men at some time or other, and it wasn't a big deal. But for Hugh it was a big deal. I suppose it threatened his confidence.

It was useless for me to say anything reassuring. That

only made him angrier. He had flung out of bed and got dressed without looking at me. Then he had turned on the TV, leaving me lying there feeling sorry for him but also, if I'm truthful, hurt and rejected.

I'd told myself that things would be better in the morning, but he had been annoyed again, this time because he had overslept and I had taken too long in the bathroom. He had rushed to work after swallowing only half a mug of coffee.

I had been a little late for work, too, but it didn't seem to make much difference whether I was there or not. I was filling a gap in the HR department now, and I seemed to spend most of my time making photocopies.

"Hel-lo? Jaki?"

"Yes?"

"I said, is that OK?"

"What?"

He sighed. "My parents and then the cinema?"

"Sorry. Yes – yes, of course."

***

The Markham-Hunts' house breathed prosperity. Solid and spacious, it had been built in the 1930s with its own tennis court, landscaped garden and rockery, with a view over the river to the church tower in the distance. The interior was always spotless and the central heating was turned up a little too high. The furniture was modern but not very comfortable, a gaudy abstract painting hung over the fireplace in the sitting room and a number of silver cups from golf tournaments stood on a high shelf. What always struck me was the absence of books. My parents' sitting room held two tall, wide bookcases, stuffed tightly with books, but here there was only a small glass-fronted one, and it seemed to contain volumes arranged in series. I had never approached close enough to read the titles.

Hugh's mother, with impeccably streaked blond hair and scarlet nails, had been talking to me at length about the arrangements for the wedding, the venue, the guest list and the flowers. I knew that all these matters would have to be organized, but she seemed so much in her element and that I felt I needn't interfere.

"I must give your mother a ring," she said. "She should come over for coffee very soon so that we can discuss everything properly. She said that you were taking care of your wedding dress. But what about the bridesmaids?"

"Uh ... I'm not sure. My sister – "

"I thought that shell pink would be ideal. You will be in white, of course."

"Oh, maybe not pink," I said hastily. I thought of Maya's face.

Just then, Hugh's father entered the room, carrying the local paper. It was obvious where Hugh got his looks, although his father was considerably heavier and his eyebrows were bushier.

He put the newspaper down on the coffee table and served the drinks. We all had G&Ts, which he made very strong. I remembered that I had eaten very little for lunch, and wished that I had consumed several slices of bread to counteract the alcohol. Too late now.

"So," he said, "how is our future daughter-in-law?"

What was I supposed to say? Hugh and I were next to each other on the sofa, and he put his arm round my shoulders.

"Blooming!" he said. I shifted awkwardly.

I felt as if I were under inspection.

"Blooming, hmm," nodded Mr. Markham-Hunt. "And very active? Almost, I might say, an activist?"

He tapped the newspaper lying on the table.

I had no idea what he was talking about until Hugh reached for the paper.

"Page 6," said his father. "A whole article with your byline, Ms Jacqueline Saunders, and a couple of photographs. If it weren't for the content, perhaps I should congratulate you."

I gasped. The article that I had spent so much time writing was there, in print, together with two of Gavin's photographs. I'd known that he was going to the newspaper office, but nobody had told me that he had persuaded them to accept it.

I felt a thrill. This might make readers pay attention.

"How did you know that was me?" Again, I hadn't used my real name.

"My dear girl, you imagine that I know nothing about you, if you're to marry my son? Saunders was your mother's name."

He had been checking up on me.

Outrage spread through me, but just then my phone beeped with a text. "Take a look at the Herald," it said. It was from Martha.

"You're very eloquent, I'll give you that," said Hugh's father, "but all this is over-dramatized and biased. Climate change? Trees communicating with one another? It's all nonsense, of course. You're talking about a piece of land with some trees on it, that's all. This is Oakfield. You're not saving the planet, you know. You're just disregarding the vital economic need for the new road here, not to mention the wasted potential of an old house with a single old eccentric living in it. Totally unreasonable, totally."

I couldn't let that pass. I started to tell him about the importance of ancient woodland, about carbon sinks, about photosynthesis, about trees that warned other trees of danger, about trees that nourished their young saplings through their roots with precious sugar. I began to rant about roads and traffic eating up the little that remained of the natural landscape. I accused firms like Sacs de Luxe of thinking about nothing but profits and bonuses. I said that the house belonged with the trees and would completely lose its character if they were destroyed.

I interrupted him several times and I think my voice was getting quite loud. Hugh no longer had his arm around my shoulder and I noticed out of the corner of my eye that he was talking quietly and earnestly to his mother on the other side of the room.

I remember shouting, "Think global and act local! We're destroying the planet, and I want to preserve this small part of it."

"All right, all right, babe," said Hugh. I was standing and

he took my empty glass. "We know you feel strongly about all this, but we'd better go if we're to catch that film."

His mother was smiling uneasily, twisting her gold bangle around her wrist.

His father rolled his eyes and shrugged his shoulders, as if to say, "What's the point?"

"Can I have that paper?" I asked.

"Take it. I certainly won't want to read it again."

We left.

As we walked down the drive, Hugh said, "God, Jaki. Did you have to embarrass me like that? I don't know what's got into you these days."

I said nothing. Time was when he would have made a joke, or tried to find out how I really felt.

***

The dress was nearly finished.

I stood in front of the cheval glass, gazing at the reflection of a slim girl with long fair hair who looked very unlike me, clad as she was in a shimmering fall of white silk that caught the morning light in its folds and emphasized curves that I didn't believe I had.

Lily was kneeling on the floor pinning the hem when we heard the front door open, and a second later Gavin walked in.

He stopped and stared. "Wow," he said. "Just – wow." I couldn't make out the expression on his face.

"There," said Lily, sitting back on her heels. "What do you think?"

Exclaiming that it was perfect, wonderful, I grabbed my clothes and hastily went into the gloomy dining room next door to change. My hands were shaking. I had felt Gavin's eyes on my body like a bolt of electricity going through me.

When I returned, Lily was suggesting a coffee in the kitchen, and we passed through the green baize door and along the corridor. The robin and two bluetits flitted out of the window as we entered.

"I liked your article," said Lily, spooning coffee into the

filter paper. "I felt that you really understand how much the trees and the house mean to me. But what will they mean to other people? I don't know that anyone will care much about an eccentric old woman living alone in a big house."

I heard the echo of Hugh's father's words.

Gavin cleared his throat. "I was thinking about that aspect of things," he said. "I think the idea will capture people's imagination. They are going to be curious about you, Lily."

Lily looked hunted for a moment. She fingered her amber beads. "I suppose it's only natural," she said slowly. Her eyes were very dark blue in her pale, lined face. "I can't hide away forever."

"Would you, say, agree to be interviewed?" I asked.

"That's the thing," said Gavin. "I was on the phone to the paper, talking about striking while the iron's hot, and so on. They've had quite a lot of inquiries and they'll publish some letters to the editor. They were talking about sending someone to interview you, but I said – well – I said I knew somebody who could do it very well."

"Oh?"

"I meant you, Jaki."

"Me!"

Lily looked relieved. "Oh, that would be fine. I wouldn't mind talking to you, Jaki. We've talked so much already, and you're an ally."

"I don't think they would pay you, mind," warned Gavin.

"That doesn't matter," Lily and I said in unison. We smiled at each other.

Of course I would do it. It might be effective in winning support – and I could ask Lily some questions that I had been longing to ask for quite some time.

***

Maya and I were sitting on the floor in front of the fire, as we used to do when we were children. Grandad was in the armchair, his hands resting on the handle of his stick. Hugh had been invited over, but he had cried off, saying that he had promised to meet some colleagues to discuss the forthcoming negotiation in Paris.

"So what do you think of Jaki's article?" asked Maya. The paper lay, folded back to the appropriate page, on the table at Grandad's elbow.

"Very interesting. Very well written," said Grandad. "Hrrrm. Have you ever thought about a career in journalism?"

I hadn't. But why not? I had to find something to do, and scarcely anyone else seemed interested in my future working life.

I pointed out that this was my first attempt, that I hadn't had any training, that there were probably qualifications required. But Grandad brushed these objections aside.

"Anything is possible if you want it enough. If you're good, somebody will snap you up."

"She's going to interview Lily Green, the woman who lives all by herself in the Rajah's house," announced Maya, hugging her knees.

"Excellent. I hope that will be published too."

"I can think of lots of questions to ask her," said Maya. "Like: are you a witch? Like: why do you always wear black? Like: why do loads of birds come flying behind you in the street?"

"Do they?" I was surprised. True, birds came into Lily's kitchen and seemed remarkably tame, but after all, she fed them. "Have you seen this happening?"

"Well, not actually seen," admitted Maya. "But some people at school have seen it."

"Hearsay is a dangerous thing," said Grandad. "I hope you don't go spreading gossip."

"No, but," said Maya, "that house in the forest is really weird and creepy, just like a witch's house in a fairy tale, and she's going to let me explore it next time I go."

"I must admit it sounds intriguing." He cast a glance out of the window at the bleak afternoon. "Ah. I miss walking in woods. Even walking in the garden is not so easy now."

"Yes. Grandad nearly fell over again," Maya told me. "You know the tree with the roots that are pushing up the paving stones? He tripped. He didn't fall, but Mum and Dad are talking of chopping it down."

"What!" I sat up straight. "Not the magnolia tree? They can't!"

Only last spring, when I had come home for a few days, the bare branches had been covered in pointed buds, promising a mass of blossom. Somewhere there was a sketch that I had made of it.

"No, no," protested Grandad. "They mustn't cut down a tree because of me. Certainly not. Don't worry, Jaki. I won't let your parents do anything drastic. If necessary, I'll simply stay indoors," he added sadly.

"Duh," said Maya. "Why is it always so difficult to do things? If you had a car, Jaki, you could drive me and Grandad over to the Rajah's house and he could go for a walk in the woods with Lily, and me and you could explore the house. Wouldn't that be cool?"

True, if I had a car, many things would be easier.

"I wonder if Hugh would drive us," I said.

Maya snorted. "He's too busy trying to get promoted. Anyhow, didn't you say that he's in favour of this horrible road that's going to smash right through all the trees and ruin the place?"

"Well, he has reasons," I said. "The firm … His father …"

Maya leaned forward and covered her face with her hands. "Oh my God," she said. "And to think you're going to be a lady who lunches, and goes to business functions and posh dinners with him. What a life."

"Oh, Maya, shut up! It won't be like that!"

"I bet you it will."

"Now, now," said Grandad. "We none of us know what the future holds in store. I don't like to see you two girls quarrelling."

Dad came into the room as we glared at each other.

"Why don't you buy Jaki a car?" demanded Maya.

"Pascal, with your contacts in broadcasting, couldn't you give Jaki some assistance, if she decides to go in for journalism?" said Grandad.

Dad held up his hands under the onslaught. "What's all this? Journalism? Are you serious?"

"Actually, I might be," I said. "What we really need for this operation is some publicity on the radio."

"Splendid idea," said Grandad.

"Well, well," mumbled Dad. "We'll see."

***

I was walking along the corridor at the office, a sheaf of papers under my arm, when my phone rang.

"Hello? Hello?"

Somebody was talking, but the line was very bad.

"Hello?"

"It's Martha," crackled the voice. "We need to talk. We've had a blow."

"A blow? What kind of blow?"

Martha said something unintelligible.

"Hello? You're breaking up. What kind of blow?"

"I said," said Martha, her voice suddenly louder, "Trees First have let us down."

"In what way? How have they let us down?"

"What?"

"HOW HAVE THEY LET US DOWN? THEY HAVEN'T CHANGED THEIR MINDS ABOUT THE ROAD, HAVE THEY?"

A door in the corridor suddenly opened and Hugh stalked out.

"Ssh!" he hissed. "Keep the noise down, can't you? We're in a very important meeting and everyone can hear what you're saying. And I think the chairman recognized your voice. For heaven's sake, Jaki!" He turned and whisked back into the meeting room.

I stood rebuked. I felt like a child scolded by its father. What was I doing here anyway, carrying pointless bits of paper from one floor to another?

I hurried on and found the door ajar to an empty meeting room, where I stood by the window that looked out on to the car park. We had been cut off, and I called Martha back. This time the line was clearer.

"I thought we ought to let you know right away. We were counting so much on Trees First for help. After all, they're a nationwide organization. This seems so unreasonable."

"Can you tell me what they've done?"

"Well, they were all set to campaign for us. They have a budget. They were going to send someone round to check on Oldwood, but when they read Gavin's report they changed their minds. They said they can't give us their support after all."

"Why not?"

"Because – you won't believe this – because when he listed all the various trees, he included the horse chestnuts. And they say that they will protect only native trees, not foreign imports. Horse chestnuts came from India originally, so ... "

"Lily did tell me that. That's awful. They're still trees, aren't they? That's discriminatory!" I said. Horse chestnuts reminded me of Paris.

"Isn't it? So we have to decide what we do now. Can you come to our place tonight for supper and a council of war?"

I had been going to cook steak for Hugh tonight, but the tone of his voice just now still rankled. In any case, he usually came in late. Well, he could fend for himself, or go out to eat. He often did anyway, money being no object for him.

"OK. What time?"

***

Entering their house, chilled after my bike ride, I was met by a delicious smell of cooking. It was the second time that I had been at Gavin and Martha's, and I had already met several environmental activists there. This time there were three there already: Sam, Ryan and Lucy.

"Great, we're all here," said Gavin. "Chuck your parka anywhere – on the sofa. Oh, you didn't need to bring a bottle!"

"Lovely," said Martha. "We all like French wine and it will be perfect with my boeuf en daube."

The food was as good as it smelt, and Gavin poured the wine, joking about getting his next job as a waiter. At least, I hoped he was joking. I knew that Martha worked part-time in the local hotel, the George, but they surely couldn't have a large income. Was he looking for another office job? How long, I wondered, had they lived in this bungalow? And how long had they been together? But those were not the sort of questions I could ask tonight. The atmosphere was warm, casual, friendly, and the lamplight glowed on the cushions whose covers Martha had woven on her loom.

By the time we had cleared our plates, everyone was tossing around ideas about the drive to save Oldwood and fight the road scheme. Bitter remarks were made about Trees First's decision to quit. "Speciesist lot," said Gavin. "Hey, that's difficult to say." We all had a go at pronouncing 'speciesist', after which the conversation became more serious.

"We need to concentrate on fundraising," said Lucy, who had very short hair tinted blue at the tips and round-framed glasses.

"How much have we got so far?" asked Sam, a tall, athletic type.

Gavin and Martha took out some paperwork and there was a discussion about figures. Basically, the answer was, "not enough".

"Lily contributes what she can," said Gavin. "But dressmaking can't bring in much cash, and that house must need a fair bit of maintenance."

I remembered that I hadn't yet paid her anything for my dress. I made a mental note to ask her about the price.

"She must have inherited some money. I have to say, she fascinates me," said Lucy. "Living there all alone."

"She's very independent, but she does need help."

"If only we could get somebody famous to back us," said Ryan, the quiet one.

"Yes, we've thought of that before," Martha agreed.

There was a short silence.

Suddenly, an idea struck me.

"I may know somebody," I said. All heads turned in my

direction. "She's not exactly famous. Well, it was a good few years ago that she had songs in the charts, but I think her records are still available."

"Who's this?" demanded Lucy.

"Have you heard of Stella? She's my aunt. My father's sister."

Gavin's and Martha's eyes lit up, Ryan and Lucy looked blank, and Sam looked puzzled for a moment and then leaned forward enthusiastically. Then some of her song titles were mentioned and after a few minutes everyone could recall something about her.

"*Rain in Another Country*! I absolutely love that song," said Sam. "My father used to play it in the car. Hey, do you think you could recruit her for us?"

"Didn't she sing in French?" asked Lucy.

"Yes, and English too."

"Yes, but," said Gavin, "Hasn't it been years since she sang in public or made a new album? Doesn't she live in France?"

It was true. My aunt Stella had known plenty of ups and downs, typical of showbiz, I supposed, and I believed that she had been 'down' for quite a while. When I was spending my semester in Paris, I had seen her quite regularly. She had encouraged me in my academic work and I knew that she would always be there for me if I needed her, but she had been withdrawn, depressed, unwilling to go anywhere. After three marriages, one of which had ended in divorce in LA, and the other two in widowhood in France, disappointment with life was scarcely surprising. After a period of brilliant success, first in a duo with a star singer called Zorinda and later solo with a different backing group, she was now something of a recluse.

I told them a few details, and there was more reminiscing about 'vintage' music.

"When will you see her again?" asked Ryan.

I didn't know. She had come to England for my grandmother's funeral, looking very pale and subdued. I remembered that she had spent some time shut up with Grandad in his study, and then had returned to France shortly afterwards. What had Grandad said recently? That he was hoping to see her?

"I wonder if she would come over if I asked her," I said.

"Do. And try to get her interested in all this," urged Martha.

I said I would try. It was a long shot. Why would Aunt Stella feel concerned about a piece of woodland in a part of England where she had never lived?

The conversation moved on, and other tactics were discussed, including crowdfunding, although Sam was dubious about that.

"If the worst comes to the worst, we'll pitch a camp," said Gavin. "We'll climb up into the trees and won't come down, so that they can't be felled."

"Oh!" I said. I shivered. "I couldn't possibly do that."

"Why not, Jaki?"

"I don't like heights. I'm terrified of heights, in fact. I think I told you that before."

Gavin looked at me thoughtfully, his eyes greenish grey with flecks of hazel, his face lean. "But trees are all about height. Growing upwards towards the light. Think of the birds, up there in the canopy, under the sky, and the treetops all swaying in the wind. It's beautiful up there."

"I'm sure it is, but I'd rather be at ground level."

"Hmm. I wonder if you could change your mind. I'd love you to feel differently."

What was that to him? I thought defensively. I had always been scared of heights. I might love the shapes of trees and know how important they were to the ecosystem, but that didn't make me want to be up there on top of one.

In my parka pocket, my phone buzzed with a text message and I stood up to check it.

What time are you thinking of coming home? Some of us have to get up early.

I hadn't thought about Hugh since arriving. Now I felt guilty, and began hastily making excuses and getting ready to leave.

"I'll run you over there," said Gavin. "It's too windy to

cycle. You can stick the bike in the back of the van."

We left to a chorus of goodbyes and voices urging me to contact Stella. I was sorry to go, but it was true: the hour was late, and although the Sacs de Luxe offices stood silent and empty, their neon lights off, they would be waiting to engulf us tomorrow morning – to engulf me, and no doubt to welcome Hugh as if he belonged there.

***

Hugh and I lay in bed side by side after rather perfunctory sex. The modern bedside light made a circle on the ceiling.

"I'd say that was a six," he said.

"Or a five," I said, and immediately regretted it.

He shifted irritably. "You don't seem to realize how tired I am with all that's been going on. Meetings, negotiations … We have to win the Paris contract, and then there's the takeover threat."

"Mmm," I said, trying to sound sympathetic.

"Are you making plans for this wedding, anyhow? You could even start house-hunting. I absolutely haven't got time at the moment. But you always seem to be off with your revolutionary friends, whoever they are."

"Not really revolutionary. Just concerned about – "

"Yes, about the road scheme and that old house. You keep talking about that. And babe, are you deliberately trying to get on the wrong side of my parents? Because if you're not, you could have fooled me."

"Of course I'm not." I got out of bed and began to dress. "But your father is so – so money-minded."

"Money-minded! He cares about what's best for the economy, and so do I. And what's good for local business is good for you and me. You'd better not forget that." He sat up, his hair tousled.

"Oh, you don't need to boast about your family's money. I know you're rolling in it, you always have been, whereas I'm bowed down with debt."

"I mean the firm. The future of the firm!" he snapped.

Then he sighed. "Just don't talk like that, babe, OK? You know we'll both be comfortably off, and we're not students any more. You'll have a nice house, good clothes and stuff. You won't have to work if you don't want to, you'll have time – "

"Time for what? Coffee mornings? Shopping? Time is what I want now. Time for something worthwhile. For my own interests."

"But don't you see that your so-called interests are diametrically opposed to our interests?"

"Oh, don't twist words. I'm not talking about things that are in my interest. I mean what interests me!"

Before we knew it, we were having a row. Of course we had had rows before, but nothing serious, and after some shouting and tears we always made it up with passionate sex. But sex hadn't been so great recently, particularly for Hugh. I knew he was under a lot of pressure. Perhaps he was also feeling stressed about the wedding. Well, so was I, when I thought about it. I wished our mothers were not so keen on organizing a grand occasion. However, it was hard for me to feel sorry for him. Why couldn't he see that I really cared about saving Oldwood from this criminal plan to build yet another road, when most of the country was tarmacked over with roads, and the main purpose of the road was to boost Sacs de Luxe's profits? Surely he could see beyond the bottom line?

Eventually he also got dressed, stopped answering me and slammed out of the flat.

I half expected to hear his key in the door five minutes later. He would come in, kiss me and say, "Come on, babe. Let's not quarrel. We can work this out."

But he didn't come back.

***

It always surprised me that Lily left her front door unlocked. Gavin, Martha or I could walk in whenever we felt like it, and apparently she wasn't afraid of intruders. Of course, we always phoned her beforehand.

Now, with my little electronic recorder in my bag, I was coming to interview her for the local paper.

"They couldn't spare one of their reporters," Gavin had told me. "They're on to some story at the moment. Something about a huge bird that has been seen around the town."

It didn't sound like a very important story, but then, Oakfield was not a large town, and if it meant that I had a proper journalistic assignment, then that was fine by me.

"Lily?" I called as I stepped into the hall.

Silence. Nothing moved, and the air was still, scented as always with a hint of rose and jasmine. The clock ticked. Was that a faint sigh? Old houses made strange quiet sounds, the timbers shifting, perhaps mice behind the panelling.

"Lily?" I called louder.

"I'm upstairs," came her distant voice. "Come up."

It was the first time that I had climbed the wide staircase, my feet clumping on the oak treads, the banister smooth under my hand. I passed a half-landing and found myself in a corridor of closed doors. I walked along the soft carpet and turned a corner, and there a door stood open.

Lily sat sewing in a low chair where the morning light streamed through the window. White silk flowed over her knees. This must be her workroom: a sewing machine on a table, a dressmaker's dummy, another cheval mirror as tall as an arched doorway with Art Nouveau tracery at the top, and around the walls a number of ornately carved wooden chests and cabinets.

She looked up as I entered and removed her gold-rimmed spectacles.

"I've been thinking," she said, "about what I could possibly say in an interview. I can't believe that anyone will be very interested."

"They will!" I said with conviction. I told her that I had prepared some questions but that she was free to talk about anything she liked. She shook her head doubtfully, but asked me to sit down, and I perched on a carved stool.

"Is that my dress?"

She held it out for my inspection. She had been embroidering the bodice with a pattern of green and silver leaves. A vague memory came to me of something that Mum had said, about green being unlucky at weddings. What nonsense. Perhaps the bridesmaids could wear full-length green dresses. Now, that would be an interesting departure from custom.

"It's beautiful," I said. "I suppose it's nearly ready?"

"Nearly," said Lily. "But are you ready for it?"

That was an odd question and I didn't answer it. I took out my recorder, opened my notebook and ran my pen down the list of questions I had prepared for her.

"Could I ask you to speak into the microphone?"

"You could ask, certainly." I took that for a yes.

"So you've told me that this house was inherited by your grandfather, and that people used to call him the Rajah because your grandmother was Indian."

"Yes, and because of his connections with India, trading in antiques. Some of them are still here." She waved her hand at the furniture. "These are walnut wood," she said.

"And your father?"

"My father – " She broke off as if pondering. "My father was an only child. He was ... He should never have married my mother, who was French. The marriage was doomed, I think. When I was only five years old, he abandoned her and took me away with him ... I don't think she ever recovered ... She didn't live long."

Lily's voice grew quieter and full of pain. I felt guilty for probing, but journalists had to ask questions.

"You were only five! Didn't she try to get you back?"

"It was impossible. We weren't in France. We weren't in England. He took me to India, and we disappeared."

"Why did he do that?"

"To punish her, I think. He never actually wanted a child, but it turned out that he – could use me."

"Do you remember that time?"

"Remember?" Her face twisted. "Of course I do. But Jaki, I thought we were going to talk about the house and the trees."

"Yes, yes, we are. Sorry. About the house – so it's partly Victorian? Could you show me around, do you think?"

She rose and laid the dress carefully aside, a needle piercing an exquisitely embroidered green leaf. I stood to follow her out of the room, and as I glanced back I thought I saw in the mirror – but it was nothing. A trick of the light.

She took me through a concealed door on the landing and up the back stairs to the servants' attics, which still contained iron bedsteads and wash-stands, the dormer windows overlooking the treetops. Here and there, at corners, narrow doorways led to tiny turret rooms whose purpose wasn't apparent. I wouldn't have been surprised to see a spinning wheel in one of them. Then we were back in the corridor and another wing.

"This was the schoolroom, and the night nursery was next door. My grandfather had two elder sisters, Alice and Florence, both born in Calcutta. But they were long gone, grown up and married, by the time I came back here. I never knew them."

The children's rooms were very bare, with bars at the windows, but the schoolroom contained an ornately painted rocking horse which Lily told me was Indian. I stared at it enviously, never having owned a rocking horse. Had Alice and Florence enjoyed riding on it?

In the bathroom, with its black and white tiled floor, a bathtub with clawed feet had pride of place. Next door was the lavatory – "water-closet", I thought – with a mahogany seat and a cistern with a chain.

The bedrooms Lily opened one by one, giving me a quick glimpse of each. They also contained oddments of carved furniture, faded rugs, blinds pulled down. Her own room, I saw was sparsely furnished, almost Spartan. On the mantelpiece over the empty grate I noticed a small, dark statuette. I would have liked to look more closely, but Lily was already leading the way downstairs.

I knew the morning room, the library and the rather gloomy dining room with red damask wallpaper. Now Lily took me to her grandfather's study, which still contained an old rolltop desk and glass fronted bookcases. Reflections on the glass prevented me from seeing if they contained any books. There was a chill in the air and a very faint scent of tobacco. We passed into the billiard room, which no longer contained a billiard table, and into the music room, where all that remained of music were some music stands clustered in a corner and an upholstered piano stool. Apart from the occasional cabinet or chest, all the rooms were remarkably empty.

"And this is the drawing room," she said, opening another door. The spacious room had a parquet floor and plaster mouldings around the ceiling, but no furniture at all. Beyond it was a glassed-in conservatory.

"It used to contain palms in brass pots, and orange trees in tubs," said Lily. Nothing remained of them.

I noticed that there was very little dust anywhere, and no cobwebs that I could see. Again I wondered whether a cleaner came regularly from the town.

"So you see," said Lily, standing in the hall. "Oldwood Court is not what it was – no longer a family home. Over the years, nearly all its contents have been sold. Otherwise I could never have afforded to stay here."

"And you want to stay here?"

"While I can. This house was my refuge – is my refuge. It has taken me in, welcomed me. I feel at peace here – or, rather, I felt at peace. You know that things have changed."

I grimaced. "The latest is that planning permission has been granted for the new road, and an agreement has been signed with the contractor," I said. "We won't let it happen! But what about the house? What's happening about the hotel project?"

"I've been approached," said Lily wearily. "First a letter, then two phone calls, then a visit from a businessman who tried to charm me. I said no. He offered me a large sum of money. I refused again. He told me to think about it, and went away."

"This house wouldn't want to be a hotel," I said, and then wondered why I had said such a thing.

"No," agreed Lily, "but he was offering a lot of money. He seemed to know that I was reaching the end of my resources."

"So you still refused?"

"So I still refused. But if the council decides on a compulsory purchase, then it will be all over. The spirit of the place will die."

"I wonder," I said slowly, "whether the spirit of the house depends on your living in it." Was that a silly thing to say?

Lily looked at me. Her eyes were remarkably blue. "There is a bond," she said. "But a bond can also mean that one is bound, a prisoner."

The thought of Hugh crossed my mind; the marriage bond; till death us do part. My ring finger tingled. Was she talking about me?

"At present, the house and I are one. Intertwined. But if things change, they have to change for the better, don't you agree?"

"Uh … yes," I said, feeling rather out of my depth.

Lily suddenly went to the front door and flung it open, letting in a surge of fresh air, the scent of damp earth, a snatch of birdsong coming from the depths of the wood.

"It's a beautiful day," she said. "Why don't we walk among the trees?"

She took a dark grey cloak from an alcove and we set out, Lily confidently leading along one of the little winding paths. She walked quickly, unhindered by hard tree roots under our feet or the occasional bramble that clutched at our sleeves. When we came to a place where two paths crossed, she paused, looking up at a group of silver birches, their feathery tops dazzlingly white against the blue sky. My head swam again at the height, but at the same time their sheer perfection, like fountains in the air, gave me a profound feeling of wellbeing. I must try to find them again and sketch them.

"I expect you know every inch of this place," I said. "How big is it, in fact?"

"Ah, well," said Lily. "How big? That depends."

Depends on what? I thought. How many hectares?

Somebody must know, if the plans had been approved. Hadn't there been a map in the paper? But Lily was walking on.

"Here are the beeches." She placed her hand caressingly on a smooth trunk. "Seven of them here. The same species tend to grow together. Had you noticed? It's because they all help one another. They depend on one another. Under all this moss, their roots interconnect and feed one another with energy."

The roots that were visible above ground spread like fingers gripping the soil, with dark cave-like spaces between them; hidey-holes for squirrels' nuts, perhaps. Thin young saplings pushed up from the leaf mould.

"And the tips of their branches just meet, as if they were holding hands," I said, looking up. It was, I thought, as if the trees were performing a very slow dance, a dance lasting for years, so slow that we busy human beings were scarcely aware of it. Yet a chainsaw could bring down a centuries-old tree in a matter of minutes. I imagined the whole wood loud with chainsaws, the rumble of diggers, men in hard hats and high visibility jackets shouting to one another, the fertile humus of the forest floor churned up as mud. Branches still covered with leaves and buds crashing to the ground, not yet aware that they were doomed. I had seen so many reports of illegal logging.

We emerged in the clearing with the lake and the weeping willow, and sat down in the sunshine on the low wall.

"You said that the trees help one another with energy," I said, holding out my recorder. "How far do you think they can defend themselves?"

"They can defend themselves against certain things, like attacks by deer that eat bark, or infestations of parasites. But their energy isn't strong enough to defend them against loggers."

"So what is this energy, exactly?"

"Exactly?" She mused. "You could say that it's a form of electricity." She laughed a little. "I used to have a problem with electricity, years ago. It took me a long time to learn to control it."

"Control electricity?"

"A form of it, yes. Or control my relationship with it."

I wondered where this interview was going. Lily could be very enigmatic.

"What else would you, personally, recommend that we do to defend this place? To try and save it – all of it – from the developers?"

"You've already done a great deal, you and Gavin and Martha and the others, with your leaflets and petitions. I know how hard you are trying. The place is old and strong. There was another house, Tudor, on the site where my great-grandfather built the present one, and it's not entirely gone. As for the trees, he planted some of them, but the rest have been here for – oh – centuries. Ancient woodland, they call it."

"I can't bear the thought of so much destruction."

"Nor can I. I'm strong too. I can hold this place together, and I have help, but I need more help. I hope it will come. Defending it uses up my energy and is very, very tiring, you see."

How old was Lily? I wondered. I didn't like to ask.

Suddenly a male blackbird burst out of the undergrowth with a shrill alarm cry and made straight for Lily. It perched on her shoulder, gripping the cloth of her cloak, one gold-rimmed eye peering skywards.

A great dark shadow passed overhead, so fast that I barely had time to duck.

"What on earth was that?"

"Nothing to worry about," said Lily, soothing the frightened bird, which was now flicking its tail and making a chinking noise. It perched on her wrist.

Could it have been an eagle? All the trees shook in a sudden gust of wind.

CHAPTER FIVE

Something was amiss in the office.

I overheard snatches of muttered conversation. People sat staring intently at their computer screens. Apparently an email had come through from top management, addressed to all administrative staff, but naturally nothing had been addressed to me. I finished filing some invoices, delivered a bunch of photocopies to somebody's desk and stood gazing out of the window at the rain. It glistened on the roof of the workshops, in which I had never set foot. That was where the real work of designing and putting together the bags took place, as opposed to this office drudgery where I felt that I was doing nothing of any importance. I was almost transparent. What was I doing there at all? Snatches of poetry drifted through my idle mind: Rimbaud, Jacques Prévert …

The rain slid down the windows, blurring the view of the workshops and, beyond them, the warehouse and the lorry park. Should I get another coffee from the machine?

"Look busy!" came an urgent whisper, and like everyone else I hurried back to my desk and hunched over the screen. A director had entered the office at the far end and was having a consultation with two other people.

Something was definitely going on, but I wasn't sure that I cared. No doubt Hugh would tell me about it later.

I checked my personal email, as I did every day, but as usual there were no favourable replies to any of my job applications. Many received no reply at all. I had continued to scan Situations Vacant, but with less and less enthusiasm. I felt as if my student debts loomed at my back like a mountain that might one day collapse and crush me. Why did nobody want me? What was the point of my even being in the world?

Hugh wants me, I told myself.

But that evening, when I let myself into the flat and found

Hugh already sitting at his computer, he didn't look up. When I went to stand behind him and leaned forward to kiss the side of his neck, he made an irritable movement of his head. "I just … " he said. His eyes never left the screen, and he typed something.

"Just what?"

No reply.

Oh, well. I wouldn't waste time but would start immediately to type up my interview with Lily. I went to find my recorder and knocked a piece of paper off the table as I brushed past. Hugh clicked his tongue and bent to pick it up, still without saying anything.

I set up the recorder and my headphones and prepared to type. I scrolled forward and back, peered at the screen, checked the connection, turned up the volume to white noise and down again. I couldn't believe it.

Nothing at all had been recorded.

Could I remember enough of our conversation to produce a faithful record of it? I felt hot, then cold.

Hugh looked up then, his eyes like gimlets.

"Why do you keep swearing?"

"Because this bloody thing doesn't work. Hasn't worked. It fucking well hasn't recorded."

"Have you charged the battery?"

"Yes." Duh! I'm not that stupid. "Something must be wrong with it."

"Oh? Well, what do you want me to do about it? There are more serious things, you know."

"This is serious. It's really serious. I've been asked to conduct an interview that could mean all the difference between life and death for thousands of trees!" I knew I was exaggerating, but I was so upset with my electronic gadget that I couldn't help it.

"Trees!" he snorted. "Babe, I've just about had it up to here with trees. I don't want to hear any more about them right now, OK? Talk about life and death – what's been happening could really mean life or death."

"Why? What has happened? Something at work?"

"Yes."

"What?"

He groaned. "It's too complicated to explain. Anyhow, you wouldn't understand."

"I wouldn't understand? Why, because I'm too stupid?"

"No, because you don't understand anything about finance and economics. Now, please, just let me concentrate on this."

I felt dismissed. He wasn't going to explain about the upheaval that had made everyone so worried in the office. Whatever was on his computer screen was more important to him than giving me his full attention for five minutes. Sometimes it felt as if we were on different planets. Tears sprang to my eyes, but I turned away so that he couldn't accuse me of making a scene.

I would have to write up the interview, but now my thoughts were all jumbled.

I decided to go into the bedroom and try to phone my aunt Stella.

Would she be at home? Probably. She seldom went out in the evenings nowadays. In the receiver, I heard the repeated single ring tone of the French exchange, unlike the brr-brr of English landlines.

"'Allo?"

"Stella?" We had dropped the 'aunt' during my time in Paris.

"Jaki! How lovely to hear from you!"

Her voice was so full of warmth and affection that it was too much for me. I couldn't speak for a moment, and then I wiped my eyes and gulped out a few phrases.

She immediately wanted to know what was wrong, but I couldn't tell her. I didn't really know myself. There were so many things: I had no job, I didn't know where I belonged, Hugh seemed to have become a different person – and there was the awful threat hanging over Oldwood Court.

I seized on that subject and poured out the whole story: the road, the trees, the old house, Lily's plight, the need to do something.

"I know you could help," I urged her. "You're still part

of everyone's memories. Those years – you could make a comeback. If you threw your weight behind this campaign, I know we could win. You would be such a help. Please, please, Stella."

"Oh … I don't think so." I could picture her in her Paris flat overlooking the Parc Montsouris, the pale, stylish furniture, the vivid paintings on the walls, her collection of guitars.

"Please come over to England and see for yourself. If only you could see the place, you would understand. And then there's Grandad. I know he's longing to see you." I clutched at every argument I could think of, but although she was concerned about me, she wouldn't say yes. I sensed a great listlessness in her when I mentioned singing. Yet singing had been her world. Surely her world could not have changed that much?

Suddenly the bedroom door opened and Hugh stuck his head in.

"Jaki, I can hardly hear myself think with you jabbering in French at the top of your voice. Would you please keep the noise down?"

"Jabbering?"

He had never been good at languages. Oh, but was this the same Hugh who used to cycle with me to visit friends, who used to sit with us eating and drinking on the floor, who had stayed up all night with me and then made love in the first grey light of dawn – and then realized that there was only a spoonful of coffee left in the house, and we had shared it? We had made pancakes once at my parents' house, and he had insisted on tossing them. One had stuck to the ceiling. He had been fun, in those days. We had made plans to travel the world, and had argued fiercely about politics.

I felt that the world was tilting and I might slide off it.

I had to get away.

"Where are you going?"

"I'm going out for a bit. I'll leave you in peace."

***

It was nearly dark, not a good time to be cycling along the dual carriageway. I had set off at a fast pace, paying little attention to where I was heading, going over in my head the short-tempered words from Hugh, the fruitless conversation with my aunt. An endless stream of cars overtook me, their headlights throwing my shadow forward on the road, their tail lights dwindling red in the distance. I wanted to get away from that cramped flat. It was too small for the two of us. Would things improve once we had our own house? A sinking feeling of doubt hit me in the stomach, and I slowed down. I had been refusing to face it, but the fact was that Hugh had changed. He had left university a year ahead of me. He had had a year's head start in the corporate world, and I couldn't easily follow him there.

Where was I going? Half consciously I had started out on the way to my parents' house, but I couldn't go there. I couldn't face Mum and tell her that I had had a row with Hugh. She would ask questions; she would try to persuade me that I was wrong and should put things right. She had always been so pleased that I was going to marry my childhood sweetheart, and she had a soft spot for that fine boy Hugh Markham-Hunt. She thought that everything would be roses and wedding bells.

No, I couldn't go to my parents' house. Anyway, there was no room for me to stay there. Grandad was occupying my room.

Should I turn back? I hesitated, swerved slightly, and a car's horn blared at me as it shot past

My hands were cold, my head ached and I was hungry. Where could I go?

I took the next turning and came eventually to the long, high stone wall of Oldwood Court. I pedalled slowly and stopped at the great gates. It was very dark inside; the drive led away between the looming trees into blackness. What was the time? I squinted at my watch. Could I possibly phone Lily at this time of night? I would have to phone from outside the gates. I knew that I couldn't get a signal once I was inside.

The phone rang and rang. Oh God, if she didn't answer,

what was I going to do?

Then I heard her voice, faint and distant as always.

I don't know what I said, but then the iron gates were opening and I was speeding along the lime avenue. I felt that the trees were lining up to welcome me, forming a long triumphal arch above me, as breathlessly I cycled towards the yellow rectangle of a lighted window, partly obscured by tree branches. There ahead was light and warmth and comfort, and I was going towards it.

Lily didn't seem at all surprised or put out to see me. After one glance at my face, she led the way across the softly lighted hall and through the green baize door to the kitchen.

"I usually eat here when I'm alone," she said. "I was about to get some supper. Could you fancy an omelette?"

I was suddenly ravenous. I offered to help, but she made me sit at the scrubbed table while she glided deftly about, taking plates from a cupboard, whisking eggs. Just before serving the omelette with salad, she produced a bottle of Bordeaux and poured us each a glass.

"Here's to friendship," she said.

I could drink to that. Lily was much older than me, but why should that matter? I realized how distant my former friends seemed. Old friends from school and uni were scattered and leading their own lives. I sometimes chatted to people on social media, but those were not true friends. My life had become utterly bound up with Hugh, to the exclusion of other rewarding relationships – except perhaps my new-found friends, Gavin and Martha and the rest of the environmentalist crowd. Nobody at the office was on my wavelength.

"Let me guess," said Lily when we had finished eating. "You've had a quarrel with your fiancé."

I found myself pouring out feelings that I scarcely knew I had: hurt, disappointment, frustration, fear of the future.

"I feel as if things that I don't want are closing in on me," I told her at last.

She was quiet for a few moments, looking at me. "Take some time," she said. "You're safe here. Would you like to stay the night?"

I protested that I couldn't put her to so much trouble, that it wasn't necessary, that Hugh would worry if I didn't return to the flat.

"So let him worry a little. It won't hurt him. Perhaps he will start asking himself some questions. There is plenty of room here, and I can easily make up a bed."

I began to waver. Did I really want to cycle all the way back in the dark? If I did, would he rant at me for coming back so late? Would he cross-examine me? Hell, I thought, why not take a night off? Lily was very kind.

I accepted her offer.

"Oh, and I forgot to tell you," I said. "I wanted to type up the interview you gave me, but I couldn't. Nothing was recorded. It was just a blank. There must be something wrong with my recorder."

"I'm so sorry."

"It's not your fault."

"Well, I'm afraid it may be … Would you like to start again and take notes on paper?"

What did she mean by saying that it might be her fault? Gadgetry malfunctioned. All right – notes it would have to be. And perhaps she would give me some answers that I would simply keep in my memory.

"You don't have broadband here, do you? Or even a computer?"

"No," she laughed.

"So how do you – ?"

"I listen to the radio and I read newspapers. In fact, in today's paper there are some letters to the editor in response to your article. Have you seen them?" She took the folded Herald from a chair and opened it to the letters page.

Environmentalist claptrap, I read. My eye travelled down the newsprint and I saw the signature at the bottom: Aubrey Markham-Hunt. Oh, God. Hugh's father. I read the body of the letter with growing agitation. Misguided … unrealistic … retrograde … wilfully ignorant of the needs of local industry …

"He hates me," I said.

"I don't suppose he hates you, but he is certainly adopting a different angle. There may be many others who think as he does. But look, there's another letter."

The next one strongly supported our cause: The environment ... climate change ... heritage ... irreplaceable ancient woodland ... the tyranny of motor traffic.

"I think the paper is trying to be balanced, at least," said Lily.

The readership was probably split down the middle. I must try to bring them over to our side.

"I must get this interview written up. Could we – I know it's late, but – could we try to do it again tonight?"

Lily raised no objections, and I began making notes on some sheets of paper that she took from a drawer. Some of my previous questions came back to me, and I jotted down particulars about her great-grandfather and her grandfather, the history of the house, the tree species that were already in place and those that had been planted, the wildlife that had found refuge in the woods. "Red squirrels," I wrote. The carbon dioxide that the trees absorbed, and the fumes that would be produced by cars and lorries on the proposed road. Eventually I thought I had enough to make an interview of reasonable length.

I yawned and stretched. "I won't put this in writing," I said, "but don't you find it lonely, living here all alone?"

Lily gazed at me thoughtfully. "Lonely? No. But are we ever alone?"

I felt a shiver. Were we not alone? Behind me and beyond me, the house loomed, its rooms and corridors empty. Nothing moved. The lines from Walter de la Mare came into my mind, about the host of phantom listeners, thronging the faint moonbeams on the dark stair that went down to the empty hall.

"Are there ghosts? Are you ever afraid?"

"I'm not afraid of ghosts," said Lily, rising from her seat. "This house has a kindly spirit, I think. There are only shadows here."

Only shadows. Dark shadows.

"Come," said Lily. "You're tired. Let's go upstairs and I'll find some sheets and blankets."

The room she chose for me was smaller than the others, with a window flanked by heavy tapestry curtains in red and gold, overlooking the front porch. It contained a wide mahogany sleigh bed, a chest of drawers with a swing mirror on top of it, a crimson and blue rug on the floor, and nothing else. Together we put clean sheets and blankets on the bed, and she lent me two rather threadbare towels. Without more ado, she wished me goodnight.

The bedroom door closed softly behind her.

What was I doing here? How had I got myself into this situation? Could I sleep in this strange bed? I felt for my phone in my bag. I ought at least to let Hugh know where I was. Then I remembered that there was no network coverage. What would he say? Would he be furious?

I went to the window. The lime avenue stretched away towards the gates, invisible from where I stood. Above the treetops I could see pinpricks of stars. What were my troubles compared to the everlasting stars and the slow, slow, steady presence of the trees, growing together, the tips of their branches touching one another in their long and stately dance?

I might as well sleep.

***

I slept surprisingly well in the strange bed, only half waking once or twice when I heard an owl hooting.

I awoke with a jerk and went to draw back the curtains on a damp, misty morning. I wished I had a toothbrush, but I made the best hasty toilet that I could in the old-fashioned bathroom, got dressed in yesterday's clothes and quickly ran a comb through my hair. The glass in the swing mirror was mottled with age and my reflection was indistinct. I probably looked a fright.

"Coffee?" asked Lily as I hurried into the kitchen. A delicious smell of fresh bread filled the air. I knew that she made her own.

She sat opposite me, neatly dressed in her usual black with the amber necklace, sipping green tea as I breakfasted.

"Lily," I said, "I keep meaning to say this. You must tell me how much I owe you for the dress. I realize you can't have much of an income. Do many people come to you to have dresses made?"

"Some. Not so many. Some change their minds and never collect the dresses."

"Really? Why ever not?"

She shook her head. "Something scares them away, I suppose."

"But that's awful! So much work for nothing."

"I have help," said Lily. She had said this before, and I was never quite sure what she meant. "And in any case, your dress is not yet finished. There is no hurry. You must wait until you are ready."

"But – " I felt embarrassed. "How do you manage for money?"

She poured more tea. "When my grandfather left me this house, he left all its contents to me. It was full of precious antiques, and I have gradually sold them. I have tried to find Indian buyers, so that the things can go back to India where they belong. Of course, there are not very many left to sell."

"And when they are all gone, what will you do?"

She shrugged her shoulders, looking very French for a moment. "Who knows? Things will change. They always do. And I feel there may be big changes coming."

"But not the changes for the worse that we're fighting!" I said fiercely. "Heavens, is that the time? I must get to work."

I offered to wash up the breakfast things, but she wouldn't let me, and soon I was on my way, cycling back down the lime avenue, where mist lingered in the upper branches, but there was a definite hint of sun behind the clouds. The air was fresh, robins and blackbirds were singing and I could hear a woodpigeon cooing somewhere far away. Spring was surely coming. It was tempting to dismount and wander off among the trees, some of which were already coming into bud.

Instead, I cycled resolutely on to join the morning traffic

and had reached the factory car park before I thought to check my phone.

Two missed calls and five text messages, all from Hugh, demanding with increasing urgency to know where I was.

I hurried into the open-plan office and switched on my current computer. A few cursory "good mornings" came my way. I couldn't really phone Hugh and explain everything from here. If he had had his own office, I could have gone there, but he was hot-desking around the building.

Suddenly Hugh was standing opposite me, his face a mixture of relief, concern and irritation. "For God's sake!" he said. Then: "Come down to the coffee machine."

We confronted each other as the coffee machine rumbled. I didn't want another so early in the day. I remembered that this was where I had first really talked to Gavin.

When I told him where I had spent the night, he looked incredulous, but I think he believed me.

"Look, babe, I'm sorry about last night. I was on edge. Things have been quite difficult, but I shouldn't take it out on you."

"There isn't really room for two of us in the flat."

"OK, it's small, but we'll manage. When we're married, everything will be better, I promise you."

I sniffed.

"Look, tonight let's go out. Let's go and do something nice, all right?"

"I can't tonight. I have to write up my interview with Lily Green."

"Lily Green! You're obsessed with that woman!"

I began to turn away.

"No, look – all right, tonight we'll have a quiet night in, and you can do your writing. Then tomorrow we'll go somewhere, OK?"

I shrugged. "OK."

"And I'll tell you what," he added, his voice intimate, "Next week I have to go to Paris for the negotiations. You could come too. We'll have a romantic few days in Paris. How about it?"

Paris! I wasn't sure about romance, but I could go to see

Stella. I could talk to her face to face.

"All right," I said, "Lovely!" I smiled up at him. It was a kind gesture.

He gave me a quick peck on the cheek.

I wondered whether he had seen his father's letter in the paper.

***

This time I succeeded in typing up the interview. I read it through, made some corrections, read it again, made more alterations. I wanted Lily to come across as a brave defender of a precious piece of the natural landscape, with a perfect right to continue to live in her own unique house. When I judged that it would do, I emailed it to Gavin to be submitted to the editor. I wanted to phone him immediately afterwards, but I felt awkward phoning in front of Hugh, so in my email I asked whether he had a photo of Lily to accompany the text.

A message pinged back that he had a good one.

I sent him a thumbs-up.

While I was typing, Hugh had been moving restlessly around the flat, switching on the TV, switching it off again, poking at his phone, getting a glass of water. I wished he would sit still.

When I looked up, he said, "Finished now?"

"I think so."

"You know, I'm glad you've found something to interest you, I really am, but it seems to be taking up an awful lot of your time."

"Well," I said, "that makes two of us who are busy." I tried not to sound aggressive. I could have retorted that his work was taking up far too much of his time.

"So are you coming to bed?"

Just then another email pinged from Gavin. Was I free on Friday morning? he asked. He was going to Oldwood to take some more photographs. We could discuss things.

Friday wasn't a working day for me, so I said that I would meet him there.

Hugh sighed. "I thought you'd finished. Babe, are you coming to bed or not?"

I stood up slowly, hoping that it wouldn't rain on Friday.

***

Friday dawned clear and mild, a true early spring day. I left my bike just inside the gates and breathed in deeply, filling my lungs with the clean air. How could I describe the scent of it? It smelt of the morning, leaf mould, rainwater, pine needles, decay, new life, freshness. It was the unique smell of woods and forests, and in particular of this wood. The pale sunlight slanted down between the tree trunks. Birdsong echoed faintly.

Gavin hadn't said where he would be, but I felt sure I would find him, and I set off with my sketch pad along one of the winding paths.

A clump of primroses glimmered palely at the foot of a beech tree. Wood anemones shivered delicately in a slight breeze, and I thought that early fronds of bracken would soon begin to uncurl. By summer the bracken would surely be waist-high. But would it all still be here in the summer? How soon was the work of destruction due to begin?

Gavin would probably know, but there was no sign of him. I had been walking for about a quarter of an hour and could see nothing but trees in all directions. Both the lime avenue and the wall were out of sight. One could very probably get lost in here, I thought. Lily no doubt knew the place by heart, but I didn't. I wasn't worried, however. "I can't see the wood for the trees," I thought, and grinned. The woods seemed to breathe peacefulness, calm and graceful indifference to the turmoil of our human lives. Nothing mattered except their pure existence, 'Annihilating all that's made/To a green thought in a green shade,' I quoted Marvel to myself. Not that there was much green yet, apart from the moss and the ivy, but buds were swelling and preparing to burst into leaf. The Japanese took 'forest baths', I remembered reading, to restore themselves to sanity and peace of mind.

I stopped walking, to still the rustling of my footsteps.

"Coo-ee!" I called. A distant echo came back "Coo-ee!" but it was only an echo.

I could sketch some of these glades, I thought, and made as if to sit on a fallen branch. But then I heard it, not a voice calling, but distant piping. Gavin was there and must have heard me.

Guided by the sound, I made my way towards him. This time the path seemed to lead straight on, never looping around in a circle, and when I came to a group of dark yews, I saw him above me, a slight figure sitting astride a reddish horizontal branch.

"Come up," he said. "There are footholds on the other side of the trunk."

But I shook my head and said that it was too high, so he pushed his penny whistle into the inner pocket of his jacket and scrambled down, jumping the last few feet. His camera case lay at the foot of the tree.

"I call this the sacred grove," he said. "The ancients always had sacred groves. Sometimes I like to play music for the dryads."

I thought how Hugh would scoff if he could hear such a remark.

"I've noticed how trees of the same species tend to grow together," I said.

"Birds of a feather. They help one another. And these yews may have been here for a thousand years."

"A thousand? Really?" Could the wood be so old?

"Yews can live for thousands of years. You know how they grow in churchyards? Well, often the yews were there before the churches were even built."

"In the Oakfield churchyard, they're growing in a straight line. That doesn't seem very natural," I objected.

"Those are young. Maybe a few hundred years old. But have you seen the one on the south side of the church? It's magnificent, and really, really ancient."

I hadn't noticed it, and he said that he would have to show it to me.

He had submitted my interview to the paper, he told

me, but its publication might be delayed. The story about the huge bird was still making headlines, and eyewitnesses were claiming that it had at least a twelve-foot wingspan. Ornithologists were pooh-poohing the possibility. No photographs of it were available yet.

"So have you taken some more photographs yourself?"

The idea was to produce a glossy pamphlet, with extracts from my writing and an eye-catching cover decorated with a delicate leaf and branch design by Martha. He showed me some of his shots from this morning.

"We could also put in another of your pen-and-ink sketches," he said.

We were wandering on through the woodland, and as we talked I glance to right and left, always looking for the perfect subject to sketch. Catkins dangled from hazel twigs. He pointed out more primroses and said that in May there would be bluebells.

"Does your camera work properly in here?" I asked suddenly. "No technical hitches?"

"It does now," said Gavin. "It didn't at first, but when I told Lily about it, she did something. I'm not sure what. I couldn't really see. Anyway, since then it's been working perfectly."

I told him about my recording device's malfunction, and he didn't seem particularly surprised. We chatted about this and that, and I asked whether he ever got lost in here. No, he told me; the paths always led him back to a place that he knew, even though "there is no road through the woods".

"I learned that poem in school," I told him delightedly. Who was it by? Kipling, that was it.

"So did I." He looked at me thoughtfully.

It felt like a gossamer link between us. Where had he gone to school? What had his life been like before we met? I wanted to know. Don't be so inquisitive, I heard Granny say in my head.

Eventually I asked him whether he had found another job.

"Ha! A job – what's a job, these days? You know they say nobody gets a job for life any more, in this so-called gig economy. I get little jobs, yes. At the moment I'm helping a guy who goes around fixing people's computer problems."

"At least that's useful, I suppose. I wish I could do something useful."

He said nothing for a moment. Then: "How much longer are you going to waste your talents in the handbag firm?"

My talents – what talents? "I'm not really sure."

He stopped walking and faced me. "Why don't you get out of that dump?" His hazel-flecked eyes were fixed on me, two lines appearing between his eyebrows. "You could do so much better."

Could I? I wished I knew how.

He turned again and continued walking. "It's none of my business, but ... You see how the trees grow together? How they like to be with their own kind? It's how nature works. Do you really feel you're with your own kind of people in that factory?" His voice was fierce.

"Well, no, but ... I don't feel I have much choice. It was Hugh's family that got me the internship – "

"Ah," he said flatly. "Hugh."

He turned to face me again, and it was if I could feel waves of heat coming from him. Almost, it seemed, the air between us was vibrating, and inwardly I began to shake.

"Jaki," he said. "I have to say – I wanted to tell you – "

What was this? Whatever it was, I wasn't ready to hear it. I began to babble.

"In any case, I won't be in that office next week. It will be great to have a break. Hugh has to go to Paris, and he wants me to go with him. It'll be lovely to get away."

"Right," said Gavin. He trudged on for a while in silence. Then he stopped, looked at his watch and turned. "I'd better be getting back. Enjoy your trip to Paris."

"I will, I hope."

A silence.

"I'll see you around."

He walked off the way we had come, and left me standing there in the middle of the wood. He did not look back.

***

Paris in the spring, tra-la. City of romance.

I knew that it would not be like the Hollywood version, having spent enough time there to experience aspects of the capital that tourists don't always see. Even so, I felt a flutter of excitement as I packed a small suitcase for our three days away. "Take something glamorous for the cocktail party," Hugh had advised, and I had rushed back to my parents' house to try to find clothes that were more suitable than my everyday office or weekend wear. In the end, with Mum's help, I had settled for the eternal "little black dress", which I planned to wear with a Venetian necklace that had belonged to Granny, and of course I would carry the handbag that Hugh had given me.

The cocktail party was scheduled for the first evening, a Tuesday. Hugh would be busy for most of the day, but I told him that I could easily amuse myself. On the Wednesday he would have more free time, and we could meet for lunch and do something together in the afternoon. "Take in an exhibition, maybe?" he had suggested. On Thursday he had more commitments, but he had booked tickets for *Les Sylphides* at the Palais Garnier in the evening.

"Oh, you are so lucky! It's not fair!" Maya had squealed when I told her. "I'd give anything to see that. You have all the luck!"

Did I? It was true that Hugh was spoiling me. This was supposed to be a business trip, and he didn't need me tagging along. I ought to be more appreciative.

But in the forefront of my mind was the idea that I would be able to see and talk to Stella. I had hoped to see her on the first day, when I would be left to my own devices, but she told me on the phone that she wouldn't be free. I was sure that we could still arrange something.

It was pouring with rain as we arrived at the Gare du Nord late on Monday evening and joined the queue for taxis. Once on our way to the hotel, I kept turning left and right to look out at the dark streets and bright lights, the coloured reflections in the rain-soaked pavements, the familiar landmarks that appeared and slid away amid the traffic and tall buildings.

What had happened to all the people with whom I'd attended lectures and chatted afterwards in cafés? Were they still in the city, or had they scattered, like most of my other friends? At least I wasn't a stranger here. I could find my way around.

I did not feel in my element at Tuesday's cocktail party, however. It was held in one of the grand hotels, and in spite of my attempts at glamour, I felt out of place. Some of the French women there were exquisite, like effortless fashion plates, and although Hugh kept coming back to me and putting his arm around me, I felt like an impostor. He introduced me to various colleagues, some of whom I knew by sight, and we murmured polite nothings through the din of conversation while Hugh talked shop. The champagne was good and the canapés delicious, but I found myself remembering the evening when I had first spoken to Gavin. He wouldn't fit in here either, I thought. A discreet guard stood next to the skilfully lit display of handbags in all their bold, elaborately decorated plastic glory. I hugged mine close to my side. For walking around Paris on my own, I had brought an old, neutral one in my suitcase.

The hotel bed was huge and soft, with enormous square pillows, and I sank into it gratefully, glad to be rid of my high-heeled shoes. I couldn't admit it to myself, but I felt relieved when Hugh said that he was too tired to make love tonight and needed some sleep before his early start tomorrow morning. I lay awake for a while, listening to the faint clunking of the lift ascending and descending, and the never-ending hum of traffic, broken occasionally by the two-tone wail of a siren.

At breakfast on Wednesday, Hugh, impeccably clean shaven in suit and tie, drank his coffee and crumbled croissants while looking through a file and checking his phone. Our only conversation was an arrangement to meet at a certain restaurant, chosen from the Michelin guide, for lunch. With a hasty kiss on the cheek, he was off to his early appointment and I was free.

My first thought was to phone Stella. I sat on the bed in the room while her phone rang and rang, but there was no answer. That was odd. Could she be ill? Then the chambermaid knocked on the door and I went out to walk the streets.

The rain had stopped but dampness hung over everything, and the colour of Paris was the grey that I remembered. Grey pavements, grey rooftops, dark grey tree trunks. I looked more closely at the trees, which had been severely lopped back. They were planes, a good choice for polluted cities, and although their branches looked like amputated limbs, I knew that new green shoots would soon be sprouting, perhaps within a month. They had been planted in straight lines, each the same distance from the next, the foot of each trunk enclosed in a metal grid. Did they look after one another through their root systems, I wondered?

I strolled along, dodging people who were in a hurry and others who were staring abstractedly at their phones. Shop windows were full of expensive clothes and shoes, not the sort of thing that I could afford now, although perhaps after we were married … ? Maybe, I thought. Maybe not. I caught the métro to the Latin Quarter and pretended to be still a student. I walked along the Seine embankment a little way, but really I was just killing time until lunch. Gradually the mist lifted and the sky cleared to pale blue.

Although I tried several times to call my aunt, she didn't reply.

Hugh was already seated in the restaurant when I arrived. He was sipping an aperitif and reading the large menu.

"How did it go, this morning?" I asked, when the waiter had taken my coat and pulled out a chair.

He grimaced. "It's a bit complicated, babe. But let's talk about something else. Did you go shopping?"

I said that I had been trying to reach Stella, but that unaccountably there had been no reply.

"Oh?" he said vaguely.

I needed the loo, so I made my way to the back of the restaurant and down a curving flight of stairs. Piped music was playing. As I washed my hands, I wondered whether I should try Stella again, but Hugh would be getting impatient.

Walking back towards his corner of the restaurant, I had a shock.

Clarke had joined Hugh at the table, and the waiter was setting another place for him. He shot to his feet as I approached, and a variety of expressions crossed his face. It might have been funny if I hadn't been so annoyed.

"You know my fiancée, of course?"

"Indeed I do." We shook hands coldly.

"I'm so glad we've run into each other," said Hugh. "There are some urgent matters I need to ask you about. Actually, I expected to see you at the reception last night."

"Ah. I couldn't make it. I was held up at head office. Sorry you missed Fashion Week."

The two men looked at each other as if each was refraining from saying something. Then the waiter appeared, and we placed our orders. I enquired about the vegetables and the sauce that would be served with the fish that I wanted, and passed the time of day with the waiter.

"Of course," said Clarke sneerily, who had placed his own order in a painfully strong English accent, "I should remember that you are perfectly bilingual."

I bit back a retort.

"She puts me to shame," said Hugh cheerfully.

They began to discuss business matters in what seemed to me a very roundabout way. I couldn't understand what was going on, and after a while I stopped trying and concentrated on the food. It was very good, and so was the wine, but I felt on edge at the nearness of Clarke, his ugly bald head, the way he shovelled food into his mouth. So much for a romantic lunch with Hugh. I could tell that he was not really at ease either, as he was putting on an exaggerated air of geniality.

When we were finally tucking into our artistically presented café gourmand, I managed to get a word in.

"What shall we do this afternoon?" I asked Hugh. I wanted to make it clear to Clarke that Hugh intended to spend time with me.

"Why don't we all go up to the top of the Montparnasse Tower, for the view? The weather's beautiful now," said Clarke.

How dare he? What business was it of his? The very thought of being on top of that skyscraper made me feel faint.

"No. I couldn't possibly go up there. I don't like heights."

"Oh dear. I'm surprised," said Clarke condescendingly.

I turned to Hugh. Was he going to support me? But he was looking preoccupied and said nothing.

Suddenly full of rage, I stood up, excused myself and hurried back downstairs. Sitting in a cubicle, I tried Stella's number again, and this time she answered.

"I'm sorry if you've been trying to reach me. I must give you my mobile number. Yes, of course I want to see you. Could you come round this afternoon?"

"Yes," I said. "I'll come right away."

***

Crossing the Parc Montsouris on my way to Stella's flat, I began to feel calmer.

The sun was shining now, and the wide landscaped spaces of the park were soothing. Here were trees that had not been drastically pruned but which had been allowed to grow and spread, both upwards and outwards, and their trunks were thick and sturdy with the rough, ridged bark of the old. Not that they were so very old. I knew that the park had been created and the trees planted in the second half of the nineteenth century, but here were massive, stately horse chestnuts, yews and cedars, and I greeted them like friends. The whole place was artificial, of course, with a lake for swans both white and black, hills and hollows, lamp-posts and occasional statues. But in the cityscape it was an oasis where the roar of traffic was muffled.

Stella lived on the top floor of a corner building, with an iron-railinged balcony running along two sides. As I travelled up in the old, but modernized, lift, I remembered the previous times I had come here as a schoolgirl and a student. She had bought the flat years ago, but had not always lived in it. Her time in LA with her first husband, also a singer, had been relatively brief. With her second husband she had moved to Provence, where he ran a painting school; but he had been killed in an accident on his motorbike.

Her third husband, Gérard, was an interpreter, specializing in Spanish and Russian, often away at international conferences, and I think she was truly happy with him at last. They had shared this flat, and he also had a place of his own on the other side of Paris. I had liked him. He had been kind and funny, and he wrote poetry, too. He always knew the details of Stella's schedule and could tell me where she was if I tried to phone her.

After his death from pancreatic cancer, Stella had been inconsolable. The loss of her first two husbands had never stopped her from singing, but after Gérard's death a cloud seemed to settle on her and she gave no more concerts.

On the carpeted landing, the heavy door opened at the first ring, and there stood my aunt.

"Jaki," she said gravely, and hugged me.

The flat didn't seem to have changed since my last visit. It was filled with light from the windows giving on to the balcony. The furniture was modern, its sleek lines softened by green houseplants. On the walls were original abstract paintings in vibrant Mediterranean colours, three guitars leaned against one wall, and everything was scrupulously clean. I knew that she employed a Portuguese cleaner.

"Coffee?" said Stella, and I followed her into the kitchen, where she offered me a choice of filter or espresso, and I watched her as she moved around. She was not as tall as me, but still slim, in jeans and a plain dark green jumper. She had let her hair go grey some time ago, and she wore it short these days, but very stylishly cut. As she made the coffee, she explained that she had been visiting a friend in hospital both yesterday and this morning. "And I don't use the answering machine any more," she said. "Too many cold callers and nuisance messages. But let me give you my mobile number. I should have thought of that before."

We returned to the living room, where she sat on the sofa and I relaxed in a comfortable armchair. It was good to be here again.

"Was Hugh too busy to come with you?"

"Oh, much too busy."

I frowned, and she glanced at me. Then she asked after Dad and Mum and Maya, and more particularly Grandad. She really ought to phone them more often, she said, and I agreed, but I got the feeling that she probably wouldn't. She seemed rather dismayed that Grandad's house would no doubt have to be put up for sale.

"But what about all his precious books?"

I didn't know. The problem hadn't really been discussed with me, as I was so seldom around nowadays.

"He'll be so unhappy if he loses his books," she said.

"He wants to see you, too. When can you come over?"

"Oh ... I don't know, Jaki. I don't really want to go anywhere at the moment."

"I wish you would come."

"So you said on the phone. What was all that about an ancient wood, and an amazing house, and some woman who is making your wedding dress? I didn't really take it all in, the other evening. My mind was on my friend who had just been rushed to hospital."

I launched into my prepared speech. Animatedly I described the woods, the house, the threat of a hotel, the dreaded road scheme, the financial involvement of Sacs de Luxe and the vested interest of Hugh's father. I alternated between French and English, as the two of us had always done when we met, and she occasionally put in a question. I produced a copy of my newspaper article and she read it quickly.

"So you see," I said passionately, "the whole thing simply must be stopped. They want to destroy an important part of the environment and turn a unique house into some ghastly hotel for business people, and kick my poor friend Lily out of her home, and she's – well – she's such a special person. We have to stop it. There's a whole group of us fighting this scheme."

"You have got yourself into an awkward situation." Stella mused for a moment. "I can see how strongly you feel about this, but it's bringing you into direct conflict with Hugh's family and with the firm you're working for – "

"Oh, that," I said dismissively.

"And with Hugh. You say he's in favour of the whole thing."

"He just doesn't understand." I started to pinch the material on the arms of the chair. "He's so caught up in his job. He really believes in growth and profit margins and shareholder value, and all that stuff."

"And you don't?"

I shrugged. "I suppose I've never really believed in capitalism. And I can't get excited about handbags," I said gloomily.

"And are you enjoying working for the firm?"

"No! I'm just a dogsbody, anyway. Hugh is on track to become one of the hotshots. I'm just trying to earn a bit of money until I can find a really meaningful job, doing something useful. I keep applying, but no luck so far."

"But you're getting married, aren't you? This year?"

"So? I still want to work and be independent."

"Hmm. And what does Hugh think about that?"

"Oh, he keeps saying I won't have to work. I think he imagines I'll lead the same sort of life as his mother."

Stella said nothing.

"In fact, I sometimes wonder whether we're still on the same wavelength. I used to believe we were soulmates, but …" My voice trailed off. There, I had put into words a thought that had been lingering on the edge of my mind like a cloud for some time now.

"Marriage with the right person can be wonderful," said Stella. "I miss Gérard so much. Every single day."

"He was great," I said.

We lapsed into silence again, and I finished my coffee.

Stella gave herself a little shake and squared her shoulders. "So tell me more about this move to save the woods. I've always been fond of trees, but we're rather short of them in Paris. That's why I'm so lucky to overlook the park. Something is attacking the horse chestnuts, though. The leaves all get little holes and go dry and brown in the summer."

"Leaf miner," I said knowledgeably. "It doesn't kill the

trees, though."

She asked more questions, and I told her about Gavin and Martha and the others, and about our attempts to raise funds and gain publicity. This brought me to my crucial question. Would she consider lending her name to the campaign, and above all, would she stage a comeback and sing for us?

"What? No, no, no. No, that's out of the question. I'm sorry."

"Oh, please, Stella! You're a star. We need you."

"No, I'm not any more – if I ever was. No, it can't be done."

"Oh." I stared hard at the floor. Why did nothing ever succeed for me? I was bitterly disappointed. I might just as well not have come.

"I'm sorry," said Stella more softly. "I don't sing any more."

"Not ever, or just not in public?" I asked dully.

"Not in public. Oh, Jaki, don't look like that. I'll tell you what. I'll sing something for you now, if you like. Just for you."

Of course I wanted to hear her sing. In her heyday I had really been too young to appreciate her gifts and her professional success, although Dad had a collection of her CDs at home. She had been a big name, writing nearly all her own songs. I had never attended one of her concerts, but I knew she had given three in the UK, two in London and one in Manchester, and she had been on tour in France and in the States, singing in a duo with Zorinda even before she went solo.

"Come into the other room." She rose to her feet.

In Stella's study, several more guitars hung on the wall, a bookcase filled another wall and racks were packed tightly with records. On her desk beside the computer stood a framed photograph of Gérard, smiling, unaware that he was going to die, and on the wall above the desk hung an oil painting of a woman who reminded me of an exotic bird: Zorinda, dead these many years of a drug overdose.

Stella took down a guitar and began to tune it. "What

would you like me to sing?"

All song titles immediately went out of my head. Then I remembered one. "Could you sing *Rain in Another Country*?"

"Oh, that's an old one. All right."

She thrummed for a few moments and then began to sing.

How can I describe the quality of her voice, the power of it? It was clear and full. Her diction was perfect. As she sang the melancholy words, the room seemed to grow quieter around her. As she leaned over her guitar, I could imagine her with long, fair hair, similar to my own, as she had worn it all those years ago. She was an idol. Men had desired her. She had enchanted both sexes with her voice. Why had I never listened to her properly before?

As she sang, I thought of Oldwood, the rain clouds dark above the trees, the raindrops dripping from the leaves and trickling down the trunks. They were drinking the water in the quietness of the falling rain, with quiet acceptance. The sadness in the song came only from ourselves, and welled up as tears.

I brushed my hand across my eyes.

Stella played the last arpeggio and chords and looked up.

"I wrote that half a lifetime ago. A whole lifetime, in your case. It was when you were just a baby."

"When you were still working in an office?"

"Yes. God, it was a different world. What you were telling me – about your friend who lives alone and does sewing – reminded me of someone I used to know in those days. She was a very good friend."

"And have you kept in touch?"

"No." She put down the guitar and went to her desk. She picked up the photo of Gérard and stood looking down at it. "I lose the people I care about."

"You mean she died, this friend?"

"Rose, her name was. Died? I suppose she must have died. There was a terrible fire, I know that much, and her body was never found."

I didn't know what to say. Stella had had such a brilliant musical career, but she had had a lot of bad luck, and now she seemed shrouded in clouds of sadness. I couldn't think of any more arguments that might have persuaded her to come over to England, revive her career and raise public awareness and funds for Oldwood. If Gavin had been there, he would have known how to be more convincing.

We began to talk of other matters: French politics, Paris pollution, Maya and her dancing, Grandad's state of health. She grew a little more cheerful, and I was able to make her laugh with an impersonation of Clarke being patronising.

She made tea, the time slipped by, and I was startled when my phone rang.

"What time were you thinking of coming back to the hotel?" said Hugh's voice. He sounded a little testy.

When I realized how late it was, I scrambled to get ready to leave.

"Thank you for singing for me. It was beautiful," I told her.

"Oh, Jaki." She hugged me again. "I'm sorry I can't come over and give a concert for you, but you do understand, don't you?"

"Yes." I didn't.

"But of course I will come over for your wedding."

"My – ? Oh, right."

As I descended in the clicking lift, I thought about my wedding. Marriage can be wonderful, Stella had said. Of course. Of course it could.

CHAPTER SIX

Maya was shouting down the phone and I held it away from my ear.

"So *when* can I come and explore the Rajah's house? Lily said I could come, and you said you would arrange it."

"Well, I'll have to phone – "

"How about tomorrow? And then you can tell me about *Les Sylphides*, and Paris, and stuff, and all the things you get to see while I'm stuck here and our rehearsal room has been taken over by karate and it's *so boring* – "

"OK! All right! Just give me a bit of time."

Sisters! I wasn't even dressed, lingering over a second cup of coffee and reading my email while Hugh was in the shower.

He had been rather silent and withdrawn since our return from Paris. I had apologized profusely for spending so much time at Stella's instead of doing something in the afternoon with him, but he had seemed vaguely irritated rather than upset. I wondered whether he had spent the afternoon with Clarke, but didn't ask. It was his business. On Thursday I had gone alone to the Musée d'Orsay to look at the Impressionists, and then we went to the ballet in the evening. I had tried to pay close attention to the sets and the leading ballerinas so as to be able to give Maya a description, but although the dancing was highly professional, I couldn't watch it with a critical eye. I'm not a dancer, and sometimes I found myself wandering in a dream.

"Who was that on the phone?" Hugh emerged from the bathroom with a towel around his neck and his wet hair standing up in spikes.

When I told him, he said, "Why not go this afternoon? I'm sure you're itching to get back to your famous trees."

"Actually, I – "

"In any case, I have to go and see my parents, so I won't be around. Father summoned me, in fact. He says something serious has come up."

"Oh. Well, in that case … "

I phoned Lily, who had no objection, and called Maya back. She was gleeful. "Brilliant! Awesome! Dad says he'll drop me off at the gates."

Perhaps I should have wondered why Hugh's father wanted to see him so urgently, but it gave me a chance to satisfy Maya's curiosity, and I wanted to go back to Oldwood. Possibly Gavin or Martha would be there, and I could break the news in person that I had failed to enlist Stella's support. Perhaps they would have some new and better ideas about a way forward.

I was starting to feel the usual sense of peace and wellbeing as we walked together up the lime avenue towards the house. I breathed in the clean air, so different from the traffic fumes of Paris. The trees were still leafless, but their branches made patterns against the sky, not like lace exactly, because they weren't symmetrical, but perfectly harmonious.

I was expecting Maya to bombard me with questions, but after a few brief inquiries she lapsed into silence. I could hear a song thrush repeating its staccato phrases.

Then she gave me a shock.

"I had to get out of the house. I couldn't stand it, with everybody rowing and yelling, and all about you."

"About me!" I stopped dead.

"They're all in a state. But don't get me wrong, I think you're quite right to be stirring things up. But it doesn't make for a quiet atmosphere to do revision, what with Mum wailing and Dad raging and swearing, and Grandad standing up to him."

"Maya, will you please explain?"

It took a little while, but I finally learned that my interview with Lily had been published, in both the paper and the online edition of the *Herald*, that there had been more letters to the editor, the beginning of a storm on social media and a statement by the mayor, and a journalist had interviewed a spokesperson for Sacs de Luxe. Phone calls had come from people wanting to talk to me.

"That's great!" was my first reaction. "It's gathering momentum."

But apparently that was not all. Hugh's father had phoned Dad and told him in no uncertain terms that he ought to stop me from causing so much trouble. Dad had replied that I was old enough to make my own decisions, and the two men had had an icily polite row. Then, having put the phone down, Dad had sworn and shouted and stamped about, and Mum had got worked up, lamenting the creation of bad feeling between the two families when they were due to become in-laws, and Grandad had added fuel to the flames by telling Dad that he ought to do more to support me, seeing that a young person was committed to a cause for once, and moreover I had the makings of a journalist.

"Gosh," I said weakly. I took out my phone, wanting to call Gavin or Martha, but remembered that I couldn't get a signal here.

"So what does Hugh think about all this?" asked Maya.

"He … He doesn't really understand. It's complicated."

"Pfff. It's perfectly simple. He ought to be backing you. Well, never mind. I'm on your side, anyhow." Maya marched forward. "Oh, look. There's Lily at the door, waiting for us."

Lily was wearing her usual black, contrasting with her amber necklace. I thought she looked rather pale and strained, but she greeted us warmly.

"Thank you so much for letting me come to explore your house," said Maya with a dazzling show of white teeth. She can be very charming when she tries.

"I'm only too happy to welcome dancers," said Lily, as we went into the library. The table was strewn with various papers. Then the phone rang in the hall, and she left us to answer it.

"Will you come round with me? Or shall I explore on my own?" asked Maya.

"Oh, I'm sure Lily won't mind if you wander about on your own. She's already shown me over the house, and I want to talk to her about – about these latest developments."

"OK." She went out.

After a moment, Lily returned and we sat down. She shuffled some papers rather hopelessly, and I asked whether she knew about the furore I seemed to have created.

She did, evidently. "I've received a great many phone calls, and these letters and forms from the Council, and a man is coming round to see me later."

"I didn't realize it was all happening. I've been in Paris for a few days."

"Ah ... Paris." Lily looked wistful. "It's been so many years since I was there. Tell me about your trip."

I talked about the grand cocktail party, the delicious food in the restaurant, the Musée d'Orsay and the evening at the Palais Garnier. I didn't tell her about my fruitless visit to my aunt. It would have been pointless.

"Perhaps I'll go back to Paris some day," she said, "but in the meantime I have plenty to do here. I've received so many inquiries from people – members of the public – wanting to come in and see the woods and the house."

"They're bound to be curious."

"Yes, of course. I can understand that, but I don't want people trampling – Would they damage the trees? I just don't know. I keep thinking that it's selfish of me to want to save Oldwood Court for myself alone. Why should I keep it all to myself? Perhaps the time has come to let other people in."

"That depends on their motives," I frowned. "You don't want people scattering waste paper and carving their initials on tree trunks."

"Oh! Definitely not. But there must be some other way ... Already, you see, I'm letting you and Maya into my space, not to mention Gavin and Martha and the others. Perhaps I'm becoming less of a recluse."

"Are you a recluse?"

"I think I've become one, yes. There are reasons." Her voice trailed away.

How much did I really know about Lily? Very little, in fact. There was a quiet intensity about her that attracted me and made me want to know her better, but at the same time I was afraid to blunder in with too many questions.

"I think I'll go and play the piano for a while, until this man arrives. Will you be all right? Will you join your sister?"

I assured her that I would be perfectly all right, and after a moment I heard the notes of a Chopin *Nocturne* floating through from the morning room.

Among the papers scattered on the table, a copy of the *Herald* caught my eye. The front page carried a smudgy photograph of something in the sky. Was it a bird? Was it a plane? Was it a UFO? I hastily turned the pages until I found my interview, illustrated by one of Gavin's photos of the house just visible among the trees, and a head-and-shoulders shot of Lily. The address of the petitions website appeared at the end, under my byline. The letters page was peppered with headings like 'Tree-huggers' revolt' and 'Turning the clock back'. There was one from the road contractors, one from a councillor and another from – wow! – the CEO of Sacs de Luxe, describing our efforts as wrong-headed, backward looking and a threat to local business.

I was definitely in trouble. Well, that was just too bad.

I wondered where Maya was. Perhaps I had better go and join her. As I stepped out, the piano music grew louder, and I saw Lily's thin back swaying to and fro over the keyboard of the piano. The music accompanied me, growing fainter as I went upstairs.

There was nobody in the room where I had slept, and the bed had been neatly made. For a moment I felt tempted to lie down on it and try to put my thoughts in order. Nobody in the next room, nobody in the bathroom. One by one, I opened the heavy doors with their round china doorknobs, glanced inside and closed them again with a faint rush of air like a sigh, and all the time the notes of the piano floated faintly up from the library.

Then I heard quick footsteps coming along the corridor. Maya faced me, wide-eyed. "I've seen – " She broke off.
"What?"
"There's something – "

"What have you seen?" I demanded.

"Come and look," she said, grabbing my arm. "There's a whole room – a whole gallery – "

She rushed me along the landing and round the corner to the room where I had found Lily embroidering the bodice of my wedding dress. She pushed open the door.

Nothing seemed to have changed, except that now there was no sunlight streaming in. I glanced around at the low chair, the sewing machine, the various cupboards and cabinets. On the dressmaker's dummy hung my dress, the silk falling in smooth folds, the hem almost touching the floor. The silver and green embroidery seemed to be finished, and I was stepping forward to examine it when Maya stopped me.

"Through the door," she said. "So many ... "

She stopped abruptly in front of the tall cheval mirror, a puzzled frown appearing on her face as she confronted her reflection.

"What door? That's not a door."

"But it – it was a door! I saw through it."

I looked at her for a moment. She didn't seem to be joking. "What did you see?"

"So many dresses! All different colours, all on headless dummies like this one. I thought it must be Lily's showroom. A whole gallery."

A whole gallery. I approached the mirror and touched the cold glass. It was tall enough to be a doorway, with decorative Art Nouveau branches making a lattice at the top of the archway. But it was just a mirror, reflecting two fair-haired girls and the reversed room behind us, with a single dress on a dummy.

"Well, they're not there now," I said.

Maya tapped the glass, then withdrew a few steps and tried looking at it from various angles. She shook her head.

"It was there. A long gallery of beautiful dresses."

"You must have – "

"Don't say I imagined it!" she flashed. Then, more quietly, "I knew there was something strange about this house. About this whole place. It's special. I'm not surprised you're under its spell."

I didn't know what to say. Perhaps I was under a spell. I certainly felt different when I came to Oldwood. Could Maya be psychic?

Before I could ask any more questions, we heard Lily calling us from downstairs.

We left the room and hurried towards the head of the stairs.

"Don't say anything to Lily," I hissed.

"I wasn't going to."

We found Lily in the hall, standing with a portly man who wore glasses and a heavy dark overcoat. He was carrying a black leather briefcase. She introduced us to him as Mr Curtis, and we shook hands. I looked at him suspiciously, wondering if he represented the council, or if he had come with another proposal to turn the house into a hotel. Lily didn't explain anything, however.

"I was thinking of this," said Lily, leading the way to the drawing room. She flung the door wide. The shining floor stretched away to the tall windows of the empty conservatory.

"Oh," breathed Maya. "So much space. This would *so* make a perfect practice room for our dance troupe."

"Hush!" I said, embarrassed.

"The parquet is still in good condition," said Lily.

Mr Curtis nodded benignly. "Yes, yes. It has distinct possibilities."

They passed on to the dining room, leaving us standing. Maya took a flying leap into the centre of the room and performed several pirouettes. Her arm went up in a graceful movement that reminded me of the ballet in Paris. Yes, I had to admit that my sister was a good dancer.

"Wouldn't it be amazing? Especially now the karate crowd have barged in and booked our usual room."

"You really shouldn't drop heavy hints like that, though."

She pouted and was about to say something when Lily reappeared in the doorway.

"Would you like to bring some of your dancing friends here, Maya? I'd be glad if you would. I have so much room, and I don't really need it."

I couldn't help laughing at Maya's shining face. Mr Curtis hovered in the background, still nodding.

Lily was certainly letting the outside world into her space. Changes, I felt, were afoot.

***

When Dad drove up to the gates in the car to collect Maya, I thought I had better go back to the family house too, and I cycled behind the car. Dad was driving jerkily. Everyone would want to know from me what was going on, and perhaps I could calm things down.

Some hopes. As soon as I set foot inside the front door, Mum appeared, brandishing the *Herald*. "Oh, Jaki, what have you done?" she demanded, while at the same time hugging me and then shaking me by the shoulders.

Dad loomed up behind her. "You've certainly stirred things up. I don't take kindly to being lectured by local businessmen, even if you are marrying into that family."

The sound of Grandad's stick came tapping from the sitting room. "Well, Jaki. You're a brave young woman. You stick to your guns."

"I intend to," I said.

"But what about poor Hugh?" wailed Mum. "Here you are, attacking his company in public and antagonizing his family. What's got into you? Only last week I was talking to Belinda Markham-Hunt about the wedding reception, and now she's going to be so upset."

Belinda? I hadn't known that they were on first-name terms.

"I'm sorry."

"Now, don't start apologizing," said Grandad. "If you can't be principled and idealistic when you're young, when can you be?"

"It's not about me," I said. "The whole issue is so important. It's global *and* local."

"Oh, slogans," moaned Mum.

"Look," said Dad, "Instead of standing in the hall, why don't we all go and sit down? Let's try and discuss this calmly."

We moved towards the sitting room, and Maya winked at me.

I tried to remain calm, going over the same arguments again and again like a broken record, but I didn't feel that I was really getting through. Each of us was keener on putting our own point of view than on listening to anyone else. Time and again I had noticed this pattern in televised debates, and we were no different.

Mum was devastated at the breach between Hugh's family and me. "But you're so well matched, the two of you. You've been together long enough to know that you're compatible. Why do you suddenly have to make trouble now?"

Sometimes parents have a fixed idea of what their children are like. If I had changed and moved on, Mum hadn't noticed.

Dad was annoyed that his authority over me had been called in question, while at the same time acknowledging that I was an adult and my own boss, "But what about your job? And you still haven't found anything better."

At least Grandad was on my side. "Pascal, why should Jaki have to curry favour with local entrepreneurs? Surely, in your position, you could help her to get a foothold on the journalism ladder."

"I don't know what kind of influence you think I have at the BBC," retorted Dad. "At my level? You must be joking."

"Come on! Anything is possible. Use your imagination," said Grandad, thumping the floor with his stick.

"I think we should be doing everything we can to smooth this over," said Mum.

"Dad," said Maya. "Couldn't you get Jaki a little slot on the morning news programme? Just, like, two minutes, answering questions?"

We looked at her for a moment. "Yes, indeed," said Grandad. "She is very articulate."

Dad tilted his head from side to side. He looked very French for a moment, and reminded me of Granny. "If I did, that might be one in the eye for Mr Markham-Hunt," he mused.

"Oh, Dad, that would be brilliant!" I said. "We simply need to get the word out. It might bring in more public support."

"I don't think that would be a good idea at all," said Mum.

"Well, we'll see. We'll see," said Dad.

"And I," said Grandad, "would be very interested in meeting this lady – this Ms Green. You've said such a lot about her, and I read your interview with her. She sounds rather remarkable."

"Oh, she is, she is!" said Maya. "Yes, you've got to come and meet her, Grandad. We must arrange it."

Why not? I thought. Good old Grandad. I needed all the help I could get at the moment.

***

When I returned to the flat, Hugh was not there, and he hadn't left a note. I wondered whether to prepare supper, but in the end I ate some bread and cheese and an apple, sitting alone at the table and watching the news in a desultory fashion. I soon switched it off. Why were people so interested in sport and arms sales, when the whole planet was under threat? Every now and then there was some talk about plastic in the oceans or deforestation, but it was never headline news.

I looked around the flat. All the surfaces were plastic or glass or chipboard. There were Venetian blinds instead of curtains, and there was no natural wood anywhere. In fact, it was like an extension of the office. It smelt the same.

In the end I went to bed, and it was very late when I heard Hugh come in. I pretended to be asleep when he slid into bed, as I couldn't face an argument. I thought he might kiss me, but he didn't.

The confrontation took place on Sunday morning. He was up before I was, wearing his Japanese cotton kimono and making coffee when I emerged from the bedroom. I went over to him for a good morning kiss, but his lips barely grazed my cheek.

"We need to talk," he said.

"I know."

He started quietly. We had been together a long time, hadn't we? We had been childhood sweethearts. We had always been fond of each other.

Fond? I had thought we had been in love.

"But things change over time. People change."

"You've changed," I said.

"Yes, I've changed. But you, babe. Sometimes I get the feeling that you're still a student."

"Are you saying I'm immature?"

"No, no. Not exactly. But people can grow up at different rates."

"And you've outstripped me, is that it?"

He sighed. "Don't twist what I'm trying to say. It's just that we ought to be able to see each other's point of view. We should support each other through thick and thin. You know how important this job is to me, and I don't get the impression that you're supporting me in my career."

"Oh. And just how much have you supported me in what I'm trying to do?"

"But Jaki, this is just a passing phase. You're bored because you haven't got enough to do. All this tree nonsense – "

"Nonsense? You think it's nonsense that we're facing environmental disaster by destroying trees? You honestly think that selling handbags is more important?"

"Having a career *is* important. Aren't you looking for a job yourself? But that's beside the point. I don't know how this Lily Green woman has got you under her spell, but all I can say is – "

"Don't insult Lily! You don't even know her. And I have my own views. I don't always have to be under somebody's influence, either hers or yours."

He sighed again. "You're not thinking clearly. Don't you realize that you're making life very difficult for me? For both of us?"

"Well, I'm sorry, but I wish you would try to see things from my point of view here."

"Babe – Jaki – we ought to have the *same* point of view. If you can't stand by me as my wife, then where are we going?"

A pause.

"I don't know where we're going, to be honest."

"Yesterday," he said heavily, "I was summoned to see my parents. They both lectured me, particularly my father. He's very upset with you after all those things you wrote in the paper, signing yourself Jaki Saunders. Not to mention what you said to his face."

"Yes, I know. He phoned Dad and told him he should keep me under better control."

"Ah, well, of course that won't have pleased you. But can't you see that he has a point?"

"What? No! Is that what you think? It was an outrageous thing to say. Your father cares about his investments, that's all. And you're one of them. He's invested in you as a business proposition, that's what he's done."

"Of course he's invested in me. I'm his son."

"And that's the most important thing to you, is it? Your father's opinions mean more to you than mine."

"That's because I share his opinions!" His voice was louder now.

We glared at each other. Then he changed tack, reminding me of all the good times we had had, how we had always clicked as a couple. How everyone had always known that we were meant to be together.

Had they? I thought sadly of all the times recently when we had seemed to be running on parallel rails, destined never to meet. Yet I had loved him, hadn't I? He had been my boyfriend, then my fiancé. Our future was all mapped out together. But he was different now, and I supposed I had changed too.

"We can still make a go of it, you know we can," he said.

"Can we?"

"Yes, babe, yes. All I'm asking is that you make an effort."

So I was the one who had to make an effort. I poured some black coffee and drank half a cupful very quickly, scalding my throat. "I can't stop what I'm doing. Not now."

"But for God's sake, think about the consequences, will you? I've tried to explain, about my family, about my career, about the firm – why can't you understand?"

"I don't know," I said. "Maybe I'm too immature."

Just then his phone rang, and he barked into it. "Yes. Yes. Hostile, yes. Right." He rang off. "I have to go into the office."

"On a Sunday?"

"In business, things don't stop moving just because it's Sunday. I'll have a shower and go in. We'll talk again later."

He hurried into the bathroom and I finished the rest of my coffee more slowly. I tried to remember the last time he had told me he loved me.

I heard a thud and a roar of annoyance. It sounded as if he had slipped and knocked against something.

"Jesus, Jaki, do you have to leave bottles of shampoo leaking all over the floor? You never put things away! Everywhere you go, you leave a mess."

I looked around. True enough, my possessions were taking up space in the flat. Not everything was put neatly away. His books were sorted in order of height. Mine were in precarious piles here and there. If we had a house – and it would be *his* house – would everything have to be impeccably neat and clean, a place for everything and everything in its place? It felt more and more like a future straitjacket.

When he had finally rushed off to the office, with "Just give it some thought, OK?" as his parting shot – no hug or kiss – I did spend some more time thinking.

About an hour later, I phoned Lily.

"What's wrong?" she asked at once, her voice distant and echoing as always.

"Lily. Please can I come back and stay with you? Please?"

***

Again I cycled over to Oldwood Court, this time in broad daylight, the sun gleaming fitfully on the puddles. Again I followed the long, high wall until I came to the gates and let myself in.

All the way there I had been thinking furiously, remembering good times with Hugh, remembering things he had said recently, thinking of cogent arguments that would compel him to see my point of view, blaming myself for letting things go wrong between us, wondering whether I was really immature – and wanting to cry.

As soon as I was inside the gates, I felt all these thoughts falling away. The avenue led gracefully towards the house, and in the woods I could hear birdsong. A blackbird, certainly – and was that a song thrush? *That's the wise thrush. He sings each song twice over*, I remembered, as the bird repeated its staccato notes in the distance. Robert Browning had wanted to go home when he wrote that poem, and when I came to this place I had a strong sense of homecoming. Yet a few months ago I hadn't even known of its existence.

"It's all right," said Lily when I walked in. "You don't have to explain anything. You can stay as long as you like."

Her pale, lined face was so serene. As she stood there, very upright, welcoming me, I felt that she was someone who had no doubt suffered and yet had come through. She was a fighter. What were my silly problems in comparison?

This time I had brought a bag with some essentials but I mumbled that I would have to collect the rest of my stuff from the flat. Only when I was saying the words did it become really clear to me that I was moving out. Lily promised me that if necessary she would drive me there in her car so that everything could be collected.

Simple.

As she showed me again to the same room over the porch – *my* room – she said that Gavin and Martha would be coming over very soon. The room was opening itself to me and folding itself around me, the tapestry curtains framing the light from the window, and the light in turn sparkling on the little scraps of mirror that had been sewn into the embroidered bedspread. That bedspread had not been there the previous time. It must be Indian, I thought, and at the same time I felt a qualm of misgiving at the thought of seeing Gavin again. We hadn't parted on the best of terms. But here I was, and it was so good to be in the right place.

I was putting away a change of underwear in the chest of drawers when I heard Martha's voice calling from downstairs. I hurried out, and there stood the two of them in the hall below with Lily. I felt as if I was floating down the stairs.

"Hi, Jaki! Such a lot has happened since we last met." Martha was waving a brochure. Her smile beamed and her dark hair contrasted with the fuchsia pink top that she was wearing over her jeans. She was such an attractive person.

Without looking at Gavin, who hadn't spoken, I opened the brochure and saw an abridged version of my original article, some of my pen and ink sketches, some quotes from scientists on deforestation and climate change, and on every page, running across the top or down the side, a beautiful frieze of leaves and tendrils and flowers. Martha was so talented. She should have lived at the time of the Arts and Crafts Movement.

"We've done a deal with the printer," she was explaining, as Lily joined me in admiring it, "and we've got loads of volunteers for distribution. By this time tomorrow, it will be all over the county."

"Excellent work," said Lily. "Well done." A male chaffinch had flown from her shoulder to her head as she took the brochure. With a delicate hand, she removed it and it flew back to her shoulder, where it perched, preening its feathers.

Gavin had still not spoken.

"Did you have a wonderful time in Paris?" Martha wanted to know.

I glanced quickly at Gavin. His eyes were fixed on me, opaque and unsmiling.

"I … uh … It was all right. But my aunt – it's no good. I tried, but I couldn't get her to support us."

Martha said, "Ah, that's a pity. And now you've walked back into the middle of a storm, haven't you? That Mr Markham-Hunt – he was incandescent in the *Herald*. Horrible man."

Gavin coughed.

"Oh!" said Martha. "Sorry. I was forgetting. He's your

future father-in-law, isn't he? That must be a bit tricky."

"Jaki has taken refuge here for a while," said Lily in her soft voice.

Martha nodded and didn't seem to find this surprising. Lily began to talk about phone calls and letters, and the two of them moved towards the library.

As Martha turned, I noticed something: the curve of her body. She was pregnant. Why should that give me a shock? She hadn't said anything about it, but then, why should she?

I thought of her with a baby in her arms, like a madonna. Yes, she would be a good mother, I felt sure. And Gavin would be tender and protective, considerate of her feelings.

"Have you got time to come for another walk in the woods?" asked Gavin suddenly.

"All the time in the world". Were we still friends?

This time I was looking straight at him, and his quick smile lit up his face like an illumination. "That sounds good."

I thought so, too, and I wasn't sure that I meant it, but it bothered me that we had seemed to be in conflict. As we walked in among the trees, we relaxed into our easy way of chatting, drawing each other's attention to particularly beautiful shapes and colours. Most trees were not yet in leaf, but the hazel buds were showing like a green mist here and there. We inspected a round hole in a bank and speculated as to whether it might belong to a vole or some other animal.

"You've been working very hard," I said.

"So has Lily. This fight has started to attract a lot of public attention, and last week a bunch of guys climbed over the wall. I suppose they wanted to explore."

"Over the wall! What happened?"

"Lily got rid of them."

"What do you mean? She threw them out?"

He turned aside to pull a long strand of ivy from a beech trunk. "Not exactly. It's ... How well do you know Lily?"

"I know a few things that's she told me – for the interview, and about her great-grandfather and grandfather, and the house. I know she speaks French. But other than that, I don't know very much really," I said. "I know I like her."

"She has a strong effect on people, you see. Not everyone can accept it. I suppose you could say it's some kind of inner strength." He looked at me. "Or power."

"I think I know what you mean. And somehow Lily and the woods and the house are all bound up together. What affects one will affect them all."

"Right. But things are changing. Things always change and develop. Evolve."

He stepped ahead of me and I watched the way he moved, smoothly like an animal, his feet making little noise in the dead leaves on the path. I thought that Hugh would have kicked at them as he walked. I tried to tread softly too.

We were coming to the great cedar near the wall, the cedar with the wooden staircase leading into its upper branches. Gavin put on a spurt and ran lightly up the first few steps.

"Come up with me?"

"Oh," I moaned, "You know I hate climbing up things."

"Just come up a little way," he coaxed. He climbed higher.

What was I so scared of? It was a sturdily built, wooden staircase with a smooth wooden handrail. It had been there for years and hadn't collapsed. If I could climb ordinary stairs, why not these? Oh, but I was in the open air, and the tree might sway, and I might fall.

Gavin was almost out of sight among the evergreen branches. "Jaki?" came his voice softly.

I put one foot on the lowest step. I hung on to the rail, and brought the other foot up. Looking up, I could see Gavin's trainers and the legs of his jeans. Another step. Another. My head was almost on a level with his feet. Then a gust of wind shifted the branches and the sun dazzled me. I hung desperately on to the rail.

"I'm going down," I called.

Then the bright sunlight vanished. Something black was overhead, flying, circling, cutting out the sun. What was it? I couldn't look up at it.

Inch by inch I made my way down, and when I felt the soft forest floor under my feet I drew in a great breath. My hand felt sore from gripping the rail.

Gavin descended quickly and jumped the last few steps.

"That was great! You're going to do it. I know you're going to do it."

"But what was that?"

"What?"

"In the sky. Something big and black. I couldn't see – it was like a shadow."

"I don't know," he said. "There are things flying here. It could have been a drone."

He was standing very close to me and I was breathing hard. Then I felt the space between us begin to shimmer, like a mirage on a hot road, and then an inner trembling that I hadn't felt for years. Gavin stood there, lean, warm, just a little taller than me. Could he feel it? I scarcely dared look at him. I felt that my hands were shaking. It had happened once before, in Paris, and I had never seen that particular guy again.

What was it? Gavin? But Gavin was Martha's partner – and Martha was pregnant, for heaven's sake. And anyway, what about Hugh?

With a great effort, I turned aside.

"I have to go back."

"OK," he said lightly.

***

That night, alone in my room, I leaned out of the open window. I could hear little rustlings in the shrubs that gave way to the first of the trees, and the scent of leaf mould was wafted up to me. As my eyes grew used to the darkness, more and more stars appeared as pinpricks in the faintly luminous sky.

It was a relief to be alone and free. I could breathe. I could be myself. And yet, and yet ... I hadn't told Hugh that I was leaving him. Was that what I was doing? I had left the claustrophobic flat and I would not be going back. Of that, I felt sure. But was everything over between us?

I remembered our schooldays, and how I used to watch him playing tennis after school. He was our school's athletics champion. Other girls would also congregate outside the courts to watch, and I was aware that envious glances were cast in my direction when he came over to me, swinging his racquet, at the end of the match. I was proud to be his girlfriend. I had been happy, hadn't I?

The stars blurred and I found I was crying. Why? Was it because our relationship had turned sour? Was I crying for loss of the past? If Hugh walked through that door right now, would I fling myself into his arms?

No, I realized. I couldn't do that any more.

It was no good. I would have to tell him that we couldn't get married in June after all. Was marriage even a possibility? Probably not, a small voice seemed to say. Somehow, everything had been messed up, and what would happen to me now? My whole identity, I realized, had been defined as Hugh's girlfriend and then Hugh's fiancée. Apart from that, I was nothing, hollow, worthless. Mum would be so upset, and there was nothing I could do about it.

From Hugh's recent behaviour, it was clear that he was having doubts about our future together, but I hadn't wanted to admit it, and nor, perhaps, had he. Yet those doubts were also mine. We would have to talk, and – and at least agree to spend some time apart. But how could we talk? Not on the phone from here.

I had scribbled him a note before leaving, but only to say where I was going.

The only way to mend matters would be to capitulate: to abandon the road protest, to apologize to his parents, to agree with everything he said, to support him in his job, and to stand at the altar saying – No! I could not. I wouldn't renounce everything that had become so meaningful to me – this place, Lily, forests everywhere.

I moved away from the window and flung myself on the bed. The little mirrors were hard and they glittered close to my eyes.

I would phone Hugh from the office tomorrow morning.

And what, said the small voice in my head, about Gavin?

I sprang up and began undressing ready for bed. I could not, would not, think about that now.

CHAPTER SEVEN

On the way to work in the morning, I dismounted from my bike and tried to phone Hugh. It went straight to voicemail. He hadn't left me any messages.

I had barely slipped into my seat and switched on the computer terminal when high heels clicked across the floor and a slim, perfectly made up woman held out an envelope with my name on it.

"Good morning. I've been asked to deliver this to you personally," she said, and with a nod she turned and clicked away.

I ripped open the envelope.

'Dear Ms Hayward, I regret to inform you ... unavoidable circumstances ... internship will be terminated with immediate effect ... Please collect from office ... '

I read it again more slowly. There was nothing ambiguous about it. I had been fired.

For a moment I looked at the computer screen. Figures and words and the firm's logo swam around on it like fish in an aquarium.

I realized that the office was quiet and people were casting covert glances at me.

I jumped to my feet and waved the letter. "Good morning everybody! I've just been fired! I'll be leaving this dump – with immediate effect!" And I burst out laughing.

Eyes were turned away and uncertain expressions flitted across faces.

"Bye-bye! I'm out of here. Out on my ear," I shouted as I strode to the door. I remembered Gavin using the same expression.

I went to the coffee machine and pressed the button for a cappuccino, thinking to myself that I would never be able to afford another one. I now had no income at all.

133

I tried Hugh again, and this time he answered.

"I've been fired," I told him before he had a chance to ask any questions. I was giggling hysterically.

"Oh, Jaki." He sounded weary. "What next? I'm beginning to get really tired of your antics, you know."

"What antics?" I took a swig of cappuccino.

"Look, I can't talk now. I'm on my way to London. I have to be at head office by midday."

"That's all right. I don't want to talk. Have a nice day," I said, and broke the connection.

I cycled slowly to the flat. The modern concrete block was an eyesore, I said to myself, looking at it afresh. Who would want to live in a place like that? Upstairs, there were signs of Hugh's hasty departure. He hadn't even made the bed. How untidy! On looking around, however, I had to admit that most of the untidiness was due to my own belongings, and as I began to gather them together and stuff them into bags, I wondered how I was going to take everything to Oldwood. Dad would be at work so couldn't drive me. There could be no question of paying for a taxi. Lily had offered to help collect my luggage, but I couldn't expect Lily to heave bulky bags around.

I knew I would have to ask Gavin.

"I'm on a job at the moment," he said when I phoned. He told me to wait and I heard voices in the background. Then he said that he would bring the van over in the afternoon if I could wait.

Of course I could wait. What else was I going to do? I finished packing, including quite a lot of heavy articles that I had printed off the internet. I reflected that Lily didn't have an internet connection, and felt a moment's slight panic. But people had managed to live perfectly well years ago, before they felt they had to spend hours a day online. I would also manage, and I could still draw. Perhaps I could work for Lily, doing housework or whatever she needed. Somehow I must repay her for her hospitality.

When everything was ready, including several portfolios and packages of charcoal, ink, pens and brushes, the time began to drag. The longer I spent in the flat, imbued with Hugh's presence, the more alien it felt. At midday I made myself a sandwich and pottered about. Should I make the bed for Hugh? No! Of course I would not. Previously, I would have done so without thinking about it, but now I was doing plenty of thinking.

When my phone rang, I grabbed it joyfully, thinking that Gavin had got away early.

To my surprise, it was Dad. Should I tell him that I had lost my internship? But he was already talking.

"This will probably surprise you. I'm surprised myself. But I've called in a few favours, and they're willing to grant you about two minutes on the news programme tomorrow morning. It means you'll have to take some hours off work. Can that be done, do you think?"

"I'm sure it can." I would tell him later about the loss of my job. "That's terrific, Dad."

"You'd better use the landline at home. Mobiles are too unreliable, and if you start breaking up then that will be the end of it. You just have to get your point of view across very clearly and concisely, and we don't know at what time they'll contact you to go on air."

I was full of gratitude, but he brushed off my thanks. "It may not go too well, but it's worth a try. Your grandfather can't say I haven't put in a good word."

Good old Dad! I took out a sheet of paper and began jotting down the most important points that needed to be made. But how much could I possibly say in two minutes?

When Gavin eventually rang to say that he was downstairs, I hastily pushed all my luggage out on to the landing. I didn't want him to enter the flat. I couldn't imagine him in it. The door was ajar and I could hear his footsteps coming up the stairs.

For a moment I hesitated, looking back. Then I pulled my emerald engagement ring off my finger and left it on the table.

I slammed the door behind me.

***

"I'm sorry there's so much stuff," I said to Gavin.

"All in a good cause," he answered cheerfully, lifting and shoving bags into the back of the van. My bike went in last, he reversed and revved the engine, and I got in beside him. This was the last time, I thought, that I would need to cover this particular stretch of road between the office and Oldwood Court.

Gavin nodded when I told him that my job was at an end. "That's good. You're moving on. Nothing's permanent. I may be moving on myself one of these days."

"Oh." My feeling of bubbling freedom faded a little, as if a cloud had passed over the sun. I didn't ask him what plans he had. So would Martha be moving on, too? Would they move away? Could all this team effort come to an end? But surely it was too early. We hadn't yet won.

I told him about my forthcoming two minutes on the radio, and he thumped the steering wheel and grinned. "Excellent. Do you know what you're going to say?"

We discussed this as we drove along. I wanted to cram as much information as possible into those minutes, but he thought that I ought to appeal to listeners' emotions with poetic descriptions.

We were still talking about this when we drew up outside the gates of Oldwood.

"Hullo. I wonder why there are three cars parked here," he said. I alighted to open the gates, he drove through and the gates clanged shut behind us.

"Lily must have visitors."

There was no sign of Lily when we reached the house, but we were able to walk in as usual, and we carried my luggage up to my room. I looked out of the window and thought I saw the figure of a man come to the edge of the trees and then turn and disappear back among the tall trunks. Then I noticed a minibus parked a little to one side.

"There's something going on."

Downstairs again, we heard faint strains of music and voices coming from the drawing room. I peeped in. The room seemed at first glance to be full of children in leotards, all leaping about. In fact, they were only seven, six girls and one boy with glasses, and I recognized Maya. Music was coming from a mobile device on the floor and they were dancing. At the side of the room stood Lily, watching them, and next to her was a shorter woman with straight grey hair in a fringe, who occasionally shouted an instruction or intervened to alter the position of an arm or leg.

Lily saw us and came over.

I said, "I didn't know you were letting Maya and her friends practise here. I hope she hasn't been pestering you."

"Not at all. It was a recent decision, and I'm glad that somebody is making good use of all this space. Madame Walenska was pleased, because there has been some conflict over the hall where they usually practise, apparently."

Madame Walenska glanced alertly in our direction at the sound of her name. She stopped the music and explained something in a strong accent to her pupils. Maya waved briefly at me. The dancing resumed.

"There are some guys in the woods. Did you know?" said Gavin as we stepped out of the room.

"Ah, yes," said Lily. She drifted towards the front door. Looking out, we again saw a man on the point of emerging but then melting back among the trees.

"Who are they?"

"They told me they were surveyors," said Lily. Her eyes were narrowed as she watched them, and she raised one hand slightly. Again the man appeared, paused and turned back. "They've been here for quite some time."

"How long should it take to do a survey of the woods?" asked Gavin.

"I really couldn't say." Again Lily's right hand went up, her fingers pointing briefly towards the trees. "They've been here for – oh – at least four hours."

"Four hours!" Gavin looked from Lily to me and back again. "Might they need some help, do you think?"

"Help? Perhaps." I couldn't quite tell whether Lily was smiling. "Are you feeling sorry for them, Gavin?"

"Not sorry, no. But – well – perhaps they might want to call it a day?"

"Some people would be happy to spend an afternoon walking in the woods. It depends on their motive," said Lily. "But if you like, perhaps you could escort them to the gates." She turned back to the drawing room, the sound of music and the thump of feet.

"Can't see anyone now. I wonder where they are," said Gavin as we set off.

"Why don't we walk around the house? We might spot them on the edge of the trees again," I suggested.

The spring grass was growing quite high, like a green robe with a rich border of daisies and dandelions, as we made our way around the irregular exterior of the building. So many additions and extensions seemed to have been made to it over time that it was hard to know exactly where we were. We passed the old kitchen garden, now neglected; skirted the yard with the stable buildings, and found ourselves after a while just below the terrace and the conservatory of the drawing room. I took my eyes off the trees to glance in at the dancers. They all seemed to be wearing green. I paused. Hadn't their leotards been a different colour? Anyway, there they were, still dancing. But surely there were more of them?

Puzzled, I was about to point this out to Gavin when he grabbed my arm.

"Look! There's one of the guys again. Let's go."

Again a man had appeared on the edge of the wood. He turned back and we hurried across the grass towards him. At first he was on a path, and apparently he couldn't hear us moving towards him. Coming to an oak tree, he left the path and walked around the tree. Then he turned and walked back around it. He did this three times, carrying what looked like a theodolite.

"Hullo!" shouted Gavin, but the man seemed not to hear him. He returned to the path and set off quickly in another direction.

We hurried after the man's retreating back and at last caught up with him near the yew grove.

"Hi," said Gavin, moving around to face him.

"What? Oh, thank God for that. Listen, mate, can you show us the way out of here? What is this place, a labyrinth?"

"Not really, when you get to know it."

"Get to know it! It's impossible! I've been going round and round."

"How many are you?" I asked.

"Three, and we all seem to be lost in here. It's incredible. I don't even know where they've got to now. Nige! Andrew!" he shouted.

Faintly, two voices answered him, one from the right, the other more distant to our left.

"Why don't we just follow this path, and I think you'll be all right," said Gavin.

After a few minutes, two men came walking towards us from different directions, and this time they saw us. They seemed very worked up.

"What the fuck is this place? We should have finished hours ago."

"Nothing works! Bloody laser won't work, GPS won't work, no phone signal."

"All these shitty trees! I could swear they change places."

"Yeah, there's one particular tree that I keep seeing, whichever way I go!"

"It's a hellish place, I tell you. I won't be coming back here in a hurry."

The one who was apparently called Nige, his face red and sweating, turned to us. "Can you get us out of here? Sharpish? We're really late."

"No problem," said Gavin. He led the way along a path and they followed us, muttering.

It was not long before we emerged into the lime avenue, within sight of the gates.

"Well, bugger me," said the first man. "I could swear this exit wasn't here. I've been this way umpteen times this afternoon and there was nothing but trees in front of me."

"It's true, woods can be confusing when you don't know them," I said in what I hoped was a soothing voice.

"At least the cars are still there," said Andrew, as they strode out of the gates towards them.

"Did you want to speak to Ms Green before you go?" I asked.

"No! No! There's no need."

"No need at all."

"We'll be on our way."

Car doors were slammed and engines revved, and within seconds they had all driven off, two towards the town and one in the opposite direction.

Gavin and I walked more slowly back towards the house. For a while, I said nothing. Then, "That was weird."

"Yep."

"Why couldn't they find their way out? It was so easy."

"Did you notice anything about Lily, while we were standing there?"

"Lily? She was … You mean … "

"I mean," said Gavin, "that nothing about Lily surprises me."

I had a great many unanswered questions, but as we approached the house the young dancers came pouring out excitedly, with Lily and Madame Walenska following. I counted the children. There were indeed seven, now dressed again in their usual jeans and sweatshirts and carrying backpacks. We shook hands with Madame Walenska, and Maya was bubbling over with enthusiasm.

"Thank you again, Lily. This is such a great place."

"You're very welcome. I'll look forward to your next session," said Lily, and they all piled into the minibus.

Maya leaned out. "Good luck tomorrow, sis! I'll probably be at school, but Dad said he'd record it."

Gavin looked at his watch and said that he had better be getting home. Perhaps Martha would be cooking dinner, I thought. She was a good cook, but I could only do basic recipes. He would be hungry and she would be waiting for him.

Lily and I went back into the house together.

It seemed very quiet.

***

"You don't need to say anything about me on the radio," said Lily. "I'd rather you didn't."

We were sitting in armchairs on either side of the fireplace in the morning room, after a simple supper in the kitchen. The tall window was open and the cool scents of a spring evening floated into the room as the light faded. I had told her about the radio slot, and how I would have to get up extremely early to be at my parents' house in time.

"All right, I won't," I said. "It will be very short, in any case. But why not?"

"Because it won't help to draw attention to an eccentric old woman living selfishly all alone in a place too big for her."

"Selfish? Lily, you're one of the least selfish people I know."

Lily raised one hand horizontally and rocked it to and fro. I knew that French gesture, expressing doubt. "Even so, I know I ought not to keep this place to myself. I've said so before. Others must share it."

"Well, you seem to have let in quite a few others today. Maya and her dancers – thank you for that! – and those poor surveyors."

Lily sat still and said nothing.

"It was strange," I said. "They were cursing and swearing because for some reason they couldn't find their way out."

"Woods have their own personality, don't you think? And if they don't like trespassers … "

"You mean you didn't know they were having trouble?"

Her face was a pale oval in the gloom and I couldn't read her expression.

"It was naughty of me." Was that just a tremor of laughter in her voice? "Of course I knew they were there. I ought to have gone and rescued them, but the children arrived … "

"I shouldn't think those men will be back in a hurry. They were really rattled."

"No, but I expect they will try another way to conduct a survey. I'm told they may use drones next time."

Drones? I thought them very sinister, unmanned eyes in the sky, spying on everything. Had that been a drone passing over us near the cedar? Were drones in use already?

"But tell me what you are planning to say on the radio

tomorrow. I'll be listening."

I outlined a few ideas and we discussed what might have the greater impact: the importance of trees in preventing climate change, or their role in ecosystems generally, or their sheer, peaceful, slow beauty.

"You're lucky to have a kind father who is doing his best to help you," said Lily. She sounded wistful.

"Unlike your own father, you mean? You've mentioned him. You told me he took you to India when you were a child."

"He did." There was a long pause. "Biologically, he was my father. Morally he was not."

"Oh. Did he ill-treat you?"

"Oh, Jaki." Her voice was as soft as a sigh. "I don't usually talk about all that. But as you're a friend now … "

"Don't tell me if you'd rather not," I said hastily.

Another pause. "Shall we light the lamps?"

"No, don't let's," I said. "I like sitting here in the dark. It's peaceful."

Lily shifted in her chair. After a moment, she said, "He exploited me. He made money out of me."

I stiffened. Horrific thoughts of child prostitution flickered through my mind.

Lily noticed my reaction. "No, no. Not that. But he turned me into a travelling show. For him, I was like a performing animal, and he took me around the villages, the city suburbs, places where people were easily impressed. Before we were in India, we moved around the Middle East. We were in Egypt for a while. I had no choice."

"But – but how were you performing? Were you singing? Dancing?"

"Not singing. Not dancing either. You see, there were certain things that I could do, and others that just happened around me. And if he beat me, more things happened. Stranger things."

"What kind of things?"

"I can't really explain. As I said, I don't usually talk about those years. They were painful."

"I see."

I did not see. I wanted more details, but hesitated to probe.

"The thing is – people like mysteries and wonders. They even like to be frightened. They will pay to see what seems like magic and clever conjuring tricks performed by a small girl."

"Were you performing conjuring tricks?"

"No."

The silence lengthened between us.

"It was a long time ago," said Lily at last. "After I escaped, it took me years to gain some kind of control. But I'm all right now, I think. And I envy you your kind father."

"Lily, are you really all right? I'm sorry if I've been asking awkward questions."

"I suppose I'm embattled, with all that has been going on." I could hear the smile in her voice. "But all right, even so. And friends can surely ask each other questions."

"It sounds as if you were friendless. A prisoner. And you say he beat you. It must have been terrible."

"Ah, but much later I had – a friend. One very good friend."

Was she talking about a lover? I wondered. Had there ever been a man in her life? Had she ever considered living with a man or marrying? But I couldn't continue to ask personal questions. In the darkness, I touched the naked ring finger of my left hand.

"But that's enough about me." She rose from her chair. "Hadn't you better be getting to bed, if you're to be at your parents' at dawn?"

***

The square lawn in front of my parents' house was thick with dew as I let myself into the garden and wheeled my bike along the path to the back of the house. I leaned the bike against the wall and then stood speechless, gazing in wonder at the magnolia.

It was in full bloom. Semi translucent, pearly pink flowers were held out like chalices all along the branches as if to catch the morning light. The whole tree resembled a graceful candelabra, the perfect waxy flowers opening to the sky. There must have been at least a hundred of them. Had I seen the tree in such glory a year ago? Surely not. I had sketched it, but I must have been at uni, worrying about exams and essays during the crucial days of its flowering, before wind and rain came to batter the blossom. Today, as the sun rose, windless and tranquil, it was at the peak of its beauty. A single blackbird was singing.

"Jaki?" My father had opened the back door.

Both my parents were up and dressed, the kitchen smelt of coffee and toast, and Maya was tossing orange peel into the bin.

"I wish I didn't have to rush off, but I can't miss the bus," she grumbled.

Grandad emerged from my old room in his dressing gown, with grey stubble on his cheeks, but under his bushy eyebrows his eyes were bright and alert. He nodded a greeting.

The radio was on, as it always was in the mornings, broadcasting the early news programme, and Dad kept moving towards the phone in the hall and then returning to the kitchen. "Now, it may not happen at all," he warned. "They said that you could only be fitted in if it was a fairly slow news day. You may just be lucky."

Maya left in a hurry, giving me a V-sign and banging the front door.

"Are you going to read something out?" asked Mum.

"No, no, she mustn't read. Listeners can always tell if you're reading a script. You have to be spontaneous, Jaki. Oh, and relaxed. And just put the stuff across. And try not to say 'um'."

Was that all? I hadn't been feeling particularly nervous, but now I could feel my heart beginning to thud. I grabbed a glass of water from the sink.

Grandad sat down at the table and we heard a war reporter, the business news and the sports results. The programme presenters seemed perfectly at ease, joking with one another. But they did this every day. Suppose I suddenly became tongue-tied?

I was listening with half an ear, but then one of the presenters said, "Spring is here at last and trees are turning green. But in some places, trees are under threat ... "

"This will be it," said Dad

When the phone rang, my heart lurched and Dad had grabbed the receiver before the second ring. He passed it to me, and someone was giving me advice, then counting, and then, "On air."

" ... her name is Jaki Saunders. Good morning, Ms Saunders."

After that, I was on some sort of automatic pilot. I was gripping the phone so hard that my hand ached, but the words poured out of me. Deforestation, landslides, illegal logging; the beauty of trees, the largest living things that we see every day; the lungs of the planet, indispensable to wildlife, irreplaceable.

The presenter cut in several times. Had I had any scientific training? Wasn't I, rather, an artist? Wasn't I very young and idealistic?

I answered him with facts. I answered him with passion. "We are working to save, not just this particular, really special wood, but the planet as a whole. We're working for the future, for the rising generation," I told him.

"I'm sure we could go on talking about this all day," he chuckled, "but I'm afraid we've run out of time. Jaki Saunders, thank you very much. And now the weather forecast with – "

I put the phone down gently.

Dad, Mum and Grandad were all in the hall, watching me.

"I thought you kept your end up pretty well," said Dad.

"Well done. A good effort. Poets are the unacknowledged legislators of the world," said Grandad.

"Why did they say your name was Saunders instead of Hayward?" asked Mum "Do you often use my maiden name?"

"It was better that way," said Dad. "I didn't want anyone to start saying that I'd been pulling strings."

"Except that you had pulled strings, of course. Thanks, Dad," I said, and laughed. I moved into the kitchen and sat down at the table, my legs collapsing under me.

"Have you had any breakfast? Do you want some toast? Coffee? An egg?" Mum demanded.

I was suddenly hungry. As I ate and drank, the others commented and analysed, expressed surprise at what I had said and suggested things that I hadn't said but could have done. Mum didn't care for that particular presenter because he interrupted too much. She was sorry about my pretty wood, but if the new road eased the traffic congestion, she would be satisfied, she said.

"Oh, Mum! The more roads they build, the more the traffic increases. It's a proven fact."

Dad looked at his watch. "I must be off. What time do you have to be at work? Can I give you a lift?"

"Uh, no."

Conversation took a different turn. I had to admit that I would not be going back to the office. I had been sacked.

Oh, well, I thought: I might as well tell them everything. Baldly, I announced that I had moved out of the flat. That Hugh and I were very probably separating.

All eyes were fixed on me and there was an uncomfortable silence.

"This is a bit abrupt, isn't it?" said Dad.

"No. It's been coming on for some time."

Dad raised his hands. "It's your decision, Jaki love. I hope you're not making a mistake."

When he had gone, I was left at the table with Mum and Grandad.

"Well," I said. "Do you think I'm making a mistake?"

Mum said wearily, "It doesn't matter what I think, does it? If you've made up your mind, you'll have to live with the consequences."

"I know."

"But you don't realize how hard it is for parents to stand by and watch their children messing up their lives! I thought everything was settled. I thought you had a happy future ahead of you. I was even starting to dream about – about grandchildren. Now it's all up in the air."

"I'm sorry," I said, and it was true. I was sorry to have upset her, but I didn't regret what I had done.

"Now, Lisa," said Grandad. "Hrrrm. Let's not over-dramatize the situation. Nobody owns their children, and they have to make their own decisions and their own mistakes."

"Yes, but who's going to pick up the pieces when it all goes wrong?" Mum's voice went up in a wail.

It was my turn to sigh. Clearly, they thought I was going off the rails. Why couldn't they believe in me? In my commitment to what I was doing?

"Jaki still has her family," said Grandad. "She knows we'll always stand by her if she's in real trouble."

I shot him a grateful glance.

"I'm going to speak to Belinda Markham-Hunt," said Mum, rising heavily to her feet. "Somebody will have to cancel the arrangements for the wedding reception. It's all been a dreadful waste of time. And another thing," she said, looking back as she left the kitchen, "What about your wedding dress? Have you even thought about that?"

I hadn't. Life was getting very complicated. How could I pay Lily for the dress? How could I even pay rent to Lily? She couldn't be expected to let me stay at Oldwood Court indefinitely for nothing. I hadn't any income. I still had massive debts.

Grandad read my thoughts. "You'll be in some financial difficulties, of course, at least for a time. We must find a solution. Hmm. This Ms Green, now – I'm interested in meeting her. Maya has been full of praise for her. 'Awesome' is the word she used, which I fear conveyed no information whatsoever." Grandad, a poet, was a stickler for correct English.

"I'm sure she'd like to meet you. I could give her a call – " Then I remembered that my phone had been switched off to ensure that it didn't ring when I was talking on the radio. I fished it out of my bag and found half a dozen missed calls and three voicemail messages from Hugh. I knew I would have to talk to him and make everything clear between us, however uncomfortable that might be.

There was also an email message.

I sat, open-mouthed.

"Something wrong?" asked Grandad.

"No. Yes. I don't know. I've been called for a job interview."

It was for a post in the Sales and Communication Department of a large electronics firm. It was my first job interview, after all the hundreds of CVs I had sent out. But it was for a job more than sixty miles away.

***

"I can't believe you're doing this," said Hugh.

We were sitting in a pizzeria on the far side of town, a place where nobody who worked for Sacs de Luxe was likely to see us. When I had phoned him, he had insisted that we meet for lunch to "talk things over", and I had pottered about in my parents' house for the rest of the morning, chatting a little to Grandad. Mum didn't tell me what Hugh's mother had said, but she went around looking like a wet week, until at last she said, "Jaki, you know I only wanted you to be happy. All I've ever wanted is for you to be happy, and to find the right man."

"I know, Mum," I said, and squeezed her arm. "I'll be all right."

After that I felt a little better, until Hugh swept up to the gate in his car and tooted the horn. He wouldn't come in.

He drove in silence until we found a parking space, and barely spoke until we had ordered pizzas. Then he put both hands on the table.

"I can't believe you're doing this. There must be something wrong with you. What's happened to you, babe – Jaki? Tell me. It's that woman, isn't it?"

I bristled. "Lily has nothing to do with this. I've made up my own mind."

"This tree business. It's incredible. I don't remember you ever mentioning trees before."

"There weren't many trees where I lived before. There

weren't any woods, let alone forests."

"Yes, but when we were students you never talked about trees."

"I'm not a student any more. I've moved on."

He went off into a long spiel about the past, how much we had in common, what fun we had had, what plans we had made for the future.

"The thing is, they were your plans," I said. "They weren't mine. I just went along with them, but I've changed. Our wants and aims aren't the same."

"But we talked about what we wanted."

"About what you wanted. Oh, we talked about films and exams and friends and shows, when we were at uni – but when did we discuss really serious plans? You always assumed that I wanted the same as you."

"But you did," he said. "You agreed to marry me, for God's sake."

"That was a mistake. I'm sorry."

He held his head in his hands for a moment. "Jaki," he groaned, "you can't do this to me. This is a very difficult time professionally, and you've stirred things up. People know that you've lost your internship, and I don't know how to face my parents. What's got into you?"

I looked at my distorted reflection in the blade of my knife. "I'm sorry. Perhaps I've grown up. Perhaps I don't believe in what you're doing, and I can't simply stand by you and accept everything that you want any more."

"So you're prepared to chuck everything away for the sake of all this – this standing timber?"

Standing timber! There was no answer to that. I glanced around and wished that I were somewhere else. Our pizzas arrived but I wasn't hungry.

"Look," he said in a conciliatory tone, "Let's not rush things, OK? I can accept that you need some space. Some time to think. I'm prepared to wait."

"I don't think there's any point."

He nodded patiently. "Just give it some thought, babe. Let's not take any drastic action. We don't need to get married right away."

"I probably won't get married at all. Ever."

He took a bite of his pizza. "So is it sex that's the problem? Tell me. I always thought everything was fine, but if you feel you'd like to be more experimental – "

"No!" At that moment, the thought of sex with Hugh, let alone 'experimental' sex, made me shudder. Yet he was the same person, an attractive man. Anyone would say that he was a good-looking guy, tall, fit, curly-haired.

"That's what I thought," he said. "I felt sure we were fine. I know I make you happy."

Happy! Was vigorous and methodical love-making all it took to make me happy? But I wasn't going to embark on a discussion about sex in a pizzeria. There were other people at nearby tables. How could I convince him that I was serious?

"So let's forget about all this nonsense, shall we? Take all the time that you want, but I know you'll come to your senses. And please, please don't give me any more stress. Things are bad enough at the office."

"Hugh, I'm doing this for me. I'm not doing it to cause you stress."

"But you are causing me stress! What about all that stuff in the paper? How was that going to go down at work, when the whole future development of the firm depends on this new road? It's no wonder they terminated your contract. And now you're out of a job, so what the hell are you going to do on your own? You can't even hold down a simple internship." Irritation was starting to get the better of him.

"As a matter of fact," I said, stung, "I've just been called for a job interview."

That interested him. He wanted to know the name of the firm, and he told me that it was reputable and that if they offered me the job, I ought to take it.

"Thanks, but I really don't need your advice."

"Oh, Jaki! You're being so childish. Really, I've had just about enough of it."

"And I've had enough, too." I stood up to leave.

"Wait! Where are you going? I'll drive you."

"It's all right," I said. "I'll walk."

Would he follow me? I wondered as I strode out into the street. No. He continued to eat his pizza. He hadn't said that he couldn't live without me. That wouldn't have been true. And he had not said, not once, that he loved me.

CHAPTER EIGHT

It was a long walk back to my parents' house, and when I reached the town centre I sat on the low wall surrounding the churchyard and took out my phone.

Six or seven messages told me that people had heard me on the radio. Congratulations! they said. Martha asked me to call her, but as I was only two streets away from the George Hotel where she worked as a receptionist, I decided to drop in and see her. There was nowhere that I needed to be. Having lost my job – or apology for a job – I now felt as if I was playing truant.

Martha glanced up welcomingly from behind the reception desk as I stepped into the old-fashioned hotel. She looked radiantly healthy, and I could tell that she would be popular with the guests. Some people found jobs that suited them, I reflected.

"You were great! You crammed such a lot into those few minutes. More than two, wasn't it? I thought the presenter was patronising, though." She put on a posh voice: "Have you any scientific training, my dear? Aren't you very young and idealistic?"

I grinned. "He was, just a bit. But I went on talking, trying to beat the clock."

"You did. I hope loads of people were listening."

A man handed in his room key and they exchanged pleasantries. Then the phone rang and Martha talked to someone about vacancies.

"Did Gavin hear me?" I asked as soon as she was free.

"Yes, he did. Hasn't he been in touch?"

Then three foreigners, apparently German, came in with suitcases, and Martha was busy. I was in the way, and left. But I did wonder what Gavin had thought.

I was nearly at my parents' house when my phone rang. Would it be Gavin? But it was Martha.

"Sorry you had to rush off. We got busy all of a sudden. But Jaki, apparently there's been a phone call and I've just been told that your wedding reception has been cancelled. Can that be right?"

I'd almost forgotten that the reception was to have been held in the George Hotel. That showed how real the prospect had been for me.

"Quite right. The wedding is off."

"Oh, I'm so sorry."

"Don't be. It was my decision. I'm a free agent."

"Oh! Well, in that case ... " Her voice trailed off.

"By the way," I said cheerfully. "You're expecting a baby, aren't you? When's it due?"

"In November. Wow, Jaki, you're observant. I didn't think I was showing much yet."

"And how does Gavin feel about it?"

"Gavin? Oh, he's happy enough."

"He hasn't said anything to me."

"No, well, we haven't told many people yet. Lily knows."

Lily knows many things, I thought. "Anyhow, congratulations. I hope it all goes smoothly."

"Thanks, Jaki. Fingers crossed. I'm excited – yes, madam?" I heard a woman's voice in the background. "Sorry – I'll have to ring off now. I'll see you. Bye!"

The town was busy with delivery vans and shoppers and the air smelt of petrol. It was growing unseasonably warm and my feet ached. For a moment I thought about going down to the river and sitting on one of the benches provided by the council, and just watch the water flowing past. Nobody needed me now, nobody was expecting me, and it didn't matter where I was.

But I would have to return to my parents' house and collect my bike.

***

As I cycled slowly up the avenue, the lime trees formed towers of vegetation on either side, and their lower branches stretched downwards to form shady bowers like caves. Only a few days of warm weather had brought out the new leaves, still small and a tender green. What shade was it? Of course, I thought: it was lime green. Later in the summer the colour would be darker.

I heard the gates open again behind me and Lily drove up in her old banger. She waved as she passed me and I followed her round to the courtyard and stables where I usually left the bike.

"I went into town to collect some more bird food," said Lily, opening the boot, "and I had to see Mr Curtis."

As if on cue, sparrows, tits, finches and starlings flitted and fluttered around her, some perching on her shoulders and then flying up to roofs and gutters.

"Just be patient," she told them. "You can't be that hungry. It's the spring. There should be plenty of natural food around."

I helped her carry sacks of birdseed into the kitchen and stow them in a cupboard.

Lily turned to me, her eyes very blue in her pale face. "You look exhausted. Drained. Have a seat. Do you want to tell me?"

So I sank into a chair, and I told her as much as I could. She had heard me on the radio and said that it had been a good performance, but admitted that it might not yield any results. People listened to items on the radio and immediately moved on to the next subject and forgot what they had heard.

Then I told her that I had lost my internship and hadn't any money.

"I should be paying you rent," I said.

"Don't worry about that. You can help me here in the house."

"With housework, you mean? I thought you had help already. Everything looks clean."

"With housework, after a fashion," said Lily evasively. "There are different kinds of help. The house needs ... clearing."

In that case, it would soon be completely empty, I thought. Since Lily had already got rid of so many antiques, it looked the opposite of cluttered, but I didn't argue.

"And the dress," I said unhappily. "The wedding dress. I haven't paid you for it, and I won't be needing it now."

"Ah."

"I'm sorry, especially after all the work you've done on it. But you see, I've split up with Hugh. I told him today that I'm not going to marry him."

Lily looked thoughtful. "How did he take it?"

"He – he seemed more irritated than upset, to be honest. As if I was behaving outrageously."

"He didn't plead with you to stay with him?

"Not at all! He didn't – " My voice broke, but I recovered. "He didn't say he loved me. I get the feeling I've been sleepwalking all this time."

Lily stood up and began to make tea, as she often did in the afternoons. She flavoured it with cardamom, which gave it an unusual flavour that I had come to appreciate.

"But the dress," I said. "It's all been a waste of time, and I must pay you. Would somebody else buy it, do you think?"

"No." She poured me tea in a delicate china cup. "It's definitely your dress. But don't give up just yet. With a few alterations, it could be a party dress. A ball gown."

"Oh! When am I likely to go to a ball?" I sounded like Cinderella.

"You never know."

I thought I did know. The future was a blank, with nothing to celebrate – unless we won our battle against the road scheme, of course, but at present that seemed increasingly unlikely.

We sipped our tea in silence for a few minutes. Outside, a thrush was singing loudly.

"When you've finished your tea," said Lily, "why don't you go for a long walk in the woods? I always find it helpful when my mind is in turmoil. Take a forest bath." I wondered whether she had already been to Japan. "The trees do something. You'll feel better, I promise."

So, in the afternoon sunlight, I walked out of the house and into the trees.

Oldwood never failed to surprise me, although I flattered myself that I was getting to know it. In some places the vegetation was a tangle of briars and brushwood and the path twisted and turned. In others, the path led almost straight, to places where the great silvery trunks, particularly of beeches, rose unencumbered, like columns in a cathedral, from the brown leaf-littered ground, with the sunlight slanting between the columns. I came upon one such place now, where high above me the fresh, new beech leaves were suspended horizontally as if floating in the air. I heard a cuckoo call, and then another, half a tone lower, farther off. The migrating cuckoos must return to this wood every year. So many birds must rely on this place for nesting sites and food and were not expecting it to be swept away. A few minutes later, the path curved, and a mass of bluebells among fine blades of grass stretched ahead of me, like an azure lake or a fallen shard of sky. I fell to my knees and inhaled their subtle scent.

How had I come to this point in my life? What was I going to do? I felt empty, yet there was so much to think about. Too much.

Sleepwalking, I had said to Lily, and that was what I must have been doing for a long time, pretending to myself that all was well between Hugh and me, when clearly it wasn't. I had been carried along unquestioningly by everyone's expectations, including my own, but I had been heading towards something that I didn't want. Why had I not realized it earlier? Had I been in love with Hugh? I'd thought so. What was more, had he ever been in love with me? Everything had been taken for granted and nothing had been looked at squarely.

What a fool. Here I was, a university graduate, and I'd even written a thesis on the romantic poets, but I hadn't a clue when it came to real life. Well, I'd burnt my boats with Hugh. Did I regret that? No. I actually felt huge relief. But it didn't solve anything. I was broke, and I didn't know where I was going.

I stood up and walked on. Here were the horse chestnut trees, the 'foreigners', perhaps planted by Lily's great-grandfather. They had even more new leaves than the beeches, besides their cones of fluffy white flowers which had not been visible a week ago. I pressed my hand against a tree trunk, tough and cracked like the skin of a very old man.

What I felt was passionate love for these trees, for all these trees, and the thought that they might be felled to make space for a road was, quite simply, unbearable. They and the old house must remain, together and inseparable.

But although there was a whole crowd of us working on the protest, a strong team, could we possibly succeed? What could I do? I could sketch and write, and I'd talked for a few minutes on the radio. What did that amount to? Almost nothing. It was all ephemeral. I had no real power, and no independence either, since I didn't have a job.

What about the new job interview? I would have to reply. How would I even get there? I would need to look up bus and train timetables.

My brain was busy with logistical details as I turned back towards the house, and at the same time I noticed that new bracken fronds were beginning to unfurl, like green shepherds' crooks. The whole appearance of the woods was changing, developing, reaching out towards summer.

What was that? I could hear something, and it wasn't birdsong.

It was the piping of Gavin's penny whistle, and at a turn of the path I saw him walking towards me through the dappled sunlight. I felt a sudden weakness and my heart thudded.

As we approached each other, he pushed the whistle into his pocket and smiled without speaking. We stood facing each other. Then he took my left hand, and with his thumb he stroked my naked ring finger. I looked into his face, hoping that my trembling wasn't visible, and he raised one eyebrow.

"I've broken off the engagement," I said huskily.

"That's what Martha told me. I couldn't quite believe it."

I withdrew my hand. "I didn't hear from you after that radio interview. I wondered whether you'd listened to it."

"Listened to it? Of course I listened to it. You were great. But then I had to rush off to a job, and I was stuck for at least four hours. A guy had a virus and a WiFi problem and he was in a rage … But then I sent you a text and I left a voicemail message."

"Oh, thank you. I didn't get them because I was already here."

"Right, and there's no coverage here," he nodded. "This place is extraordinary. But you knew that, of course."

We were strolling side by side, our footsteps synchronised. As we emerged on to the grass, the sunlight cast our long shadows ahead of us. Two outlines: Gavin and me. I was still shaking inwardly, confused and unsettled. I tried to remember the name of the boy in Paris who had produced that effect on me, brief though it had been. His name wouldn't come to mind. I had shut out the episode, just as I had cut myself off from the nameless boy, because I had been Hugh's girl then, pure and faithful.

I had to do the same now. Not only was Gavin with Martha, but he was going to be the father of a child! My reactions were making no sense.

" … sorry to be in such a hurry, but I wanted to apologize." Gavin was saying something and I hadn't been attending. I saw that his van was parked in front of the house.

"Apologize?"

"For not calling you straight away after you'd spoken on the radio. I wanted to, but this guy kept me on the line. So how about I buy you lunch tomorrow, at about 12.30? There's a new vegetarian place." He described where it was in the centre of town. I must have walked past it this morning without noticing it.

"I … "

"Good, that's settled, then. See you tomorrow." He jumped into his van, turned it swiftly and drove off along the green avenue of limes.

Lily was standing just outside the front door. "I told him you were in the woods. Are you feeling better?"

"I – I think so."

We stood side by side, looking towards the trees.

"The light is so beautiful at this time of day," said Lily.

"Golden. And the shadows are not as dark."

"Oh, Lily! I don't know where my life is going. I feel I've been living in the shadows for years, not seeing things clearly."

"You will," said Lily. "You'll find your way. I need to let more light into this house, too – light and life."

***

In the morning I washed my hair and dried it with a very old, clunky hair-drier, and put on a white shirt and a clean pair of jeans. In town, I had just fastened the bike to some railings and was walking towards the new vegetarian café when I heard quick steps behind me and Gavin caught up with me.

"I could see your hair a mile off," he said.

The place calling itself Crunch was rather trendy, with house plants and handmade pottery, bare wooden tables and selections of quiches and salads chalked up on blackboards. I looked nervously at the prices, and Gavin noticed.

"Choose whatever you like. I got a fat fee for that long job yesterday."

I asked whether he was vegetarian, and he said, "Not yet," but that he was tending in that direction. The older he got, he said, the more aware he became of human mistreatment of the natural world, and industrial farming was an abomination. He referred to various writers on the subject, and I asked him what he had read at uni.

"Life sciences," he said, with a grimace. "But there were no openings. That's why I've had to fall back on IT. In any case, it's almost impossible to find a permanent job nowadays."

"Yes. The gig economy. It seems our generation are the unlucky ones."

"True. But would you want to be back at Sacs-de-bloody-Luxe? I hear you … uh … left under a cloud."

"Summarily dismissed," I said, "and I imagine it was because I was taking initiatives against the firm's interests. They want the road."

"If that was the reason, it was a badge of honour. But they may also be cutting down on staff for other reasons."

"Oh? What have you heard?"

"There was a profits warning. I think they may be in trouble."

Could that be the trouble that had been making Hugh so tense? The question crossed my mind – but I was not going to think about Hugh.

"I've been called to a job interview," I told Gavin, and his eyes seemed to darken when I told him about the post and where it was.

"Do you foresee a career in international sales of electronic equipment?"

"I don't foresee anything, but I think I ought to go. I never seem to get beyond the application stage."

"Can I ask why you applied for that particular job?"

I shrugged. "They have connections with various French-speaking countries in Africa, and they want someone with fluent French. But to be honest, you get to a stage where you start to apply for absolutely anything."

He nodded. "I know. But you still go on hoping to find something meaningful. A job where you can make a difference, help to put right some of the things that are wrong with the world."

"That's it! But I haven't found anything – except our campaign against the road. That's definitely meaningful, even if I'm not earning a living."

He put out a hand as if to grip my arm, but withdrew it again. "I'm so glad you joined us. What would we have done without your talents?"

I felt myself beginning to blush, but a very young waitress came to take our order, and after that we talked of other things: his childhood, his abandoned dream of being a musician, my earliest attempts at sketching, films we had both seen and books we had read. I felt that I had his full attention, and he didn't check his phone even once.

Returning eventually to the subject of the protest, he told me that a delegation had been to a meeting with the town council, at which Lucy (with the blue hair) had been quite outspoken. Sam had been more diplomatic, but the result had been deadlock.

I felt rather put out that I hadn't been invited. He read my thoughts.

"We thought it better not to ask you, because of your close connections with the firm and the Markham-Hunts."

"But that's all over," I said.

"Completely finished? Really over and done with?"

"Yes," I told him. "That's all behind me now."

After that, he said nothing for a while, but whenever I looked up, his green-grey, hazel-flecked eyes were always fixed on me.

"Are you in a hurry to go anywhere?" he asked as we left the café.

I said I wasn't. In fact, the afternoon was a blank. Nobody needed my presence anywhere.

"You remember that I offered to show you a very old yew tree in the churchyard? Maybe we could go."

The churchyard of Saint Michael and All Angels contained ancient, grey stone tombstones, some of them leaning at odd angles. There was no room for recent graves. When Oakfield residents died nowadays, they were buried in a cemetery on the outskirts of the town. We walked up the path lined with tall, neatly clipped yews leading to the south door, but these were not the trees that Gavin wanted to show me. The high square tower loomed above us, and the stone gargoyles in silhouette opened their beaks and spread their wings. Again I felt a slight dizziness and looked down. Were they supposed to represent all angels? They seemed more like devils to me. Of course, I thought, there were such things as fallen angels.

We walked around the massive tower to the south side of the church, where the tombstones were grander, some of them boasting statuary, and at once I saw the tree that Gavin had been talking about. My few excursions into the town had never taken me to this particular spot. Otherwise, how could I have missed it?

The great girth of its reddish, fluted trunk held up a huge

and spreading canopy of dark branches. Gloomy, full of shade, and yet not entirely dark. On the ends of all the twigs with their small, sombre leaves were rounded bunches of bright emerald. The new leaves were sprouting, young and brilliant, all over a vast and ancient living organism.

"It's – " I glanced at Gavin. "I was going to say: amazing. But that's not a good enough word." Awesome would have been a better word, I thought, except that Maya and her friends used it to describe anything and everything, so that it had lost its meaning.

We sat down on the flat tombstone of one William Fry, who had died in 1757. I hoped that he would not have minded.

"I've always loved yews," said Gavin.

"You told me that they can live for thousands of years. I wonder how old this one is."

"I expect nobody knows. Every part of them is toxic, by the way."

"Why do you think they always grow in churchyards?"

"Some people say they've been planted in enclosed spaces so that horses and other animals can't browse on the leaves and be poisoned. Others say – well … "

"What?"

"That they keep away evil spirits."

I gazed up into the dense branches. "I don't feel that it's malevolent," I said.

"No. Trees never are."

"They're not, are they? I've never felt threatened by trees. They're just big and old – and slow. Living on another time-scale from us. And yet it takes no time at all to cut them down."

"Some are sacred," said Gavin softly. "Yews in particular."

"Yes." I could feel that this yew had a definite presence. Others must have felt it for hundreds of years.

"Are you a church-goer?" he asked.

I told him that I had been baptised, like most people, but that religion was not really part of my life. My parents didn't attend church, and in fact I had never set foot in St Michael's, which always seemed to be locked in any case.

"I'll tell you what," said Gavin, "we'll go in now. I know the verger – Pete – we were at school together. And he told me that any time I liked I could go up to the top of the tower. Usually it's closed to the public."

"Oh! But – " I bit my lip. "You know I hate heights."

"Jaki, I know you think you do. But come up with me. I promise you it'll be worth it. We need to be far-sighted. To broaden our horizons."

"Are you talking metaphorically?" I demanded rather crossly.

"Metaphorically and literally. We can probably see Oldwood from up there. Come on – don't be a wuss."

A wuss! How dare he? I wasn't going to be called a wuss, but still I hesitated.

He held out a hand, I took it without thinking, and he swung me to my feet. The tingling sensation travelled all the way up my arm. I followed him dumbly back to the south door, agonizing over choices, afraid of heights, afraid of the future, afraid in some ways of Gavin himself.

We stepped over the threshold into the church through the south door, down two steps into the gloom and the musty smell of damp and old hymn books, where the wooden pews on either side of the aisle faced the altar and the east window with its hovering dove. The afternoon light shed violet patches from the stained glass on to the sturdy pillars.

Pete, the verger, came bustling to greet us, and in no time he had unlocked the door behind the font which led to the spiral staircase.

I followed Gavin up the first few stone steps and stopped.

"I don't think I can – "

"Yes, you can."

"I don't think so. Oh, please."

"You can, Jaki. Do you want to hold on to me?" He looked back and down at me, his face half hidden in the dim light of the staircase.

"No," I gulped. "No, all right. I'll – I'll follow you."

Up and up and round and round. We passed the closed door to the ringing chamber. We passed the belfry. If that great bell had suddenly struck the hour, I thought I would have died. Up and up, round and round. Perhaps there was no end to this staircase, or perhaps we would emerge in another world, like Jack and the Beanstalk. And still Gavin climbed untiring ahead of me. My breath was coming in short gasps. I willed myself to continue onwards and upwards. This was mad and pointless. Why was he doing this to me?

At last there was brighter light ahead. Gavin stepped out of the arched doorway, and I followed. The sky was huge and open and I felt as if I were drowning in space. I closed my eyes.

Gavin's hands were on my forearms. "Easy now, easy," he said, as if gentling a horse. "Take your time. Get your breath back."

After a few moments I opened my eyes and released myself from his grasp. I looked around and gasped. The top of the tower was not even flat, but consisted of four sections with a shallow gradient sloping up towards the centre. The walls were crenellated, and between the crenellations yawned empty space.

"It's OK," said Gavin. "You're perfectly safe. Look, if we go and stand in the centre you'll be well away from the edge. You can't possibly fall, and then we'll have a good view."

I edged towards the centre as if walking on ice. Only then did I dare look beyond the battlements.

Gavin was talking in a matter-of-fact voice. "So on this side we can see the roofs of the old town, with tiles and chimneys, and then farther away there are the housing estates and the blocks of flats. Can you hear the traffic on the motorway?"

I could hear the wind in my ears, although it wasn't a windy day.

He moved to the edge and leaned over. "From here you can see the cars looking like toys, and people like marbles with their legs scissoring forwards and backwards – what?"

I had crawled after him and grabbed his sleeve. "Please come away from the edge! Please!"

"All right. I'm quite safe, though."

He didn't resist, but moved back to the centre with me and stood gazing towards the horizon.

"And then you see in that direction what used to be farmland. Well, it's still agricultural, but just look at those endless seas of yellow. Oil-seed rape, and no hedgerows. I bet there's very little wildlife. No wild flowers, no bees, no other insects. Just money growing, really."

I forced myself to look, squinting against the brightness of the light. There was one small group of trees in the distance, but otherwise I could see only sheets of plain yellow or plain green.

"It looks like a desert," I said.

"A desert, sure enough. And now look, if you just turn in this direction," he gestured, "way over there we should be able to make out the treetops of Oldwood. Yes! Can you see?"

"Yes. Oh! I hadn't realized that some parts of the wood were on a slope. I thought it was mainly flat."

"I wish I'd brought binoculars. I don't think any part of the house is visible from here."

"I can see – What's that? Something above the trees."

Gavin peered at the thing apparently hanging in the sky. He narrowed his eyes. "Wow. I think it's a drone. Yes, look – it's swerved off. It is a drone."

"Lily said they might use drones to do a survey. I hate them – horrible things, like spiders in the sky, spying."

Gavin was tense beside me. "Not for much longer. Not that one, at any rate. Look! Look what's happening!"

What was I seeing now? It appeared to be an enormous bird, flying straight towards the drone on powerful wings. The drone sped sideways, but with an aerial dip and dive, the great bird caught it in its talons. Then it flew towards us. It seemed to be coming straight for us.

"Oh, wow," said Gavin again.

I stared, transfixed. How far away was it? It was impossible to tell how large it was. Could it really be so huge, or was it an optical illusion? It continued to approach with slow wingbeats, then suddenly veered off, still carrying the drone like prey, and disappeared to our right. It had seemed black, a great black bird, but I thought I had caught just a tinge of crimson.

We stared at each other. Had we both seen the same thing? Apparently we had. After a few moments we both spoke at once, and then laughed. "Well, that was an experience. I said we ought to broaden our horizons," said Gavin.

"It was incredible."

"Why didn't I have my camera?" He clicked his tongue.

"It flew by so fast," I said.

"How are you feeling? Better? Are you glad you came?"

"I would hate to come up here alone," I admitted.

"Ah," he said quietly, "but you're with me."

With him? With him in what way? No, this wasn't how it should be. I felt an urgent need to turn the conversation.

"How is Martha?" I demanded.

"Martha? She's fine. Why?" He looked puzzled.

"I know she's pregnant."

"Oh, yes. Well, she seems to be doing fine so far. No morning sickness or anything like that, thank God. And of course she's happy about it."

"And you," I said pointedly, "are you happy about it?"

"Me? Oh, well. I suppose so. As long as it suits her. Can't say I'm overjoyed. I tend to think there are too many babies on the planet."

A shock went through me. How could he be talking so offhandedly about his own child? I hadn't thought of him as cold and flippant.

"It's going to change her life, of course," he said when I didn't reply. "Things change anyway. Nothing is ever permanent, and everyone has to move on. I'll probably be moving on myself before too long."

"Moving on?" I croaked.

"To fresh woods and pastures new." He smiled heart-breakingly, his eyes very bright.

"Why?"

"Oh, various reasons. I'll need to get out. Three people living in that small house is a bit of a crowd, you know."

I couldn't believe my ears. He was planning to abandon Martha and his own son or daughter. Did she know? She had seemed happy and confident. Trusting.

This was Gavin talking: Gavin, who had seemed so idealistic, so warm, so interesting – so much on my wavelength. Gavin, who had caused that indescribable thrumming, shimmering feeling in me which had seemed to mean something. And now revealed as so heartless. Irresponsible. Uncaring. I felt as if I had been hit by a cold wave.

I scrambled to my feet. "I must be getting back."

The journey down the spiral staircase seemed even longer than the upward struggle. I went first, treading carefully on the wider outer edges of the steps. I must not stumble. Down and down, round and round. Sometimes I touched the cold stone of the wall, and Gavin came steadily on behind me.

Safely at ground level, outside the church door, he said, "When shall I see you again? Are you busy tomorrow?"

"Not tomorrow. Not any time soon."

"Jaki, what is it? Is something wrong?"

I couldn't look at him. "There's nothing wrong with me."

"Then why?"

"Because," I burst out, "Because I've had a – a bit of a shock. I don't think we ought to see each other any time soon."

"Was it such an awful experience for you? I'm sorry, Jaki. Maybe I shouldn't have insisted – "

"It's not that."

"Then what is it?" He looked honestly perplexed, taken aback and disappointed. How could he look like that after what he had said?

"I think you don't understand," I said. I stalked off, and then broke into a run. I had to collect my bike and go back to the protection of Oldwood, to the gentle acceptance of Lily.

He didn't follow me.

***

That night, I couldn't sleep.

The bed in my room over the porch was as comfortable as ever, but I tried first one position and then another, punched the pillow, turned it over, tried counting to a hundred, tried to relax each muscle in turn. Nothing worked.

In the end, I got up, drew back the curtains and looked at my watch in the moonlight. It was nearly half past two. I leaned on the sill of the open window, breathing in the soft night air until my eyes grew used to the darkness and I could make out the shapes of trees. A cautious rustling and puffing noise made me look down, and I saw the humped shape of a hedgehog bumbling across the grass in front of the house, foraging for food. Eventually it disappeared around the corner.

Its life was simple, contented – and short. Why was mine so complicated?

How could I have been so wrong about Gavin? Why was he so committed to saving Oldwood if he was such a superficial, cold person? Perhaps he cared only about trees and not at all about people. Why had he seemed so keen to spend time with me? Perhaps it was my appearance that attracted him. After all, I was a blonde, and I knew all too well that some boys and men had a "thing" about blondes. Why couldn't I have been a brunette like Martha? But I wasn't going to think about poor Martha, expecting a baby that its own father didn't care about.

I was such a poor judge of men. I had thought that I knew Hugh, but gradually I had discovered that he wasn't the perfect partner I had imagined. Either I was incredibly naïve, or else he had become a different person. We had both changed. "Things always change," Gavin had said, and he was right. Why on earth was I thinking about Gavin again? Things changing, things changing ... I wished they would stay the same just for a little while. Just so that I could hold on to something stable and find my balance.

It was no good. Gavin's image swam back into my mind, slight, wiry, green-grey-eyed, attentive, and the feeling rose up in me again like a fountain. My skin felt acutely sensitive all over.

I wanted him. It was a feeling of desire that I no longer had for Hugh, if I had ever had it.

I wanted Gavin, and I could not have him. I must not even think about it. I covered my face with my hands and groaned.

I paced around the room, sat down on the bed and stood up again. How had I fallen into this? What a fool. And I really, really liked poor unsuspecting Martha.

What must I do? He had said that he would be going away. Then I would never see him ... oh, no ... oh, no ... Stop! He wasn't going anywhere immediately. So in that case I ought to go away myself. And abandon the campaign? Surely not. But somehow I must keep out of Gavin's way while still doing all I could to support the action.

Was that even feasible?

Of course, there was the prospect of a job with the electronics firm. That was far enough away – a good sixty miles. If they offered it to me, I would have to find digs in that town. It was much too far to commute – and anyway, I couldn't expect Lily to put me up indefinitely.

I would have to leave this place.

Deep in the woods, a bird began to sing, first some fast twittering, then warbling, then three or four melancholy, descending notes. After a pause, it began again. It was a nightingale.

Staring up at the unmoving, indifferent stars, I thought that it was the saddest song I had ever heard.

***

"If I drive you to the bus stop, you could get the number 49 at 8.17," said Dad, peering up over his glasses from his laptop, "and then you could either get the train at 9.03, but that's a stopping train. Let's see if there's a faster one."

We were both sitting at the dining-room table.

Dad was in his element, working out the best itinerary to enable me to report for the interview on time. I was grateful, because I hate timetables and logistics, but with part of my mind I was worrying about appropriate clothes, and at the same time I was looking at my tablet. The lack of an internet connection at Oldwood hadn't particularly bothered me until now, because I had been in contact with people by phone from the office or the flat, and I had got together frequently with Gavin and Martha. Now I was avoiding both Gavin and Martha, and I felt cut off. I needed to come to my parents' house to use the WiFi.

"What time do you have to be there?" asked Dad again.

"Ten-thirty."

My attention was suddenly focused on an email marked urgent. It was the sixth and most recent, all of them unread and all from Hugh.

"Since you appear to believe ... as I have repeatedly stressed ... have not even had the courtesy to answer my communications ..."

God! He sounded so pompous.

" ... you clearly have no intention of responding to my offer, made in good faith, and I can only conclude that you wish to have nothing more to do with me. You may therefore consider that our engagement is at an end. I am prepared to believe that we were both mistaken about our feelings for each other."

My heart was thumping. He was prepared to believe that, was he? Well, bully for him. I was prepared to agree with him. I could have told him that I hadn't received his "communications" because there was no phone signal or internet connection at Oldwood, but it was pointless to try to explain. He had clearly been working up to this, and after all, it was what I wanted, wasn't it? A clean break.

" – should get you there on time," said Dad.

I said nothing.

He looked up at me again. "What? Is something wrong?"

"Nothing much. Hugh has just confirmed that we're no longer engaged."

"I see." He tapped the table a few times with his pen. "Well, it's best to get things straight, isn't it?"

"Yes," I said. I bit my knuckles and burst into tears.

At that moment, Mum came into the room with the newspaper and bent over me, her arm around my shoulders. Why was I crying? What was wrong? I couldn't tell her. I didn't really know myself. I certainly wasn't crying because I'd lost Hugh. It was just that life seemed a total blank, and there was no choice I could make that would bring me any happiness. Mum rocked me to and fro, and Dad stood up, saying that he would go and print out my itinerary.

My sobs subsided and Mum went into the kitchen to make some tea, talking through the door to me as she filled the kettle. "There's something in the air. I've felt it for several days now. And my stars say today that a person close to me will have difficult decisions to make."

That was an easy enough prediction to make, I thought, though I didn't say so. Any decisions now might as well be random, anyhow. Everything was pointless.

"I hope you get this job," she said, returning with the tea. "It will be something definite. Everything else has been too much up in the air lately."

I opened the Herald as I stirred my tea. There seemed to be no more items about the great bird flying over the town. It must have been the one we had seen from the church tower, and surely other people would have noticed it. But perhaps it was yesterday's news. I flipped over the pages. Petty crime, a new petrol station, vandals causing damage at a primary school … What was this? 'No threat to Sacs de Luxe, says CEO.'

I read the article and tried to make sense of the business-speak. Half-year results had been disappointing. Economies of scale … In the longer term, building scale was key to driving profitability. No reason to predict job losses …

I read it again, but couldn't make out exactly what rumoured threats the CEO was denying. Something appeared to be upsetting the firm, but apparently all was basically well. Perhaps there had been previous articles that would have shed light on this one. Hugh could no doubt have explained it all in great detail, but some time ago he had stopped trying to talk to me about the business world, as my eyes would glaze over.

I was obviously not cut out for the business world, yet here I was, about to try to be recruited to another business. What choice did I have, though? It was my only offer and my only escape route.

As the afternoon wore on, I spent a long time online, mugging up as much information about KY Voltatronics as I could find. I must come across as motivated. I must get a foot on the employment ladder. I had wasted far too much time faffing about on that internship, where I had learned nothing worthwhile and hadn't made use of my talents. My talents? What were they? I would have to think about that. Surely I could be useful in some capacity.

I heard Maya come in through the back door and fling her school bag into a corner. There were a few words exchanged with Mum, and then she entered the dining room holding a glass of fruit juice.

"Hi. What are you doing?"

"Trying to prepare for this job interview."

"Oh." She slouched over to the window and drank a third of the glassful at one draught. "Gavin thinks you would be thrown away on a job like that."

"Gavin?" My heart turned over. "Have you been talking to him?"

"He came round here yesterday and helped me with my maths homework. It's been totally doing my head in."

"What – and you were discussing me?"

"Not particularly. He asked after you. No, we were talking about me and the troupe and our plans. He's quite interested in dancing, as well as being good at maths. He's not a bad guy."

I said nothing. I peered at my tablet screen. Had he perhaps come looking for me? How would I have reacted if I had been here yesterday?

"Are you all right?" said Maya.

Grandad came in and forestalled any answer I might have made. I again explained what I was doing, and then Mum asked whether I would be staying for supper. No, I said, I had better get back to Oldwood and have an early night. I collected my papers together, including Dad's itinerary, and he said that he would pick me up at 8 o'clock tomorrow morning, just outside Oldwood Court.

As I was collecting my bike, Grandad came hobbling after me.

"I'll walk with you as far as the gate," he said.

His stick tapped as we walked along the path. Petals were falling from the magnolia.

"Are you quite sure you want this job?" He stopped at the gate, his eyes under his bushy eyebrows looking straight into mine.

"Oh, Grandad. What else am I going to do? I have to find some kind of a job. I can't go on just floating on the surface of life, and staying free of charge at Oldwood – it's not fair to Lily."

"Yes, it would be only fair to pay rent."

"If they hire me, I'll need to pay rent near the office. I'll have to find somewhere to live, and I don't suppose I'll be earning much on an initial salary."

"Quite. That's what I was thinking. Now, about rent and living expenses. I'm prepared to make you a monthly allowance – "

"Oh, no, you mustn't – "

"Wait!" He held up one hand. "I intend to do this, Jaki. I'll be occupying your room for the foreseeable future, and my house is to be sold. It will go on the market this week, and if I find a buyer quickly, money is not going to be a problem."

"Your house? But what about – "

"The contents? Everything must go. I'm at an age now when I should be letting go of possessions, not clinging to them."

"But what about the garden that Granny loved so much? And your books!"

He looked briefly at the ground. "I regret the books. But they must be sacrificed like the rest."

"I'm so sorry."

"Don't be. It will give me pleasure to help you. You are the rising generation."

Speechless, I flung my arms around him, feeling how thin and fragile he was, and he patted my back.

"But I shall be sorry if you abandon your battle to save the trees. I admire your commitment, you and your friends. Believe me, everything that has changed in history comes from individuals making a stand."

CHAPTER NINE

Inside a glass cubicle, divided from the busy open-plan office by partitions, I sat on a low chair. On a higher chair, facing me across a desk, sat a carefully made-up woman in a navy business suit. I had already taken a written test which involved writing a piece of sales copy for a new component of overland vehicles, first in English and then in French. Luckily I had been reading up about precisely this new gadget, and I praised it lavishly, warning potential customers that it would not be long available at such a competitive price and urging them not to miss this unique opportunity. I didn't find it difficult to write such stuff, although I didn't believe a word of what I had written.

My interviewer had been firing questions at me, and after such an early start I was feeling seriously in need of coffee, but I summoned up all my play-acting resources. I was keenly interested in the firm, I told her. My skills, although not directly related to its activities, were highly suitable, in particular my ability to draft in two languages. I was someone who had drive, and I thought it essential to be a good team player. In five years' time, I would hope to have developed my abilities and usefulness to a whole new level.

Ms Jackson suddenly switched to French (with a strong accent) and I fielded some more questions without difficulty. Then:

"What would you do if you had a budget of a million pounds?"

For a split second, I thought: I would buy Oldwood Court and save it, and then I would travel the world and plant a million trees.

That was not the kind of answer that she wanted.

"I would start by travelling to all the countries of French-speaking Africa and launch in-depth research on their needs in the field of electronics so as to draw up an initial plan for the next five years."

There were a few more questions, while phones rang and people moved quickly to and fro behind the glass partitions, but at last the interview was over. Ms Jackson escorted me to the lift, this time making small talk about the weather and the difficulties of parking near the office. With a quick professional handshake, she left me.

I shot through the lobby and out into the roar and fumes of traffic. Farther along the street I had noticed the entrance to a shopping centre, and I went in search of coffee. Concrete buildings loomed above me, plate glass windows reflected me as I walked, dodging other people on the pavement. There were no trees in this street. If I got the job, I thought, I would be walking along here every day. I would need to find a flat or at least a room to rent, probably somewhere on the outskirts of town. What was the bus service like? Ms Jackson had also mentioned the possibility of travel to Senegal, Mali or Togo if I made the grade. That would be an adventure. I had never been to Africa – I had never been anywhere, really.

In the neon-lit shopping centre, surrounded by loud music, garish artificial colours, footsteps and voices, I sipped a scalding cappuccino from a cup the size of a small bucket. Had I made a good impression? Had I screwed up the whole thing? In any case, it was in the lap of the gods. If they took me on, I would be starting a whole new life, and that was what I wanted, wasn't it? No more Hugh, no more Sacs de Luxe. Independence. If Grandad helped me at first, I would definitely pay him back as soon as I could.

But what about Oldwood, Lily and the campaign? For a second I felt the soft woodland air around me and saw the leaves moving. Then I was back in booming noise, a plastic table, bitter chocolate powder in the shape of a letter on the foam of the coffee. How could I abandon everything? It would surely be possible to go back at weekends and join the others. A compromise might be possible, despite the distance.

But what about Gavin? I took another gulp of coffee. If he were to walk up to this table right now, I would …

No. I couldn't see him. I had to avoid him. Of course, I could abandon the whole fight for Oldwood. I had already abandoned Hugh. And perhaps Gavin would not be there. After all, he was prepared to abandon his partner and his unborn child and move on, just like that. He was prepared to give up the fight for Oldwood, apparently. Abandonment was the name of the game.

Then I thought of Grandad saying that he admired our commitment. Was it all a farce?

It didn't really matter what I did. Nothing mattered.

***

June had arrived, but the weather wasn't summery. All night and all morning it had poured with rain, and now, in early afternoon, the sky was still overcast above Oldwood Court.

I had been wandering disconsolately from room to room until the minibus had arrived, bringing Madame Walenska, Maya and her dance troupe, and I had taken refuge upstairs. Faint music and thumping sounds wafted up from the drawing room. I had joined Lily where she sat at her sewing machine, now making green tunics for the dancers, who were planning to put on a show.

"I can't settle to anything," I complained.

"Sit and talk to me," said Lily.

"All right ... but I need to be doing something."

I glanced towards the tall cheval mirror. In it I could see only the reflection of the room, but the colours of the walnut cabinets were dark and gloomy. My wedding dress, still on its stand, hung like a headless ghost. I looked away.

"Lily, could I draw you?"

She threw me an amused glance. "If you like. I can't sit still and pose for you, though."

I fetched my sketchpad and charcoal and began her portrait. The broad outlines, the sewing machine, the working figure, were easy enough. Outside, rain dripped from the gutters.

I had described my interview to Lily and she had not

said very much, but she knew that I was waiting for news. Nothing had come from KY Voltatronics, although a whole fortnight had elapsed. Every day I had cycled over to my parents' house to use the WiFi, check my email and find out if anything had arrived through the post. Nothing. Perhaps they wouldn't even let me know that they had appointed another candidate.

I also checked social media to find out how the Oldwood operation was going, and scoured the local paper for news, but it seemed that nothing much was happening. Even Sacs de Luxe was not in the news.

I was in limbo.

Once, while stopping at traffic lights, I had caught a glimpse of Hugh's car. He was at the wheel, but he didn't see me, and he was not alone. I caught the outline of a dark-haired woman in the passenger seat. So he hadn't lost any time in finding a substitute for me. Or perhaps she was just a colleague? What did it matter, I told myself crossly. I had no need to think about him.

I worked on my sketch. Lily's attitude as she pushed the fabric through the machine was not difficult to draw, but her face was another matter. I couldn't capture her features. Perhaps it would have been easier to draw her back view. She looked up.

"You and I are alike," she said comfortably. "We both need to be making something. Why don't you move all your artist's materials into the old schoolroom? That could be your space, if you like."

"Thank you. It would be lovely to have space to work," I said. "But I may not be around much longer if I get that job."

"Do you really want it?" She stopped sewing.

"I ... What else am I going to do?"

"Nel mezzo del cammin di nostra vita," said Lily, and I stared at her. Was she suddenly speaking Italian?

"What?"

"That was a quote from Dante. Perhaps you are lost in a dark wood right now. I hope the way will become clear for you. I'm sure it will, Jaki."

I had been vaguely aware of a vehicle arriving outside, and now I heard the drawing room door opening and releasing a surge of sound. I heard Maya's voice shriek, "Gavin!"

Gavin. My heart lurched and I stood up abruptly.

"I think it's stopped raining. I'll go out and walk for a while."

Lily nodded calmly. "Don't get lost."

I nipped down the back stairs, the plain stone staircase up which servants must once have toiled, carrying coal scuttles and cans of hot water. I emerged in the empty kitchen and let myself out into the yard. From there I headed for the trees, avoiding the drawing-room window. Gavin's van was parked at the front of the house.

The ground was wet underfoot and soon my shoes were soaked through. Branches and leaves dripping with rainwater brushed against my clothes, and I shivered, but I kept going along the paths, turning left and right at random. I couldn't face Gavin and I would wait until he had gone. Perhaps he would come looking for me? No, he surely would not.

Hazel and sycamore, ash and beech and hawthorn, their different shapes rose up on either side, thick with leaves gleaming and wet. Birds flitting in the leaf canopy overhead sent down showers of raindrops, although the rain itself had stopped. I walked with no particular direction in mind. Eventually I came to the grove of yew trees, looming and black, and I remembered Gavin playing his pipe to the dryads. Walking around the tree in which he had been sitting, I noted that there were lateral branches that could provide useful footholds. He must have placed his feet in them.

Suppose I just climbed up a little way? Not far. Not high, but just a little way.

Up on to one branch. Then another. If he could do it, so could I. My hands gripped other branches, and I saw more possible footholds ahead. Perhaps just one more. Then another. The tree was almost like a ladder. I hauled myself up, hand over hand, scraping my knees, almost slipping but not quite. I was climbing in a kind of dream. The reddish branches with their fine dark leaves like combs were becoming thinner and more supple as I climbed higher, and then almost unexpectedly my head emerged from the foliage and I realized I was at the top of the tree.

Other treetops stretched away from me, some higher, others lower, as far as I could see. Where was the house? It must be behind me, but I didn't dare turn around. Where was the stone wall? Ahead and to right and left stretched the trees. A gleam of sunlight pierced the clouds and I caught a glint of water. That must be the lake. A crow, cawing, flew with steady wingbeats into the distance, but it was definitely a crow, not the great bird that we had seen. The tree moved very gently under me, creaking, like a boat on the swell of the sea.

Where did the woods end? Where did the outside world begin? It was impossible to tell. Perhaps the whole of the world was, fundamentally, forest. Thousands of years ago, it must have been so. I was looking farther afield, towards new horizons, but I could see only the trees.

My head was in a whirl. I had never before climbed a tree to the top, yet here I was. I should be feeling fear, vertigo and nausea, but I felt nothing of the kind: only a great questioning, a craving, searching for an answer to a question that I had scarcely formulated. The trees meant something. They must mean something.

But now I would somehow have to get down.

***

A few days later, I was sitting in the old schoolroom, working on my sketch of Lily. I wasn't happy with my first attempt and had started again, drawing again the seated figure in the room with the carved furniture and the tall cheval mirror, but leaving Lily's face blank. I felt I would need a number of tries before I got her features right.

Now and again I pushed down the nose of the colourful wooden rocking horse, and he nodded as he rocked, encouraging me.

I was just thinking about cycling over to my parents' house

yet again, when I heard a car drive up to the house. I stood and peered down through the barred window. I thought it might be Lily returning in her old banger.

A taxi had just halted on the gravel sweep and its doors were opening. Maya bounced out of one door. A stick poked out of the door to the front seat, followed by a pair of thin legs in trousers, and Grandad's bent figure straightened itself. Then the remaining door opened and a woman with sleek silver-grey hair emerged. She pulled a guitar case after her, and stood gazing upwards. I banged on the window, but it wouldn't open.

I rushed down the stairs, through the hall and out of the front door.

"Grandad! Stella!"

Maya was jigging about gleefully as Stella paid the taxi-driver and he drove off.

Grandad said, "Your aunt has paid us a surprise visit, and I felt it was high time that I made the acquaintance of Ms Green."

Then Stella was hugging me, laughing, and saying that she had come over from Paris on the spur of the moment. She had heard my interview on the radio and had been thinking for some time about me and the wonderful house and woods that I was so anxious to preserve. "I've even started on a new song," she said. The theme was trees, and she had decided that she had better come in person to see this possible source of inspiration.

She gestured up at the ornate façade, with its turrets and pilasters and Virginia creeper spreading over one wall. "This is an extraordinary place."

"Let's go in!" said Maya impatiently. "Come and meet Lily."

"As a matter of fact, she's out," I told them. "She had to go into town on some kind of business, but I expect she'll be back soon."

I led them into the morning room, where Stella propped her guitar against an armchair and headed straight for the piano. She sat on the stool and touched the keys delicately.

"What a beautiful instrument."

Grandad lowered himself into the other armchair and told me how delighted he was that Stella had finally decided to visit. He had booked a room for her at the George. "The charming receptionist there tells me she knows you."

"Yes, that's Martha." I swallowed. I didn't know what to say about Martha.

"Yes, she's one of your activists," said Stella from the piano stool. "She told me how it has been going. She said you've started crowdfunding now, which seems like a very good idea. You simply must save this amazing place. And the woods! I do hope your Lily will let me explore."

"Here comes Lily now!" shouted Maya from the window. "Her car has just gone round to the yard."

We all waited. Stella spun round on the piano stool. Grandad grasped his stick and prepared to rise to his feet.

Distant sounds came from the back of the house. A door closed. A faint draught blew into the room like a sigh. Footsteps came lightly along the stone passage, the green baize door creaked, footsteps crossed the hall, and the door opened.

Lily stood in the doorway, upright, black-clad, her hair snow-white, with a bluetit on her wrist and a greenfinch on her right shoulder.

Nobody spoke. The silence was almost palpable.

Then Stella stood, frowning, and took a step forward.

Lily also took a step into the room. Her hands rose.

Then both women were half running, half stumbling towards each other, the birds took off and flew back into the hall, and my aunt and Lily were embracing.

"Stella! At last! After all these years!"

"Rose! Is it really you?"

Rose? What did this mean? Could Stella have mistaken Lily for somebody else? Clearly not. They were acting like long-lost friends, gripping each other's arms, beaming into each other's faces, wiping away tears and making incredulous noises.

I stood watching in astonishment, and so did Maya,

'gobsmacked', as she told me later. Grandad stood leaning on his stick and swaying slightly, and eventually he cleared his throat and said, "Ms Green?"

Then both women turned to him and urged him to sit down, introductions were made, we were all asking questions and giving explanations, and gradually things began to make sense.

It seemed that long ago, when I was just a baby, Stella had known Lily in Paris. But in those days she had been called Rose. For reasons that weren't clear, she had changed her name. "A rose by any other name … " quoted Grandad. Rose was the great friend that Stella had mentioned to me, but she had completely lost touch with her and thought that she must be dead. They would both have been young in those days – possibly about my own age. I tried to imagine them together in Paris.

"And Jaki," said Lily, turning to me, "You reminded me so much of Stella, but you said your name was Saunders. If you had said Hayward, I would have known at once that you were related."

"Really?" said Grandad, raising one eyebrow.

"Yes. Sorry, Grandad. It was nothing personal."

"Ah, well. 'What's in a name?' Your aunt Stella never used her surname professionally, either."

That was true. In showbiz she had been known simply as Stella.

The conversation turned to her career as a singer, with Stella being modest about her trajectory, but Maya, Grandad and I all prompted her to mention her triumphs in France, America and England and the success of her various albums. Had Rose – Lily – not heard about her?

"I've been – quite out of touch with the world. Living in obscurity," said Lily. I began to think of her as Roselily. "But I always knew you were gifted."

"It was you who encouraged me. I don't think I would have dared to do anything with my songs if you hadn't pushed me. But that was all such a long time ago. I've retreated into obscurity, too."

"Oh, but you mustn't!" said Roselily sharply. "Not when it's important. You must come out into the light."

Stella looked at her doubtfully. "I have been working on another song recently. I'm not quite sure … "

"Play it for me!" I had never heard Lily – I mean Roselily – speak in such a commanding voice.

Obediently, Stella took her guitar out of its case and tuned it. Perched on the arm of the chair, she began to sing.

The lingering ballad in Stella's clear voice told of the slow growth of trees, the branches dividing and reaching out, the leaf buds opening. She sang of the world's forests, falling and dying for humankind's financial gain. Sometimes she broke off, saying, "That's not quite right." Sometimes she hummed instead of singing words. I found words coming into my head of their own accord and thought that perhaps Stella could use them.

Now Roselily was at the piano, picking out an accompaniment to Stella's guitar. She began to sing a little, wordlessly. Their two voices rose and blended.

"We could do something with this," said Roselily, as Stella played a final chord.

"We could. It's coming. But how about this bit?" She played a series of downward arpeggios.

"I think it needs – " Roselily played a few notes in a minor key.

"Listen to us! It's just like the old days," said Stella, delighted. "Do you remember when we played Bach? *Jesu, joy of man's desiring*?"

"Of course I do." Roselily launched into the tune and both their voices soared effortlessly.

Maya and I had been sitting on the floor, listening, and we looked at each other wide-eyed. Grandad was nodding in a satisfied kind of way.

Maya nudged him. "Grandad," she said in his ear, "They're busy. Come and look at the rest of the house."

I went with them across the hall and into the library, where Grandad gave a whistling sigh at the sight of all the half-empty bookshelves and the broad oak table in the centre of the room. It had always been his dream, he told us, to have a great library like this. Surely it should have contained collections of leather-bound volumes, tooled in gold. What had happened to them?

"I think Lily – I mean Rose – had to sell most of the books, and most of the furniture and the Indian antiques, just to make ends meet," I told him. "Her grandfather left her the house – the whole estate, in fact – but he didn't leave her a fortune for its upkeep."

Maya was keen to show him the drawing room where the dance troupe practised. "All this space!" She pirouetted on the parquet. "It just needs a barre along that wall. Then it would be perfect."

"Come and see the old schoolroom upstairs. She's allowed me to spread out all my drawing and painting materials. That is, if you can manage the stairs," I added anxiously.

"There were stairs in my own house. I'm not quite an invalid yet," snorted Grandad, climbing slowly with a firm grip on the mahogany banister. Floating up from the morning room came the sound of Stella and Roselily now singing *Flocks in pastures green abiding.*

He looked through my latest sketches of trees, and went over to the window. "I can quite see why you and your friends want to save the wood. It has a look about it – as if it had been here forever."

"For hundreds of years, at any rate. And it all means so much to Lily – Roselily. The trees and the house together."

Grandad had turned back to the room and was examining my several attempts to draw Roselily sewing. "No face?"

"I can't get it right."

"Yes, she has a most unusual face. Her features seem to change as the light changes. Quite a remarkable woman. She is not someone who would pass unnoticed in a room."

I could only agree with him. No wonder Stella had never forgotten her.

Maya was sitting on the old rocking horse with her eyes closed, rocking forwards and backwards. "I could go on a dream journey on this horse. All the way to India and back."

"Oh!" said Grandad suddenly. "Jaki, my dear, I nearly forgot. This letter came for you." He fished an envelope from the inside pocket of his jacket.

KY VOLTATRONICS. The capital letters on the envelope seemed to shout.

I ripped it open as piano and guitar notes, singing and happy laughter drifted faintly up to us.

I had to read it twice. Then I folded it.

"Well, what does it say? Have you got the job?" demanded Maya impatiently.

I swallowed. "Yes," I croaked.

They wanted me to start work in ten days' time.

***

Later that evening, Roselily, Stella and I were relaxing in the great leather armchairs of the morning room. As dusk fell, Roselily had lit three tall white candles and placed them in brass candlesticks on the wide hearth. The windows stood open to the summer evening air.

Grandad and Maya had gone home, leaving Stella behind because, as she said, there was so much to talk about. Roselily said that she would run her back to the hotel in the car, but Stella said no, she would phone later for a taxi. We had eaten one of Roselily's usual frugal suppers in the kitchen, which suited me fine. She seemed to live on eggs, bread and cheese, fruit, nuts and a few vegetables that she grew in a corner of the old kitchen garden. Then we had taken our green tea into the morning room.

I had told them over supper that KY Voltatronics had offered me a job, and at once their eyes were fixed on me. There was a short silence.

"Well, congratulations, if it's what you really want," said Stella.

"Yes. Well done. I'm glad they seem to appreciate you," said Roselily.

Somehow, they didn't sound very enthusiastic.

"I've been looking for a job for ages. I need to be able to

earn my own living. I'm sure I can make a go of it," I said firmly, trying to convince myself. "And anyway, it's only as an assistant, and only for a six-month trial period, initially."

"But what about your commitments here? You seemed so passionate about – "

"I still am! I'm not giving up. I intend to come back every weekend."

"It's a long way," murmured Roselily.

There was another short silence.

"Anyway," said Stella, "I would like to help now. Count me in, Rose. I still have quite a few contacts, and some favours I could call in. I might even – ha! – I might even 'make a comeback'. I could do a fundraiser."

"Oh, Stella!" said Roselily and I together.

"Well, I'm not making any promises, but my manager thinks it's a possibility. And Rose, now I've found you again, it feels like fate. It must mean something."

"Perhaps," said Roselily. "Why not?"

"And to tell the truth, all this enthusiasm and commitment – Martha and Jaki, and even Maya – well, they put me to shame. I feel I can't stay moping alone in Paris forever when I could be useful, and when I still have some life in me."

We talked about Stella's songs and concerts and record labels, and I was glad that the conversation had turned away from KY Voltatronics. I would think about that later.

Now, as we sat quietly in the morning room, I could scarcely see their faces, only the shapes of the two women, Stella lounging with her left foot on her right knee, Roselily upright and elegant as always. A crescent moon slid slowly into view in the upper corner of the window, and a dog barked, very far away.

"So, Rose," said Stella, "will you tell me what happened to you?"

Roselily sighed. "Where shall I start?"

We had lapsed into French by now, the language that those two had spoken to each other all those years ago.

"I never asked you questions, did I? I suppose I was too taken up with my own affairs."

"No, you were discreet, that's all. And I might not have found it easy to answer questions in those days. Everything was still so fresh and recent."

"What had happened to you, Rose? Why were you in Paris in the first place? Do tell me," pleaded Stella. "If you want to, that is. I've always wondered, always."

"I was escaping," said Roselily. Haltingly, she began to talk about her past, as the tall flames of the three candles gleamed and wavered against the dark hearth. Her father, as she had told me, had paraded her across India and around other countries in the Middle East as some kind of performing act. At last, with the help of a French diplomat, she had broken away from him. The diplomat had taken her to France, where she said she had family, but it had been difficult to track them down. Her mother was long dead, and her uncle, her mother's brother, had never had anything to do with her. However, once found, her Uncle Sébastien and his wife had been obliged to take her in.

I felt that there were a number of pieces missing from this jigsaw.

"Were they kind to you?" I asked.

"Kind enough. But they thought I was peculiar. Things happened around me."

"Yes," said Stella. "I remember."

"I'm sure you do. It was very difficult for me to make friends. Really, you were the only person who accepted me and treated me like a true friend."

"We were friends. But I still don't understand … "

"And there were the birds, of course. They always accepted me."

Stella suddenly laughed. "I remember Jacques."

"Dear Jacques."

"Who was Jacques?" I asked. Perhaps Roselily had had a lover, after all.

"He was a crow."

"An unforgettable crow."

I was silent. These women had memories that I knew absolutely nothing about.

Roselily went on to say that she had gone to school in Paris, but then had taken up dressmaking. After a time it had become absolutely essential for her to move out of her uncle's flat, and he had eventually found her a place to rent on the other side of the city.

"Why did you have to move out? Did your uncle want to get rid of you?"

"It wasn't that. He ... he had a son. His name was Grégory. Oh! I should never have done it. I couldn't control things, in those days."

"Did he – ?"

"He was obsessed with me. He wouldn't leave me alone. All the time, he – it was impossible – but I should not have done it."

"Did you hurt him?"

"Yes. Badly." She didn't explain further.

"Olivier told me something about that. He said he was disfigured," said Stella.

"Oh – Olivier! I haven't thought about him in years," said Roselily. "I wonder what happened to him."

"So Olivier never did find you?" Stella asked.

"No. But Grégory did."

Another silence fell. We were all three only ghosts in the candlelight.

"Rose," said Stella, and there was pain in her voice. "What happened to you after the fire? Where did you go? Why did you disappear? I tried to find you."

"I had to go. I was being hunted and persecuted. Everything was out of control. I'm truly sorry, but I had to disappear. Those were terrible years. I travelled around, living anonymously, hand to mouth, until at last I came to England and my grandfather took me in. I came here, to Oldwood Court, and there were the trees, you see. The trees drew me in. The trees were ... And then my grandfather told me that my father was dead."

"And I was travelling, too, in those days," said Stella, "globetrotting and singing, because you had told me that I could and that I ought to do it. But you never knew about me, and I never knew about you, and now – "

"Now we've found each other again," said Roselily's voice out of the darkness.

"Unbelievable. Is it just a coincidence?"

"When certain things happen," said Roselily, "some people call them coincidences."

***

Two days later, Stella and I were walking together in the woods. Roselily had gone into town again on some mysterious business errand, so I offered to show Stella a few of my favourite places. The weather had cleared and the lime trees were tall domes of scented blossom, alive with bees. We walked along the paths in dappled sunlight, the air warm. Small clouds of gnats hovered over our heads, and a tortoiseshell butterfly flew ahead, alighted on a plant, flew ahead again as we approached, almost as if it was leading us farther into the woods. Overhead, the leaf canopy shushed quietly like waves on a shore. We could hear birdsong, and the sudden screech of a jay.

I took her to the lake with its weeping willow, its reflection perfectly inverted in the water, and to the solitary oak, and then to the place of the tall, smooth beeches, where earlier I had found a carpet of bluebells. The bluebells had finished flowering and the glade was full of all the long grasses of high summer.

"Oh, look! A squirrel!" Stella pointed. Like a flame, it ran up a beech trunk, turned head downward and looked at us, and then disappeared around the other side of the trunk.

"This place is pretty much a wildlife sanctuary," I said.

"For wildlife – and for wild people, perhaps. I'm so glad Rose found a sanctuary here … But of course, it's under threat now."

"It would be criminal to destroy all this for the sake of traffic," I said fiercely.

"Oh, I agree. Living in Paris, I've had quite enough of traffic, and there aren't enough trees to absorb the pollution.

They even cut down a big plane tree near my flat the other week because they wanted to widen the entrance to a showroom." She kicked a pebble. "I hate the sound of chainsaws."

"So Lily – Rose – I'm going to call her Roselily now – "

"That's a pretty name."

"Anyway, she used to live in Paris and you knew each other." I pulled a long stem of grass from its socket and bit off the sweet end. "Why have you never mentioned her?"

Stella looked thoughtful. "I don't really know. I suppose I felt guilty."

"Guilty?"

"Things were bad for her. She was being harassed by several men, including a guy called Olivier that I thought I was in love with … Incredible! What did I see in him? Anyway, things were complicated and got worse, and instead of standing by her, I went to England and left her. People hated her and were afraid of her."

"Afraid? Why?"

"As she said, things happened around her."

We walked slowly on, and I waited for her to explain. We came to another oak, this one squat, ivy-clad and hollow, with branches like stiff hair rising from the top of the trunk, and I told her that this was Maya's favourite, because it reminded her of Tolkien's Ents. "I think everyone finds their own sacred tree or grove here," I said. I thought of Gavin in the yew grove, playing his pipe to the dryads, but I didn't mention him.

"Which is your sacred grove?"

I took her up to the rise where the silver birches grew, slim and delicate, their leaves dancing in the lightest breeze and their trunks purest white against the blue of the sky.

"Beautiful," said Stella. "I think mine would be the beeches. I wonder which would be Rose's favourite."

"She has a cedar not far from the gate," I said, and shivered. Had the sun gone behind a cloud? "She loves all the trees, though."

"I feel there's a spirit in these woods, and the house has its own personality. They're both special."

I returned to the attack. "So what sort of things happened around her?"

Stella ran a hand through her hair. "Well, she attracted all kinds of birds. They were delightful, in fact."

"Yes, she still does, and I think it's charming. But why would that have made people afraid?"

"The birds weren't the only thing. Have you heard of poltergeists?"

I stood stock still as she described some of the things that occurred. Objects flying about. Light-bulbs exploding. Her piano playing by itself. I had heard vaguely of such phenomena, and I could see why people might be alarmed. Perhaps I would be scared myself if I experienced them.

"I think she must have got over it by now," I said. "I haven't witnessed anything like that."

"Got over it? I wonder," said Stella. "Does one get over such things? But perhaps she's more in control after all this time."

"She did tell me that she used to have a problem with electricity."

"Electricity! Yes, she certainly did."

"But that was in the past. She seems OK with it now."

"I hope you're right," said Stella, walking on. A bramble tore at her sleeve and she released herself. "You see, Jaki, people with special gifts can be very fragile. Vulnerable. Rose needs help."

"I know."

"I let her down before. I abandoned her, and I'm not going to let her down this time. I've decided. I'm going to do everything I can to help her save Oldwood Court, the house, the woods – even if means appearing in front of an audience again."

***

In the days that followed, I was very busy. I had to sort out what I would need when I started work, organize a suitcase, get my hair cut, check train times and bus timetables. Dad helped me to book into a B&B that was only one bus ride away from the office of KY Voltatronics. Respectable clothes needed to be washed and ironed, because at my interview I had realized that jeans and trainers were not the dress code.

These preparations meant that I spent more time at my parents' than usual, and meanwhile word had got around that Stella was back in England and actually staying in Oakfield. All Maya's friends came round asking for autographs, which surprised me, because they would have been toddlers when Stella was a really big star, but apparently Maya had been doing some boasting. Then a journalist and a photographer from a national newspaper arranged to come and interview her, and Mum went into panic mode because the house didn't look tidy enough. But Stella said that she would do the interview at the hotel, to the delight of the manager. Phone calls came from France, and when she was in the house her phone never stopped pinging with text messages.

I was rather on the sidelines of all this turmoil, although Mum fussed a little about laundry and Grandad again offered cash to tide me over until I received my first salary.

The clocks ticked on remorselessly. The days passed quickly.

In a slight lull, I sat at the dining-room table flicking through the local rag. It contained a photo of Stella shaking hands with the mayor ("He doesn't yet know what I'm going to say about his road," she grinned when she saw it), and on another page a photo of Sacs de Luxe's premises caught my eye. 'No comment, says CEO' ran the headline. It occurred to me that perhaps I could sell the flashy handbag that Hugh had given me. Then I remembered that my heeled shoes, the ones I had worn to the reception in Paris, needed to be repaired.

Stella and Grandad emerged from the sitting room, where they had been deep in conversation.

"Help!" I said. "I must go into town and get my shoes repaired. I hope they can be done by the weekend."

"I'll give you a lift," said Stella. "I need to get back to the George."

She had rented a car and drove it everywhere, although

at first she found it tricky to drive on the left.

Parking is not always easy in Oakfield, but we found a space in Chantry Lane behind the church, and I nipped through the churchyard to All Soles, the shoe repair shop. The assistant shook his head at first, but then relented and said they could be collected on Saturday, and I made my way more slowly back to the car, thinking that I would soon be gone, and on my way glancing up at the gargoyles and then towards the great spreading shape of the yew on the south side of the church. It stood dark and motionless. How much it must have seen over hundreds of years. How petty our ephemeral concerns must seem to it.

My philosophizing stopped abruptly when I saw Stella standing beside her car with a small crowd around her.

I recognized Lucy's blue hair at a distance. Martha was there, and Sam, and Ryan, and four or five other supporters of the campaign, and they were all talking and animated.

"Hi, Jaki!" exclaimed Martha. "We haven't seen you for a while. How are you?"

I glanced hastily around, but Gavin was nowhere on the horizon.

"We're so excited to meet your aunt at last," said Sam, his eyes sparkling.

"And she's coming to join us," put in Lucy.

"We're all going for a drink in the Three Lions. You must come. Stella's willing to talk strategy with us," said Martha.

"Well … "

"Oh, come on, Jaki," said two or three people at once.

Reluctantly, I let myself be persuaded. I kept glancing around to see if Gavin would appear, and I was itching to ask where he was, but couldn't bring myself to pronounce his name.

In the Three Lions, the attention of drinkers at the bar was immediately riveted on Stella, and while we were noisily moving tables and chairs, the landlord himself came over to take our orders and to collect an autograph for his wife.

There were two main topics of conversation: progress of operations to save Oldwood, and Stella's plans to make a comeback. Ryan was busy peering at his phone and checking figures. He announced that we had reached nearly 100,000 signatures on the petition, and we all cheered.

"Where have you been?" asked Martha, who was sitting next to me and sipping tonic water while the rest of us drank beer or cider. "I've seen your posts on social media, at any rate. Things are gathering pace. But have you been hiding? Even Gavin hasn't seen you, or at least, he hasn't mentioned you."

I shifted uncomfortably. Everyone else was talking. "I had a job interview. And now I've found a job."

"Really? Congratulations. I hope it's local."

"No. It's sixty miles away."

"Oh! Oh, Jaki! That's bad news for us." Martha's brown eyes were wide.

Sam, sitting on the other side of her, turned solicitously. "Bad news? Is something wrong? Watch out, you're spilling your drink." He gently took the glass from her.

"Jaki's leaving us."

"Really?" Sam frowned. "Gavin will be sorry."

Gavin! He was talking casually about Gavin and at the same time so close to Gavin's partner that their arms almost touched. What was going on here? Her pregnancy was showing now, a neat little bump. Perhaps Sam was trying to comfort her for Gavin's heartless desertion. Had he gone already?

Suddenly I stood up. "I must just … "

They probably assumed that I was going to the loo, but I made for the door. Just as I pushed it open, there was Gavin, about to enter the pub.

"Oh!" We both stood poised. I let the door swing closed behind me.

"Jaki," he said, and gripped my arm. And there it was again, the warmth, the trembling. "Have I done something to offend you? I don't understand. Please tell me."

I couldn't meet his eyes. Instead I looked at the pattern of his shirt, a fine green and brown check.

"If you don't know, then I can't … Anyway, it's not about

me … Just – how can you be so faithless?"

"Faithless?"

I looked up at him now, and his eyes were genuinely perplexed. Those eyes. That lean face.

"It doesn't matter." I broke away from him. "In any case, I won't be sticking around. I leave next week."

"God, you're not really going to work for that bloody electronics firm, are you? What about the campaign? What about saving Oldwood? What about Lily? What about – "

"Oh, please shut up! I'll still do what I can."

"What, at a distance of sixty odd miles? Don't fool yourself."

"You can talk!" My voice rose. "Why shouldn't I leave this place, when you're moving on yourself? You said so."

"That's different. I haven't told you – "

"I don't want to know! Different? What – one rule for me and another for you? That's rich."

"Jaki – "

I turned away and began to walk quickly down the street. Damn him. I broke into a run.

CHAPTER TEN

I had never felt so tired, not even when I was revising for finals. KY Voltatronics clearly believed in throwing new recruits in at the deep end.

I was working on the floor below the one where I had been interviewed, but the office was also open-plan, with glass partitions, telephone conversations and people striding around. The atmosphere was much busier than at Sacs de Luxe, although the surroundings of chrome and plastic and strip lighting were similar. It would have been helpful if I had been familiar with the software that everyone was using, but it was new to me and I found myself on a steep learning curve.

On the first day my boss, Ms Jackson, had introduced me to various people in quick succession, but only now, some three weeks later, was I gradually putting names to faces. Most of the staff were young and seemingly dynamic, although some of the line managers were middle-aged.

"Great to have you join us. I hear you're quite the linguist," said Kylie in a loud and enthusiastic voice by the water-cooler.

Elegant Diana, a brunette with arched eyebrows and thin crimson lips, who was passing in the corridor, threw me a chilly glance. Did she roll her eyes? I couldn't be sure.

Apparently something was going on there.

I had attended several lengthy meetings where everyone talked in the sort of jargon that Hugh used to spout. In fact, several of the men reminded me of Hugh: young, thrusting types, who clearly thought that what they had to say was very important. And no doubt from the firm's point of view it was important: sales strategies, sales figures, market share, competition, cost-effective approaches. Sales of electronics were the centre of their universe, and if I was going to succeed in this job, then they should also be mine.

I did my best. I wore the uniform and tried to look the

part. I walked swiftly from place to place. I was deferential to Ms Jackson and to directors. If I still felt like an outsider looking in, that was because I was so new. I must concentrate and try harder – and try to make friends with my co-workers, although that wasn't so easy, particularly where the women were concerned.

I once found myself alone in a lift with one of the men from Human Resources. "Gorgeous hair, darling," he remarked. "Oh, sorry. Was that a sexist remark? I do apologize." He laughed loudly and I thought it better to say nothing.

At first I had worn my hair shoulder-length as usual, but soon I began to put it up in a chignon. I wore stud earrings, straight skirts or formal trousers, high heels. By the end of the day my feet were sore, and it was a relief to change into sandals for the trek home on the stuffy bus.

"Home" was still the plain and characterless B&B, with its low-wattage bulbs and two pastel pictures of landscapes on the walls. At weekends I had been so busy looking for somewhere more permanent to rent that I had not had time to return to Oakfield. After the meagre B&B breakfast with its tiny packets of muesli, miniature pots of industrial jam, sliced bread and watery coffee, I would set out on a search. I saw so many unsuitable and depressing places, some in run-down blocks of flats, others miles out of town. Nothing appealed to me, and I didn't want to consider flat-sharing. After all, I wasn't a student any longer.

When I had been a student, I had lived in a city not unlike this one, but the atmosphere hadn't weighed on me so much in those days, perhaps because I knew it was only temporary. After graduation, Hugh and I would do great things together. How far away those dreams seemed. And how far away Oldwood Court also seemed, almost like a dream itself. Tramping along hot pavements in the midst of traffic fumes, wailing sirens and neon signs, I would sometimes have a vision of the peaceful woods, smell the clean air and hear birdsong. Then it vanished.

One big advantage of urban living was that I always had a phone signal. However, talking to anyone on the phone was another matter. I tried several times to call Roselily, but she always seemed to be out. The school holidays had started, and Maya had gone to Benidorm with a friend's family. She sent me photos of beach scenes. Dad rang me once and talked at some length about the difficulties of finding a buyer for Grandad's house and the hassle of putting books and furniture into storage. Just before he rang off, he said something about Sacs de Luxe that I didn't catch because a massive lorry was passing, but he added, "Just as well things didn't work out with young Markham-Hunt." Then we were cut off, and I wondered what he meant, but not for long. I didn't want to think about Hugh. I received a few updates from Ryan about the petition and the crowdfunding, but nothing from Martha. Perhaps she saw me as a deserter.

And nothing at all from Gavin.

I wasn't as addicted to my phone as most people seemed to be. Maybe I had grown accustomed to not using it while I was at Oldwood. Here, nearly everyone in the street tended to weave about as they walked with their eyes and thumbs busy on their phones, or else they marched quickly to and fro, to and fro, going nowhere, talking into their phones in carrying voices.

I missed having conversations face to face. True, I was often called upon to act as an interpreter at KY Voltatronics when one of the African representatives came over on business, and that was hard work, especially as the dialogue was usually technical. I spent long hours mugging up French and English equivalences for electronic terms, at the same time trying to figure out the functions of these various pieces of gadgetry. They also needed me to correct reports and draft sales materials in both languages. I took to testing myself on the relevant vocabulary while eating hamburgers or sandwiches in noisy café-restaurants where music blared that was nothing like Stella's albums. Could her type of 'vintage' music make a comeback? I didn't know, and I hadn't heard from her, either. She must be busy, I supposed.

I lay on my bed in the B&B, listening to the trickling and clunking sounds of plumbing in the building and the never-ending roar of traffic. A streetlamp outside the open window cast a bleak orange light on the walls. I ought to get up, prepare for bed, learn some more vocabulary, listen to the news on the radio. Instead, I continued to lie motionless.

I had never felt so lonely.

***

In the lunch hour, I usually ate a snack while sitting at my computer. At first, when one of the other women in the office had announced that she was going out to eat, and had asked, "Anyone coming?" I had stood up, eager to be on good terms with everyone. But nobody would meet my eye. Rachel, Sarah, Sophie and Laura would loudly discuss where to go, and then leave in a bunch, ignoring me.

After this had happened several times, I cornered Kylie as we were washing our hands. I asked her straight out whether I had done something to offend the others.

She looked embarrassed and pretended to be hunting for her lipstick. "It's not your fault."

"Well, what is the problem? I'm an interloper – is that it?"

"Not exactly. Well, you were a bit unexpected. Jackson has a reputation for thinking outside the box."

"What box? They wanted someone bilingual who could write without making loads of grammatical mistakes, and I fit the bill."

"Yes, yes. It's just office politics." She ran a comb through her curly hair and wouldn't meet my eye in the mirror.

"But I want to know what I've done wrong."

"You haven't done anything."

The door opened and a woman from Accounts came through to use the loo. She glanced at us standing there.

"Look," said Kylie hastily, "Don't let it get you down. It'll blow over."

After that I stopped making friendly overtures and adopted an attitude of polite indifference. It may have been a coincidence that my computer kept developing bugs. It may have been unintentional that a message was not passed on to me that I was needed at an urgent meeting, so that I had to run along corridors and arrived out of breath to find disapproving faces around the shiny table.

A few days later, I was just leaving at the end of the day when the man who had made a comment in the lift stopped me. "My name's Dave," he said. "I'm sorry – I hope you weren't insulted the other day. I really do think you have beautiful hair."

I muttered something and turned to go, but he said, "Wait!" and went on to ask me whether I was going to the party on Saturday.

"What party?"

Oh, it was just an informal get-together, a few friends, a few drinks, maybe some dancing. If I told him my name, he could introduce me to some people. He knew that it wasn't always easy to network in a new job.

I hesitated. He had quite a nice smile, although it would have been more attractive if it hadn't shown his gums as well as his teeth – but that was hardly his fault.

What the hell, I thought. After all, I might as well go.

So it was that on the Saturday evening I put on slinky trousers and the sparkly top that I had last worn to the reception at Sacs de Luxe, and carrying a bottle of wine I made my way to the ninth floor of a block of flats in the suburbs. I had deliberately arrived rather later than Dave had suggested, as I was hoping to slip in discreetly. A blast of hot air and loud music hit me as a woman with an off-the-shoulder dress opened the door and said something that I couldn't hear. The air was thick with the smell of alcohol and perfume, although through the crowd of people dancing, drinking and talking I could see glass doors open to a balcony, and the shimmering city lights in squares and rectangles at varying heights beyond.

Dave shouldered his way towards me, took my bottle and put his mouth to my ear to ask what I would like to drink. I wasn't sure what was available, so ended up with a fancy glass of some highly-coloured cocktail. Then I had to put it down because he wanted me to dance. There was really no room, but we gyrated vaguely among other twisting and jerking bodies. To his credit, he did try to introduce me to a few people, but the music was so loud that we had to yell at one another, and I learned scarcely anything about anyone. I danced with a few more men, and tried to strike up a conversation with a thin girl who was sitting in a corner, but there was so much noise that I learned almost nothing except that her name was Jessica, after she had shouted it three times.

It was much too hot. I even missed the air-conditioning that made the office a little more bearable. At one point I made my way to the balcony for some air, but everyone out there seemed to be smoking and I nearly got burnt by a man who was animatedly waving his cigarette and holding forth about tennis. I leaned over the balustrade. Funny. Nine floors up, but I felt no vertigo.

The evening wore on, and gradually I began to smell something besides alcohol and perfume: it was weed. All right, I had often come across that at uni. I had even smoked it. What I wasn't prepared for was to be subtly propelled by Dave to a bookshelf on which a line of white powder had a huddle of people bending over it.

"Ah, no," I said. "Sorry, that's not my scene."

"What?"

"NO!" I shouted.

"Ah, come on Jaki. Don't come all prim and proper." He put his arm around me and squeezed me hard. He tried to kiss me, but I turned my head and he kissed the side of my neck. "Its good stuff. It'll relax you. Come on – you may act little miss innocent, but I know you're wild underneath."

He knew I was wild? How dare he? He knew nothing about me. He certainly didn't know that I would never be willing to snort cocaine. I remembered what it had done to a boy called Mike whom I once knew. I broke away from him, saying I needed the loo, but I didn't go to the loo. I quickly ran down to the seventh floor before calling the lift, in case anyone tried to intercept me, and once outside I hailed a taxi.

I felt guilty for wasting Grandad's money on taxis, but it seemed so quiet and peaceful in the back of the cab. Through the windows I could see buildings all lit up, groups of people drinking pints on the pavement, spilling out of jewel-lit pubs. Neon adverts jumped and flowed. Traffic lights changed and motorbikes slalomed between cars, causing my driver to swear.

When I reached it and locked the door behind me, my bland pastel room felt like a refuge. Was I priggish? Was I a killjoy? Was I wild? I knew that I was definitely not a Saturday-night reveller, but who was I, really? Was I in the right place?

***

"You can sleep in Maya's room," said Mum. "She won't be back until Tuesday."

At last the August bank holiday weekend had rolled around, I had received my first salary and I decided to abandon flat-hunting for a couple of days and go back to Oakfield. Mum came in the car to meet me off the train, and grumbled for several minutes about the traffic and the lack of parking spaces before looking at me properly and commenting that my hair looked tidier in a chignon.

I had hoped to go straight to Oldwood, but felt that I owed it to my parents to spend at least one night at their house. In any case, I had left my bike in their garage, and I would be able to cycle over there the following day. But a weekend was so short. I was longing to see Roselily again.

Mum chatted about this and that as she drove. Stella, she told me, was in France, "organizing things" with her record label, and would not be back until the following week.

Traffic slowed ahead and we came to some roadworks. Mum complained some more as we were obliged to follow a diversion. I realized that we would be driving past Sacs de Luxe, and was not particularly keen to see those rectangular buildings again. However, I was surprised when I saw groups of people assembled outside the main entrance, and some of them appeared to be holding a banner. I craned round to see what it said, but we had already gone past.

"Do you know what's going on?" I asked.

"Oh," said Mum, "I think there's been some trouble. People have been laid off, or there's a strike, or … I don't really know. Someone said something at the WI the other day, but I don't remember the details. Your father knows more about it."

"Right, I'll ask him."

"Yes, but don't bother him until he gets home. He's away for the moment, dealing with the sale of your Grandad's house."

"Oh. Is there a buyer?"

"Yes, thank goodness. A sale's been agreed. A young professional couple with children. So now all the contents have to be removed by the end of next month."

Poor Grandad, I thought. All traces of his past being broken up and dispersed. I remembered that house so well, and Granny's garden. Why did things have to change? My thoughts turned again to Oldwood and the threatened fate of the house and the woods. Could the campaign save it? If it succeeded, it wouldn't be thanks to me. I had run away.

I slumped in my seat and didn't have much to say until we arrived, and Grandad, at any rate, was there to greet me warmly. He didn't seem particularly upset about his house. Maybe it was easier to let go of things when you were old.

The following morning found me cycling up the lime avenue with the wind in my hair, wearing jeans and a T-shirtand feeling so light and free that I could have gone on pedalling for miles. God, I needed exercise in the fresh air, even if it was too hot in the middle of the day. Living in a town was stifling. Now all the trees were in full leaf and were just beginning to acquire that faintly dusty look which meant that summer had almost run its course and autumn would soon be on the way. But not yet, I thought, not yet.

I found Roselily in the library, removing books from the sparsely filled shelves and putting them into boxes. She turned to greet me, upright and elegant as always, her eyes dark blue.

"You're back! I've missed you."

We took a break to drink tea in the kitchen, where Roselily

fed several starlings which squawked and squabbled for a few minutes on the draining-board before flying out of the window into the yard. She asked about my job and I told her as much as I could, but I found that I couldn't really describe it. The whole office setup seemed so artificial and alien when I was at Oldwood; but it was a job, and I was getting paid for it. She listened carefully and observed that at least I was using my French.

"But let's not talk about Voltatronics," I said. "Why are you packing up the books?"

Roselily stood and rinsed the teacups. "You see," she said after a moment, "This place has to be cleared. Cleansed. All the clutter that belonged to the past has to go."

Just like Grandad's house, I thought. The past was being swept away.

"But you've already got rid of so many antiques." I hoped that she was not planning to sell the rocking horse, at least.

"Yes. As much as possible has gone back to India, where it belongs. Then the house can be open to light and air. And people."

"People? You're surely not going to let them turn it into a hotel, after all?"

"No, no, Jaki. Don't worry. That is not the plan at all." She dried her hands on a towel. "Would you give me a hand with the books?"

To reach the few volumes on the top shelves, I stood on the wooden library steps that could be cunningly folded in half to make a chair. I handed them down one by one to Roselily, who wiped them with a cloth before placing them in boxes. I glanced at the titles. Quite a few were by nineteenth-century French authors: poems by Baudelaire, novels by Victor Hugo and Balzac.

"I'm expecting a phone call from Mr. Curtis," said Roselily suddenly.

"Oh?" I waited for more information.

I realized that the black-bound volume in my hand was entitled Curses and Necromancy, and hesitated, wondering what was in it. But Roselily reached up for it and continued to speak.

"He has made a suggestion. We've discussed it a lot. Hasn't Gavin said anything to you?"

"Gavin?" I nearly dropped the next book. "No. I haven't spoken to him."

Roselily glanced at me sharply.

"I see. Well, there is a sort of plan, if enough money has been raised to save the house."

I waited. Then: "What sort of plan?"

"I don't know if it will work. I don't want to say too much about it just yet."

"All right, but in that case what about the woods? The trees?"

"Ah, the trees. If I could only … Well, perhaps some may be spared, even if they do build the road."

I had a vision of a wide tarmacked road, complete with high-mast streetlighting, and two-way traffic pumping out exhaust fumes as it surged right past the circular lawn in front of the house, speeding past ragged stumps of trees that had been cut down.

"You can't be serious! You haven't given up?"

"Jaki, I haven't given up anything yet. Help is available, if we're granted it. Something in the woods is still very much alive. We can hope for protection, if we get rid of … certain things."

Roselily could be very mysterious.

"A date has been fixed for work to start on the road," she announced, not looking at me.

"What! When?"

"The end of September. They intend to start by removing the gates and demolishing part of the wall. They say that half the lime trees must be felled by the end of the year."

I felt a chill. Official plans were advancing like a Juggernaut.

"I hate all this," I burst out. "It's so easy to destroy trees. Forests are being destroyed all over the world, just when we need more trees to stop the planet burning up a few years from now if we do nothing."

"It began a long time ago," sighed Roselily. "My own

great-grandfather was partly responsible for deforestation in Assam. Vast areas of forest were destroyed to make way for tea plantations, and it's still going on. So many elephants were killed. In this house, there used to be an umbrella stand made from an elephant's foot. It was one of the first things I disposed of."

I could have added a lot about deforestation in Indonesia and Brazil, but her old-fashioned landline was ringing in the hall and she left the library to answer it.

My mind full of dismay and conjecture, I ran my hand along the top shelf and grasped another book, one whose covers were loose and frayed. Several pages and other sheets of paper slipped out and floated to the floor. I descended the steps slowly. Could Roselily really be reconciled to the idea of a horrible busy road being bulldozed through the woods? I could hear her voice speaking on the phone in the hall, but couldn't make out what she was saying.

Slowly I clambered down to pick up the loose sheets. Gradually she was emptying the house, as if preparing it for something. Demolition? Surely not. Perhaps she already had other plans for 'my' bedroom, with its crimson and blue rug and the bedspread twinkling with tiny scraps of mirror. It wasn't as if I had any permanent claim to it. I didn't really live here any more. If she wanted to sell the furniture, she could. Perhaps I could sleep on the floor sometimes, I thought.

I picked up the pieces of paper and was about to place them inside the old book when one of them caught my eye. It was a yellowing newspaper cutting. At the top I read The Times of India and under it the heading: Wonderworking girl incident. Father arrested. The photograph showed a young child with long dark hair and a pale face, her eyes full of anguish.

I began to read the article. It seemed to be referring to recent events already known to readers and to some kind of festival trick which had gone horribly wrong in a village. It described the outrage of the people and praised the swift intervention of the fire brigade and the police to prevent a lynching from taking place. The photograph was blurred, but there was something familiar about the face. The child,

I read, was known as Rosheen.

I heard the clunk of the receiver being replaced, and Roselily walked back into the library.

I glanced at her and then I knew. That face: it was Roselily as a child.

I held out the article. Roselily frowned at it and sank into a chair. "Oh, Jaki. Oh dear. Where did you find this?"

I explained that it had been inside a book, and she said wearily that she thought it had been lost long ago.

I waited. Then, "Can you tell me about it?" This, surely, was the heart of the mystery. Hints had been dropped, but I had never found out what had really happened.

She examined her hands, her long pianist's fingers resting on the surface of the table. "Tell me. Do you find me strange and frightening?"

"No," I said stoutly. "You're not like anyone else I know, but you don't frighten me."

"But I used to frighten people. And intrigue them. My father knew that, and he profited from it. He used to take me around the villages, and I would ... The more he beat me, the more strange things would happen around me ... I'm not sure you can understand that."

"I think so." I remembered what Stella had told me. I felt a faint quiver of unease. "What sort of things?"

"Perhaps I shouldn't tell you. I've kept it secret for years."

"Please tell me, Lily – Rose – Roselily. I hope you can trust me."

She sighed. "Things would fly about. Objects would appear and disappear. There were lights and flames. People sometimes felt as if invisible hands were touching them. My father pretended that he was orchestrating it all, like some kind of ringmaster in a circus, but he wasn't in control."

"Were you in control?"

"I was a child, Jaki. How could I be in control? I was a freak."

A silence. "You're not – " I began.

"Then this happened. Afterwards, my father was arrested,

and that was when I managed to escape. But it was dreadful, dreadful."

"What happened?"

Her voice shook. "I didn't mean to. He had hurt me so badly, and I was so desperate to get away. It wasn't deliberate but it was unforgivable."

"Did you cause some damage?"

"Oh, yes. I didn't mean to, but I did it. In the square where I was performing, there was a sacred peepal tree, venerated in the village."

I could hear the clock ticking in the hall. I waited.

"I set fire to it."

"How? Did you have matches?"

"No. It happened. Can you understand that? Because of me, it caught fire." Her dark blue eyes bore into mine. "It burned like a torch, Jaki. I burned a holy tree."

***

What would I have done without my phone? It was a lifeline, my connection to a world that I had left. When Stella texted me to say that she would be passing through on her way back from a trip to London, and suggested that we meet for lunch, I felt a thrill of excitement. Normally I had only an hour for lunch, but I asked Ms Jackson if I could make up the time in the evening, and she agreed, especially after I had explained who Stella was. She had seen her being interviewed on television.

When we met in the ground-floor lobby, several people had already approached her and she was fielding questions about her plans. Was she soon going to give a concert? Apparently she was.

We escaped from the building, and she took me to a little French restaurant in a sidestreet that she had found online. Sitting at a table in a corner, we were suddenly transported to France. The waiter was French, the menu was in French (with some funny translations into English) and we both fell naturally into speaking French to each other.

She remarked that I scrubbed up well, and it was true that I probably looked quite different from my casual Oakfield self.

How was I getting on in my job? I shrugged, and told her that I was doing my best. She looked at me speculatively, and talked about recording sessions while we ordered and then waited for our food.

The blanquette de veau was delicious and made a welcome change from the cheap snacks that I had been living on. We talked about the family and about Grandad's house, and how he seemed reconciled to the idea of losing it. We reminisced about Christmases years ago.

Then, over a café gourmand, she said: "You do know that I'm going to do a gig – in Oakfield?"

"Oakfield? No! I … I've been a bit out of touch."

It was to be held in the Assembly Rooms and the proceeds were to go to the Oldwood campaign. "I've been talking to the mayor, and I persuaded him that it would be good publicity for the town. I also approached the county council."

"But what did the mayor say about the road? Apparently they've already fixed a date."

"Surprisingly, not a lot. I was expecting more opposition, but he said vaguely that things were changing in the area. Maybe there's still hope."

"Wow, that's brilliant, Stella!"

We talked about possible dates for the concert, which would certainly be on a Saturday, and I resolved to be present. Roselily must be so pleased at this news, I thought.

"The mayor's wife is a fan of mine, which helps. But I flatter myself I'm quite a good negotiator. This concert will be a scoop, I told him, before the new album comes out, and before we organize a concert in London. 'But,' I said, 'all this only on condition that the funds raised go towards the Oldwood plan.'" She put down her coffee cup and beamed jubilantly.

"And did he agree?"

"Not in so many words. But I sensed something."

"You've achieved a lot," I said. Myself, I was out of the scene. But getting Stella involved was what we had hoped for, wasn't it? Perhaps I had been some kind of catalyst after all.

"Maybe, but you and the others did all the groundwork. Do you want another coffee?"

I looked at my watch. "I'll have to be getting back to the office. But how is the rest of the movement going?"

"Haven't you been talking to any of the lead activists? Martha? Or Gavin?"

My heart turned over at his name. "No."

"Call them. They know you're busy, but I'm sure they'll be glad to know that you're still committed. They're such a nice bunch of people, too. I've been to Gavin and Martha's house several times. I love Martha's weaving. She says she will make a winter scarf for me. And Sam! He's such a fan, which I'm surprised about, but there you are – even young people are turning back to the old style of singing, with proper words and melodies. I'm in luck, I think."

"You seem so much happier than when I saw you in Paris."

"Oh, I am. You know, I think that was a turning-point, when you came to see me. I was really at a low ebb. But now - I haven't felt like this since before Gérard died. And I'm putting one of his poems to music, as well. I think it will be good."

She was on a roll, and I was glad for her. I only wished I could feel equally positive.

"How about you? Have you done much drawing recently?" she asked.

"Hardly any. I don't have time, and I'm too tired at the end of the day. I've made one sketch of some rooftops and lampposts from the window of the place where I'm staying, that's all. I had started a portrait of Roselily, but I haven't finished it. It's still in Oldwood."

"Oh, you must finish it. You must finish something that you've started."

That could have several meanings, I thought gloomily.

"When will you be coming down again?"

"I don't know. It's a slow journey. And I can't take time off."

"Try. All work and no play – and Rose says she misses you."

"Is she all right? She told me – " I broke off. Had Roselily ever told Stella about that crucial incident in her childhood?

"What did she tell you?"

"Nothing, really."

"Well, she'll have plenty to tell you when you come." Stella waved a scribbling hand at the waiter, and he hurried over with the bill. "And now I must let you get back to your demanding job."

***

That evening, I sat on my bed, scrolling through the latest posts on the website. A photo that had attracted a lot of interest was an early shot taken by Gavin, a beautiful perspective of one of the paths and the trees in bright, translucent leaf. He had got the perspective just right and captured the moment when the sunlight highlighted the detail of the oak trunks. Added to the foreground, a white notice with aggressive red lettering demanded: WOULD YOU BULLDOZE A ROAD THROUGH THIS?

They were getting along very well without me. All the same, perhaps it was time I made contact.

After pacing up and down the room a few times, and staring at my phone, I finally rang Martha's number. She answered on the third ring.

"Jaki! How are you doing? We haven't heard from you for ages."

"Well ... I haven't heard from anyone, either."

"I'm sorry. I would have phoned you, but I'd got so used to you living at Oldwood, where you couldn't get a signal. And then I thought you would be too busy with your new job anyway."

"Well, yes. But I still want to be involved."

"Such a lot has been happening." Her voice crackled down the phone, and she chattered enthusiastically about Stella for several minutes. "And of course there's the new plan for Oldwood Court."

"What new plan?"

"It's a great idea. Apparently it's been in the offing for a while, but Lily wasn't too sure about it, and of course Mr. Curtis has – oh! Hold on! Something's boiling over."

She put the phone down and I heard chinks and clanks and a hissing noise. My eyes roved around the room as I waited. Pale wallpaper, smooth paintwork, a picture of a landscape with cows. Why was she taking so long?

Abruptly, Martha came back on the line and said: "Gavin will be so sorry to have missed you. He's out."

I made a croaking noise.

"Jaki, why are you giving Gavin such a hard time? Can you tell me? He says you wanted to have nothing more to do with him all of a sudden. I mean, I know you must have your reasons, but he seems so miserable, poor guy."

I couldn't speak.

"Hello? Are you still there?"

"Sorry," I muttered. "Sorry – my phone is almost out of battery. I'll have to call you back."

I cut the connection.

Afterwards, I flipped through my mainly blank sketchbook and found the drawing that I had mentioned to Stella. Roofs, telegraph wires, chimney pots, and not a twig or a leaf to be seen.

I tore it up.

***

I was leaving the office building after another exhausting day of complications and computer problems, a day when nobody except Ms Jackson had spoken a friendly word to me. I was just stepping from the antiseptic air-conditioning of the atrium into the humid heat and petrol fumes when Diana marched past me without a glance.

"Goodnight," I said.

She ignored me.

Suddenly I had had enough. I caught her up.

"Diana. Can I have a word?"

She stopped and glared at me, her black eyebrows inverted Vs. "What's wrong with you?"

"With me? I don't know. Is something wrong with me? Why are you so hostile?"

She snorted. "Get out of my way, please. I need to go home."

"Can I buy you a drink first? It's hot." I would miss my bus, but so what? Nobody was waiting for me.

"A drink? Why would I want to have a drink with you? We're not buddies, you know." Her eyes were narrow slits of incredulity.

"So what's the problem? I don't get it. I'll just have to suppose that there's something wrong with you." I made as if to move away.

"Oh! I'm not going to stand here and be insulted."

I turned back. "OK, then will you stand here and just tell me why you've been so unfriendly ever since I arrived?"

A bus drove past deafeningly, and home-going office workers passed us swiftly in both directions, paying no attention to us as we stood there on the pavement. We might have been rocks in a stream.

Diana's face had turned pink. "So why the hell would I be 'friendly'," her fingers sketched quotation marks in the air, "after what you've done, barging in, stealing my promotion? Oh, I know why it happened. You needn't kid yourself that you were the best candidate. Everyone knows about Jackson. She likes blondes. And picking you was one in the eye for Harris." Mr. Harris was another senior executive. "Oh, I know what goes on."

"I swear I know nothing about any of this. I applied – "

"Yes, and pulled strings, didn't you? But I know more about you than you think, Ms Jacqueline Hayward who goes swanning off for long lunches with celebrities and pop stars while the rest of us do the work."

"You mean Stella? She's my aunt."

She rolled her eyes. "Oh, very funny. Ha-ha. And my uncle's the Prince of Wales."

"But it's true! She is my – "

"Listen, I don't give a fuck who your influential contacts are. I know about you. My Daddy knows Mr. Markham-

213

Hunt, big shareholder in Sacs de Luxe down in your part of the world. Name mean anything to you?"

I said nothing. I felt as if she had punched me in the stomach. How had Hugh's family caught up with me here?

"Ah, I can see it does. I know you were a troublemaker and they had to let you go. So you'd better watch your step."

"But – " Where could I begin?

"Sorry." She brushed me aside. "I can't waste time talking. Some of us have lives, you know." She stalked off and was swallowed up by the crowd.

I stood for a few more moments. So that went well, didn't it? I thought. Office politics. Yet I had tried so hard to do my job and be on good terms with everyone. Welcome to the corporate world.

***

It was late afternoon on Saturday when I pushed open the front door of Oldwood Court. I had spent most of the day at my parents', feeling guilty that I had been neglecting them. Maya was still suntanned from her holiday in Spain, but beginning to groan about the approaching autumn term at school. Autumn? It was still high summer, although today had been very windy, with threatening clouds piling up in the west.

I could hear music. I peeped around the door of the morning room. Roselily was at the piano, Stella was perched on the arm of a chair, playing her guitar, and – Gavin. Gavin was standing in the curve of the grand piano, playing his penny whistle. Nobody was reading sheet music in this trio of musicians. They seemed to be having a jam session. The sound was interesting but rather confused, and as I stood just outside the door they wound it up with a flourish and all burst out laughing.

"That needs some work," said Gavin.

"Creative chaos," agreed Stella.

I moved forward hesitantly and was welcomed by everyone, although Gavin hung back and I couldn't look at him.

Roselily, rising from the piano stool as I put down my bag on the floor, said, "It's good to see you again, Jaki. I wasn't sure whether you were coming this weekend. We all miss you."

That was nice to hear.

"But tonight I'll have to leave you on your own. I'm going out with Stella and I may be back late. Will you be all right?"

"Of course."

I looked to Stella, who said, "I've persuaded Rose to come to a rehearsal. We'll soon be ready for the concert, but she doesn't want to come to the event itself."

"It's not that I don't want to come," protested Roselily, "but you know I don't like crowds. A rehearsal, with just you and the musicians – that will be perfect."

"Couldn't I come too?" I asked, rather plaintively.

"Sorry! No," said Stella. "I want you and the others to be at the concert on the night, when we've got everything right. I want it to be a surprise."

"I can't wait," said Gavin. The sound of his voice vibrated through me as I turned away.

I took my bag up to my room, and by the time I had come down again and Roselily had explained that there was food for supper in the kitchen and I must help myself, Stella and Gavin had both gone outside. Roselily took her grey cloak in case it grew chilly later, and in fact gusts of wind were beginning to make faint hooting noises in the window-frames. I assured her that I would be fine. I would read, and I might go to bed early, I said. It had been a tiring week.

It felt strange to be in the house alone in the evening. I had been alone plenty of times during the day, when Roselily had gone out on various errands, but she had always returned before nightfall.

I made myself some sandwiches with Roselily's home-made bread in the kitchen, drank cold water and then took a cup of tea into the morning room. Through the window I could see tree branches thrashing in the wind, and above them the sky darkening.

I sat in the armchair where Stella had been playing her

guitar, and switched on a lamp as the light began to fail. I had brought a newspaper but the print began to swim in front of my eyes, and I let it slide to the floor. I leaned back and closed my eyes to rest them.

I awoke with a jerk. How long had I been asleep? It was completely dark and I couldn't see the face of my watch. The lamp seemed to have stopped working. I reached forward and pressed the switch, but nothing happened. The bulb must have gone.

The wind had really risen now and was buffeting the windows, wailing in the cracks.

As I stood up, my foot touched the mug that I had left on the floor and I nearly upset the tea that I had forgotten to drink. It was stone cold. Holding the mug, I groped my way to the door, intending to switch on another light and throw the tea away in the kitchen sink.

But I stopped, aware of the carpet under my feet and the empty space above me, the high ceiling and the dark staircase leading up to empty rooms and gloomy passages. An extraordinary noise was swirling around the house. It was only the wind, but it sounded like many wordless voices in close harmony.

I managed to find the green baize door and to make my way cautiously along the stone passage to the kitchen. My hand reached for the light switch. Click. Nothing happened. The storm must have caused a power cut. My eyes were beginning to adjust to the darkness and I was able to make out the dim shapes of table and chairs and to tip the tea into the sink. But what was I going to do without any light? I couldn't read. It might be hours before the power was restored.

I supposed that I would just have to go to bed, although after my unplanned nap I wasn't feeling sleepy. On the contrary, I felt hyper-alert, and there was far too much noise going on. Then I remembered my phone and its flashlight application. It was upstairs in my bag.

I felt strangely reluctant to tackle the stairs in the dark, but I told myself that I had been up and down them so many times that I could surely negotiate them with my eyes shut. I made my way back to the hall, keeping one hand on the wall all the way. The green baize door closed very quickly behind me, startling me. Of course, it was on a spring.

Up I climbed, blindly, holding the banister, cold wood under my fingers. On the first landing, I paused. What was that? It sounded like voices coming from the dim far end, where the corridor turned a corner towards Roselily's sewing room. Surely she and Stella would not have come home in pitch darkness without trying to find where I was. I strained my ears, but the wind was howling. There it was again. It sounded like voices, murmuring.

One foot behind the other, I walked to the end of the landing and turned the corner. It was even darker here, but I saw that the sewing-room door was very slightly ajar.

"Roselily?" I said. "Roselily, is that you?"

No answer. I pushed open the door and gasped as I saw a shimmering white figure. Then I laughed as I realized that it was only my dress, still displayed on the dressmaker's dummy. The next moment, the laughter dried in my throat.

A pale glow was coming from the tall mirror. I felt the hairs on my arms stand up as I looked at it. This was the mirror that had scared Maya, and yet when I had returned with her there had been nothing unusual about it. Now I could see something that was not the banal reflection of the room. I was looking down a long gallery, and on either side were headless dummies wearing long dresses, pale blue, pale green, mauve, nothing bright in the dim glow, and the far end of the gallery was swallowed up in blackness. Then, as I watched, paralysed, something shapeless started to move in that blackness. It began to swirl slowly and to send out long feelers. It was like smoke, and it was coming towards me.

With a gasp, I stumbled out of the room and slammed the door behind me. The slam seemed to reverberate through the house.

Light, I must have light. I tried to run along the corridor but tripped over something, possibly a crease in the carpet, and fell. Behind me I could hear the murmuring again, and always the senseless howling of the wind.

I was desperate to reach my room, but as I came to the top of the stairs another noise was added to the din. Somebody – or something – was knocking on the front door.

I bit my knuckles. Roselily must have locked the door for safety as she went out, but she would have her key. Normally it was never locked, and I need only turn the handle to enter the house. It could not be Roselily who was knocking. So who? The sound came again.

Knock, knock, knock.

Could it be a rapist who had learned that I was alone in the house? If I opened the door, I might be confronted by a maniac who would strangle me. If I didn't open the door, I was trapped in this house where something horribly strange was happening.

What could I do? My thumping heart was making more noise than the wind.

Then I thought I heard a voice, very faint. It sounded like "Jaki!"

I nearly fell down the stairs, tripped again in the hall but somehow found myself turning the bolt with shaking hands.

The door opened, and on a huge gust of wind the person who had been knocking was blown in. It was Gavin. We struggled together to push the door shut.

"Jaki? Are you all right?"

"I – I – I – " I couldn't speak. My teeth were chattering. He was there, but I could barely see him.

"I knew you were alone, and I thought you might need – "

"There – there's a power cut," I stuttered.

"Yes, I saw that all the windows were dark. Luckily I had a torch in the van."

He shone it briefly in my face, dazzling me.

"What is it? You look terrible."

I couldn't tell him.

"Come on. I seem to remember there are candles in the morning room." He grabbed my hand and led me, showing the way with the bobbing circle of light from his torch. His hand was warm and I gripped it convulsively. Once in front of the empty hearth, he let go, and I felt bereft. He was kneeling on the floor.

"Ah, here we are." He had found a box of matches, and after several attempts he lit one of the three candles, then carefully lit the other two from the burning wick, but the flames guttered and wavered in the draught that was coming down the chimney. Dark shadows around the walls also moved and wavered. The uncurtained windows were like black mirrors reflecting the flames of the candles and the vague shapes that were the two of us, while through the reflections I could see the wild trees, their branches rising and falling like waves.

"Some storm," he said, looking up at me with his familiar half-smiling expression. "I didn't know you were so scared of storms."

"It's not the storm," I managed to say. "I heard – I thought I saw – "

"Shadows," he said soothingly. "Lily always said that this house was too full of shadows."

"It wasn't just – Argh! Look out!"

On the far side of the room was the tall cheval mirror in front of which I had once stood, swathed in white silk, when first Lily had agreed to make me a wedding dress. On another occasion, Maya had been dancing and posing in front of it when suddenly something had spooked her.

Now the same dull light was glowing in it, the same phosphorescent radiance as in the mirror upstairs. Something was swirling in its depths. Something dark and amorphous. Was it? It was a coil of smoke.

"Smoke!" I shouted.

Gavin was on his feet. "Smoke?"

It was coming out, coiling and billowing. At the same moment, a whistling gust of wind came down the chimney and all three candles blew out.

I was rooted to the spot. What was on fire? What could we do? What was happening? Oh, God, I thought, please help me. I never pray, but I prayed now.

The smoke was uncurling like the tentacles of an octopus in the depths of the sea.

In that instant, something occurred outside the window.

A beating of wings. There was a flash, like lightning, and we both saw, spreadeagled against the window panes, a huge bird, its great wings outstretched and knocking against the glass. As it turned its head, I saw the fiery glare of one eye. The wind shrieked.

"It's trying to get in!" I yelled.

"Should we let it in?" shouted Gavin.

"No!" I screamed. In my terror, I clung to him. I was in his arms. "Oh, what's happening?" I sobbed.

"I don't know." He held me.

The bird was still there. The smoke seemed to be filling the room, fogging the darkness.

Then we both heard the front door opening.

Roselily's voice called, "Jaki? Jaki!"

At that moment, all the lamps in the hall came on, and the lamp beside the armchair also sprang to life again, dazzling our eyes. The reflections in the windows receded.

Where was the bird? I couldn't see it.

Roselily swept into the room in her grey cloak. She walked toward the cheval mirror, and it had resumed its normal appearance. There was no smoke.

Had there really been smoke?

"Oh, Roselily. I was so scared," I quavered. "I saw something upstairs … "

"What did you see?"

"It was … I don't know."

"Let's go up."

Roselily led the way, and Gavin and I followed her. The staircase and landing were now fully lit. I pointed towards the sewing room, and Lily strode in.

Wherever she went, lights came on. She swung her cloak towards the mirror as she turned, and there was no strange radiance. No gallery of dresses. Nothing – only the reflection of white-haired Roselily, tall and severe, and me, and Gavin, who was still holding my hand.

CHAPTER ELEVEN

I don't remember much about the rest of that night. I know that Gavin left, Roselily continued to say reassuring things that I didn't really take in, and eventually I went up to bed. I remember hanging my T-shirt over the swing mirror on the chest of drawers. Then, surprisingly, I must have fallen almost immediately into a deep sleep.

The early morning sunlight woke me. The events of the previous evening came flooding back, and I could almost convince myself that I had had a nightmare. But no, they had been real. Yet the furnishings of my familiar room, the tapestry curtains, the crimson and blue rug, seemed so comfortingly ordinary in the daylight. This was Oldwood Court, which had begun to seem like home. Could it really be a frightening place?

The whole atmosphere felt airier as I descended the stairs. The storm seemed to have blown itself out, like a great cleansing force.

I found Roselily sitting at the kitchen table, drinking tea. She looked drained, her cheekbones prominent in her pale face.

"I'm so sorry about last night," she said.

"Well, I – I don't understand."

The morning sunlight gleamed on the cobbles of the yard outside the window, and sparrows and tits flitted around the bird feeders. On the window-sill, two baby sparrows with tufts of down on their heads fluttered their wings and cheeped, no doubt a late brood. A male sparrow, black bibbed, came and poked food into each gaping yellow beak.

The kitchen looked just as usual. No disturbance had taken place in here.

"Things got a little out of control. But believe me, you are quite safe here. Nothing can hurt you." "But what did I see?"

"Shadows, only shadows."

I sat down and poured myself some tea. "I'm not sure – " I began.

"Sometimes," cut in Roselily, "it's the past that revisits the present, or not even the past. What might have been. Or what may still be. But there's no substance to any of it. I'm not sure if I'm making sense," she added, as I frowned.

"So it wasn't real?"

"Real? What is real? Are feelings real? Are dreams real? Is love real? You can't weigh and measure any of those."

Love. The thought of Gavin flashed through my mind and I repressed it.

"I thought I could see smoke. A lot of smoke."

"There can be smoke without fire and fire without smoke. Nothing was burning, was it?"

"No." I wanted to talk about the gallery of dresses, but the words wouldn't come.

"This house," said Roselily wearily. "This house still contains the past. It harbours too many shadows, as I've said before. Partly because of me. It needs to be opened up to air and sunlight, and to other people. I've been trying to bring that about. Luckily I've had help."

"You mean the campaign? The activists?"

She reached out and briefly clasped my wrist. "Yes, Jaki. I don't know what I would have done without all of you young people. But I've had other help, too."

I wondered what she meant, but didn't ask.

"I haven't done much lately," I mumbled.

"You haven't been here. You've been working. But what do you think of the plan?"

"What plan?"

"You mean the others haven't told you yet?"

"Martha did mention something … But I don't know anything. Will you tell me about it?"

So, sitting there in the kitchen, Roselily told me all the details of the plan for Oldwood Court.

***

One reason for my weekend visit was Mum's birthday, today, Sunday. I had bought her a bottle of her favourite perfume, and by mid-morning I was cycling down the lime avenue. It must have rained as well as blowing a gale during the night, as the foliage dripped raindrops on me as I passed and the air smelt fresh and moist. I was afraid that some of the lime trees might have been blown down, but they were all still standing, although the ground was littered with twigs, little round fruits and leaves that had been torn off. Glancing to the side, I saw here and there half-hidden places where trunks were leaning at angles, caught up in the branches of neighbouring trees. They reminded me of wounded soldiers, held in the arms of their comrades. With luck, I thought, they were fallen but not dead.

Twigs had also been blown off the magnolia tree in my parents' garden, but luckily it, too, had withstood the wind.

"Hi, sis!" sang out Maya as I entered the kitchen.

"Happy birthday, Mum." I went to kiss her as she sat at the table anxiously watching my father, who was busy at the sink.

"Pascal, can I – ?"

"No!" said Dad firmly. "You just sit there. I may not be a cook, but I can at least prepare a salad. And then we'll have the birthday cake for dessert."

The house seemed comfortingly ordinary, the table and chairs dull and solid, the tiles on the wall above the worktops rather old-fashioned. The reminder board on the back of the door was pinned with phone numbers, fliers, old business cards, supermarket coupons, all skew-whiff and in need of sorting. There was nothing alarming here. Nothing particularly inspiring, either.

Mum was wearing a new pink blouse. Dad had bought her a huge bunch of varied hothouse flowers, Maya had spent her pocket money on a large box of chocolates – "Mainly coffee creams, your favourites," – and Grandad had given her a delicate silver necklace that had belonged to Granny.

"You're all spoiling me," said Mum, beaming. The post had brought a number of cards from friends and distant relatives, and she exclaimed gratifyingly over the perfume.

"Is Stella coming round?" I asked.

"Later," said Dad. "It'll be just the four of us for lunch."

We all adjourned to the dining-room to eat Dad's salad off the best china. Maya had helped to make an artistic arrangement of cucumber, tomatoes and radishes which was suitably admired. Then Maya fetched the birthday cake and came in holding it high, saying, "Ta-da!"

"Only one candle?" I queried.

"One is quite enough," said Mum. "It stands for one more year."

A year, I thought. So much had happened in the past year. Where would we all be a year from now?

She blew it out, we all sang Happy Birthday, and then the conversation became general. We discussed the closing down of a chain store in town, I talked a little about the graffiti and the rough sleepers that I saw every day on my way to work, and soon the talk threatened to slide into politics. So, to avoid an argument on Mum's birthday, I intervened.

"Dad, I've been meaning to ask you. What's going on with Sacs de Luxe? Has there been a strike?"

"You mean you haven't heard?"

"I haven't been around."

"And Mum heard about your ex-lover-boy," put in Maya.

There was an awkward pause.

"You mean Hugh?" I said robustly. "What about him?"

"Well," said Mum, "You won't be seeing him any more."

"I don't want to see him, thank you."

"Just as well – because he's going to China."

"China!"

"You see, there's been a takeover." This was Dad. "They've been bought out by a Chinese firm. Apparently they'd been struggling financially for quite some time, although nobody here knew about it."

"I had heard some rumours," I said slowly, "but I had no idea. So the factory – ?"

"They're closing it down. The whole place. There have been several hundred job losses. It's pretty serious."

"Whew." I took this in.

"It's made a difference to the traffic already," said Mum. "No more big lorries causing congestion."

"I suppose this will have considerable consequences for the town," said Grandad. "It seems a pity that it will result in more unemployment."

"Yes, but what sort of employment did Sacs de Luxe create? Making and selling plastic handbags for the luxury market? Is that a worthwhile sort of job, good for the community? Jobs aren't the be-all and end-all," I said hotly. "Big business can get away with anything on the grounds that it creates jobs."

"Ho!" said Maya. "When did you change your mind about jobs? You were dead keen to find a job. I didn't know you were such a lefty."

"Let's not get into politics," I said hastily. "But I'll tell you about something that really will be good for the community."

I took a deep breath and repeated what Roselily had told me that morning.

She had set up a trust, and Oldwood Court was to be converted into a community arts centre. Big plans were taking shape. It would be used for painting, writing, acting, music – "And dancing!" yelped Maya. "Yes, and dancing." There would be spaces adapted for all kinds of creative activities. Singing. Weaving. Of course, various regulations would have to be complied with. A number of alterations would have to be made.

"Won't it be very expensive?" asked Dad.

I explained that Roselily still had some savings, and the campaign had raised a lot of funds. "And then there's Stella's fundraising gig," I said. "That should bring in plenty more."

"I wonder," mused Mum. "Do you think there might be room for a knitting circle? I've always thought that would be nice. Knitting and crochet, say."

"Why not? All kinds of things are possible. It's really exciting. Roselily wants to open up the whole place so that people can follow their dreams in it. That's what she told me."

"I really must meet this lady," said Dad.

"Oh, you must! She's so cool!" said Maya.

Just then the phone rang in the hall. "That will be Stella," said Dad, and went to answer it. We could hear him talking for quite some time, and meanwhile we continued to discuss the possibilities for Oldwood. Creative and artistic people from miles around would be able to get together. It would really shake up the town.

Dad reappeared and said, "It's Ms Green on the phone." He addressed Grandad. "She wants to speak to you."

Grandad struggled to his feet and I handed him his stick so that he could go out to the phone. Maya went on chattering excitedly about the dance troupe and the show that they would very soon be putting on.

A few minutes later, we heard the tap of Grandad's stick, and he pushed open the door. He stood there, his face jubilant.

"My dears, this is the best news I have heard in a long time. What do you think? This wonderful lady, this friend of yours, Jaki, has just offered to provide a home for all my books."

"All of them?"

"All of them. They will constitute a library, for lending or research. They will be all together in that splendid house, and I shall not have to get rid of them after all!"

***

Never had I seen such a traffic jam in the street where KY Voltatronics had its head office. Gears ground, brakes hissed, engines revved, and I felt that I was choking in the smog of exhaust as I hurried to get to work on time. The day was again going to be hot, and I felt that my makeup was melting already.

Just as I was fishing my pass out of my bag to go through the doors, someone called my name.

Kylie caught up with me as we headed for the lifts. "I hear you're looking for a flat."

"Yes. Why?"

"Well, a friend of mine – " She broke off as we were surrounded by a group of men in business suits and we filed into the lift. When we emerged on our floor, I looked at her expectantly, but at that moment Ms Jackson came striding along the corridor brandishing a file.

"There you are! Now, this is urgent. I want you to go – "

Kylie slunk away as Ms Jackson filled me in briefly on the latest crisis and I had to hurry to another office and take action before I could even go to my own workstation. It was that sort of a day. There had been a problem with a sophisticated electronic circuit, and the airport authorities in Benin were furious. I hardly had time to think as the day wore on. At one point, as we rushed past each other in the corridor, Kylie hissed, "See you after work!"

By the time I left the office, half an hour later than usual, I was frazzled. All I wanted was to go back to my B&B, drink cold water and lie down, but Kylie was waiting for me in the lobby.

"At last! Now, are you still trying to find somewhere to live? Because a friend of mine is moving out, you see, and she's looking for someone to take over the lease. So I thought of you, and I said I'd bring you round tonight to look at the place. So let's go, OK?"

"That's kind of you," I said faintly.

It meant a bus journey in the opposite direction to my usual route, after which we weaved down side roads and along an alleyway beside a heavy post-war block of flats. Kylie rang a bell beside a ground floor door. It was opened by the friend, a rather overweight, red-faced woman in shorts and a T-shirt, who introduced herself as Lea.

"Come in! Sorry about the mess. I'm packing up, as you can see."

The cramped hallway was stacked with cardboard boxes, and I sniffed the air. Other people's houses always have their own peculiar smell. Could this be the place for me? Would it smell like home when I opened the door after a day at the office?

We followed Lea into the narrow bedroom, which looked out on to the alleyway. The window was equipped with an electric rolling shutter. The living room had a slightly larger window with a view of an inner courtyard and some tired-looking plants in front of a concrete balustrade. The furniture was basic Ikea. A small shower room with ugly pink tiles and a galley kitchen equipped with a microwave and a fridge completed the layout.

It wasn't just a room, I told myself. It was a flat. It bore no comparison to Hugh's modern flat, but I would be living here alone, after all. Alone and independent. I could decide how I was going to occupy the space – if I took it.

"Can I get you a drink? I'm sorry I haven't got much in stock." Lea opened the fridge and peered inside.

I said that water would be fine, and we went into the living room to discuss rent and service charges.

"It's a nice little place, isn't it?" prompted Kylie, perching on a stool.

Was it? I tried hard to imagine myself living there. I could put up posters, add a colourful rug to the scratched parquet floor. At ground level, it would always be dark, but perhaps in hot weather like this it was an advantage to be in shadow.

Shadow. A momentary shiver. "I think I could just about afford the rent," I faltered.

"It's very reasonable," said Kylie. I felt that she was eager to do me a favour.

"You see, I'm in a hurry. I'm starting a new life! I have to move to Scotland, and I want to find someone who'll take over the lease straight away. So d'you think you might be interested?" asked Lea.

I hesitated. "I can't really say straight away. I need – well, I need to do some calculations and – and talk to my family. What's your deadline?"

She sighed. "End of next week, max. Look, take my phone number and give me a ring just as soon as you've decided, will you? I hope you'll take it. It would be a weight off my mind."

Later that evening I lay on my bed under the open window, vaguely watching snippets of news on the TV perched on its high bracket. It had been kind of Kylie to think of me, even if the place was – well, certainly not my dream flat, but what could I expect on a starting salary? Perhaps I would eventually be offered a permanent post, with prospects.

I flicked from channel to channel, dismissing men with revolvers, endless commercials, sport and loud-voiced comedians. I caught a glimpse of treetops and switched back to the programme. It was a documentary about deforestation in Indonesia, and I watched with a sick feeling as huge, ruthless machines advanced like tanks on a battlefield, toppling, crushing, mowing down helpless trees that could offer no resistance. They had grown, in their slow and natural way, over the years from seedlings to saplings to tall trees, and now, in the space of minutes, they were flattened to make room for palm oil plantations. The camera panned over endless rows of oil palms, stretching to the horizon. For a moment the huge, sorrowful eyes of an orangutan, its home destroyed, filled the screen, and my own eyes filled with tears.

I clicked off the TV. Gavin had had a lot to say about deforestation. Gavin ... No, I would not think about him tonight.

Miles away, Roselily's wood was growing cooler as the day ended. The last of the setting sun would catch the domes of the treetops, and all would be quiet among the pillars of the trunks, apart from little rustling or clicking noises as seeds or caterpillars fell to the mossy floor, where invisible creatures, mice or beetles, went about their business. As it grew darker, far away would be heard the eerie call of a tawny owl.

It was so hot and airless. Even my pillow was hot. Traffic passed and repassed. It would be hard to get to sleep, but I needed to rest and to be fresh for work tomorrow.

***

Several cars and vans were parked in front of Oldwood Court. The front door and three windows stood open and I could hear hammering and voices and, briefly, the screech of an electric drill. This time I had hitched a lift from the station and walked up the lime avenue from the gates, stepping from sunlight into tree-shade and back into sunlight, carrying my overnight bag.

One of the vans was Gavin's. Stella's hire car was also there, and another van that I didn't recognize.

I put down my bag just inside the hall and listened. The place was teeming with activity. Something seemed to be happening in every room. Even the air felt different.

I turned into the library and found Grandad there with Roselily. Cardboard boxes were stacked on the floor and on the long table, and several shelves had already been filled with books that I recognized from my grandparents' house years ago. Grandad was seated at the table and Roselily was taking books out of boxes and dusting the shelves.

They greeted me rather distractedly, as if I had never gone away.

"It's such a delight to see these old friends again," beamed Grandad, stroking the cover of a leather-bound volume.

His stick crashed to the floor and I stepped forward to pick it up.

"Your young friend drove all the way to my old house to collect these books, and drove them all the way down here. I must say, he really is a very helpful chap." He ignored the stick.

"Who?" I said.

"Gavin," said Roselily from the bookshelves. "He's here somewhere."

"Oh."

"And what's more," said Grandad, "Not only are all my own books together here, but I see that Ms Green has a great many interesting works that must also be placed on display, not kept hidden in boxes. Look at this: Rabindranath Tagore! A very great writer. And what was the volume we saw just now?"

Thus Spake Guru Nanak, said Roselily with a cheerful glance. "I know we put all these away, but your grandfather insists that we should take them all out again."

"A splendid library like this deserves to have its shelves filled," said Grandad decisively. He reached into another box.

"I'll just ... " I said vaguely. I wandered out.

I could hear Stella talking to someone in the morning room, saying something about music stands, and a few chords were played on the piano.

All the doors, except the green baize door, stood open. Roselily's grandfather's study was empty, but in the billiard room beyond it I could hear more voices: Martha's, Sam's and – Gavin's. A clattering of wood on the floor.

I turned and made for the staircase, but at the same moment Maya came skipping out of the drawing room.

"Oh, hi, sis! This is brilliant. Come and see, come and see." She dragged me into the drawing room, where two young workmen with toolboxes littering the floor were fixing something to the wall.

"It's a barre," said Maya. "See? It's exactly what we need. It's like, everything's coming together. Have you seen the schoolroom? Oh, you've only just arrived. Well, come up and I'll show you."

She dragged me up the stairs two at a time and waited impatiently while I put my bag in the bedroom. Nothing had changed in there. The bedspread with its little mirrors, the lapis and ruby rug, the tapestry curtains half closed against the sun: it was all as I had expected, but big changes seemed to be happening in the rest of the house.

The schoolroom still contained desks, but three large easels had appeared from somewhere.

"Where's the rocking horse?" I asked in dismay.

"In the night nursery. Don't worry, he's staying here. Some other bits of furniture have been cleared to make space. Isn't this great, though? Painting and drawing in here, and maybe in the night nursery too. It depends on how many people are interested."

I thought of the room full of art students. "Where's my stuff? There was a portrait – "

"All in the big cupboard in the night nursery, just until everything's organized. Mr Curtis has been explaining about alterations and regulations. Plumbing, and stuff. I think there are going to be more bathrooms, bedrooms converted, that sort of thing."

"Wow. I see. Yes, I suppose there will have to be alterations if it's to be a real arts centre."

"Oh, yeah," said Maya airily. "Anyhow, it's going to be ace. Ryan and Lucy were here earlier, making some sort of calculations, but I think they've gone now. Oh, and Martha's setting up her loom downstairs."

"Yes," I said, "I thought I heard her voice."

"Come down and say hi to her and Gavin and Sam. You might be able to give them a hand. I think they're having a bit of trouble. And while you're doing that, I'll go and make some tea in the kitchen. Roselily said I could, while she's busy with Grandad. D'you want some?"

We were already on our way downstairs. Usually the place was so peaceful when I arrived.

"Uh ... yes. No. Actually, I might just go for a walk in the wood."

"A walk? Oh, well. Whatever." Maya vanished through the green baize door, which thumped shut behind her.

"Did I hear your voice, Jaki?" called Martha. "We're in here."

I would have to look in and say just a brief hello. Then I would make some excuse and escape into the wood. Already I could almost sense the shade of the branches and feel the mossy path under my sandals.

Just a brief hello.

In the billiard room, large pieces of wood were lying around, and two uprights seemed to have been screwed into position, but I saw only the people in the room. Martha, heavily pregnant, was sitting on a stool, Sam, in a bright Hawaiian shirt, was wielding a screwdriver, and Gavin held a long spindle of wood.

Without looking at it, he put it down and stepped forward, his eyes fixed on me, his palms turned outward. The lines of his body, the angle of his head – I couldn't look away. Again that humming, trembling sensation. I was afraid I must be visibly shaking.

"Jaki?" he said, and his voice went through me.

"Hello." My own voice was husky.

"Hi, Jaki," said Sam. Then, to Gavin: "Look, mate, could you just help with this a minute?"

Gavin seemed to be in a daze. A second later, abruptly, he turned, picked up the piece of wood, sank to his knees and began pushing it hard into position. His back was to me and I couldn't see what he was doing.

"No!" screeched Martha. "Wait! Not like that! I told you the treadle rail has to go in before the back beam."

"So you did," agreed Sam.

"Oh. Sorry," muttered Gavin, standing up.

I half turned. There was too much going on in the house. The wood would be so cool and quiet.

Martha laughed. "Trust my brother! When his mind isn't fully focused on something, you have to watch him."

I took one step towards the door and froze. I felt as if a huge trumpet blast had suddenly deafened me. I looked at the door-jamb, the stone flags and part of the carpet in the hall without understanding what they were.

Her words went round and round in my head. "My brother."

I heard Gavin behind me say, "I'll just take a short break, OK?"

I moved across the hall as if wading through water, heading for the open front door and the outside world.

"Where are you going?" asked Gavin's voice beside me.

I scarcely dared glance at him. "Into the wood," I croaked.

"Good idea. I'll go with you."

We said nothing else until we had walked some distance along one of the paths, and the sounds from the house were muffled and dwindling. A slight breeze shifted the leaf canopy high above us, and the sunlight sent points of light like showers of bright coins dancing ahead of us. I was trying to breathe normally. He was walking beside me.

Gavin said, "Jaki, I really, really have to talk to you."

Suddenly I stood still, covered my face with my hands and burst out laughing and crying at the same time.

"What's wrong? Jaki, what's the matter? Tell me!"

I couldn't speak. I choked. Tears poured down my face, yet I was laughing uncontrollably.

"Tell me!"

I gasped, choked again, gasped and said, "You're Martha's brother!"

"Of course I am." His puzzled expression made me laugh still more, but gradually, gulping and wiping my eyes, I was able to speak. Gradually it all came out: how I had thought he was Martha's partner, that the baby she was expecting was his, that he didn't want it and was going to abandon both of them.

"But it's Sam's! She's with Sam!" he shouted. "Did you honestly think … ?"

I looked up into his face. "Yes," I said.

"So that was why … "

"Yes."

"Oh, Jaki." His voice was full of love.

"I'm sorry. I can't believe how stupid I've been. I didn't dare – "

"Didn't dare tell me that you wanted – "

"Yes. And did you want – ?"

We interrupted each other, stopped and looked into each other's eyes.

Then I kissed him.

And he kissed me right back, for a long, long moment.

I suppose people never forget their first kiss with the person who really feels right. I never will. We stood there, our bodies moulded to each other, kissing like two people who had been dying of thirst and at last had found a freshwater stream. It was as if I had always known what his hard, urgent body would feel like. We broke away from each other, laughed in delight, kissed again, and then continued to walk deeper into the wood, his arm around my shoulders and mine around his waist.

As we walked, we kept explaining our misunderstanding, talking over each other and interrupting. "I thought you suddenly wanted to go back to your fiancé." "I thought you were coldly abandoning your own baby. I couldn't believe you were like that." "I hope I'm not like that, though I do believe there are more important things than bringing more human beings into the world." "Such a stupid thing. How could I have thought that?" "You changed so suddenly, it was a shock." "You and Martha don't look like brother and sister." "She takes after our Italian grandmother."

Deeper into the wood we walked, following the path, and came at last to my place of the silver birches, tall and delicate like fountains against the blue afternoon sky, their leaves still shimmering and green, although before long they would turn to gold. We slowed our pace, faced each other. We sank to our knees on the soft carpet of moss. Any sounds from the house had long been lost behind us. I began to unbutton his shirt, trembling still, and soon we were lying entwined together like wild creatures in a wild place, our hands and mouths exploring, responding, recognizing.

This was right. This was what we had so nearly missed, and now we had found it.

***

Even the most magical moments don't last forever. Eventually we were standing again, fastening zips and buttons, brushing twigs and dead leaves from our clothes. A mosquito had bitten me on the thigh.

A last caress, a few words in an undertone.

The others would be wondering where we were. The mundane world had to be attended to.

As we walked back, he told me that he and Martha had for years shared the little house which they had inherited after their parents' tragic death in a road accident. They had always been on good terms (unlike some brothers and sisters whom I knew), and they had a common commitment to environmental causes and to trees in particular. Each had had temporary relationships, but a big shift had occurred with Martha's pregnancy and Sam's moving in. That was what Gavin had meant about the house being crowded. He hadn't been referring only to the baby. "Sam's a good guy, though, and Martha's happy. But I do feel a bit superfluous."

We had emerged from the wood and were walking towards the house, hand in hand.

Stella and Roselily were standing on the front doorstep.

"Didn't you say, that time, that you would be going away?" I asked.

"Hello, you two!" shouted Stella. "Does this mean what I think it means?"

"What do you think it means?" shouted Gavin, grinning.

"That you're an item?"

"You could be right."

We came up to the two women, feeling a little embarrassed but still blissfully happy.

"Bless you, my children," said Roselily.

"Gavin," I said again, as we entered the house, the high-ceilinged hall and its scent of rose and jasmine, "Will you be going away?"

"Yes," he said. "I will. But not before the concert."

The concert? That was very soon. I felt a cloud pass over the sun.

***

I couldn't stay in paradise. I had to get back to the office.

Even on the Sunday, there was much coming and going at Oldwood House, and I was surprised to see my parents arriving with Grandad and Maya. Stella introduced them to Roselily, and they both asked a lot of questions, Dad mainly about the building. Mum seemed more interested in Roselily's experience as a dressmaker, and she was taken to see my "wedding" dress, still on its dressmaker's dummy. An expression of regret flitted over her face.

"It's a ball gown," I told her quickly. I remembered Roselily, my fairy godmother, telling me so.

"And do you have many dressmaking clients in this area?" asked Mum.

"I had, in the past," said Roselily lightly. "But none recently. Some women are a little nervous about coming to this place."

"Really? Surely not," said Mum robustly. "I'm sure I could get together a group of friends for a sewing or knitting circle here. I mean, if you're planning anything like that for the – um – community arts centre."

"Why not?" said Roselily. Her long fingers stroked her amber necklace as she looked down at my plump, rosy-cheeked mother. "Everything is changing here. Changing very quickly."

I had to leave Oldwood, full as it was of shifting patterns and humming activity, and get the train back to the town. Gavin also had customers waiting in Oakfield, but at least we could be in touch every day by phone. It was understood that we would get together again as soon as possible.

I sailed into the office on Monday morning, still on a cloud of happiness. However, I couldn't help finding the air-conditioned atmosphere sterile and indifferent. Everyone was busy with files and orders and invoices and technical errors and ongoing disputes. I plunged back into my own set of dossiers, but my thoughts kept straying to our time in the wood and it was hard to concentrate. As usual, the other people in the office had barely acknowledged my presence. Kylie said "hi", but Diana walked past me in the corridor without a glance, as if I didn't exist.

Depending on what I was doing, time alternately galloped and dragged.

Shortly before the end of the afternoon, Ms Jackson called me into her cubicle and told me to sit down. She turned over some papers on her desk, checked her phone and then eyed me keenly. Did she always buy the same colour lipstick? I wondered. Gavin didn't care for lipstick. He'd said so. Not that I'd been wearing any when …

"Well, Jacqueline," said Ms Jackson. "I hope you feel you've found your feet with the firm. As you know, your present contract is due to expire on … " She checked her screen. "I have high hopes of being in a position to offer you a renewal, this time possibly for one year. However – " She held up one hand to stop me, although I hadn't said anything. "Any renewal is likely to depend on a forthcoming challenge. I hadn't intended to suggest this mission to someone so junior, but as we need a very fluent French speaker, I think you may be able to carry it off. Of course, you must get a yellow fever jab."

What was she talking about? Memories of the sunlit wood receded as she explained that a team of technicians was to be sent to Brazzaville, Congo, and I would accompany them for several weeks. She went on to enlarge on the project, and I tried to take in the details. Africa! Wow! Gavin had talked about widening horizons, and I would certainly be doing that. Great tropical forests… Did I think I could cope with it? She wanted to know.

"I – well, it's a surprise. An honour, really. I would do my best," I said, uncertainly. I wasn't at all sure that I was the right person for such a responsibility. And what on earth would Diana say if she heard about it? And how many thousand miles would separate me from Gavin?

"I'll be able to confirm the details in the next couple of weeks," said Ms Jackson, rising from her desk so that I knew I had been dismissed. "Meanwhile, keep up the good work." She gave me a professional smile.

On Tuesday, nothing more was said about Africa. Wednesday was the same as usual. Instead of being warm and sunny, the weather had turned sultry and dull. How hot and humid might it be in the Congo? I thought it best not to mention my conversation with Ms Jackson to anyone, not even to Kylie. I wasn't entirely sure why she had seemed to befriend me, or whether she had some personal axe to grind. Was it simply out of the goodness of her heart that she had suggested a flat to rent? That reminded me – I had promised to give an answer to Lea.

Almost on cue, as I stepped out of the lift on Wednesday evening, my phone rang. Lea. I stood still in the lobby to answer it, while all the office workers flowed past me on their way home. She really, really needed to know. Did I want the flat or not? She couldn't wait much longer. She would have to offer it to somebody else.

I grimaced. I did need somewhere to live. It was very hard to find low rents, and even this one represented nearly half my salary. Perhaps I would take the plunge. Yes, I –

"Jaki!"

He was there, standing by the reception desk, and his face lit up as our eyes locked. He looked nothing like a city office-worker in his jeans, open-necked shirt and trainers.

"Sorry, sorry! I'll have to call you back." I broke the connection.

I ran to Gavin, who hugged me.

"Oho!" said a male voice, and Dave walked past me to the door, turning his head with one eyebrow quizzically raised.

"What are you – ? Never mind. Let's go," I urged Gavin, and we left. He had parked his van in a sidestreet, and we sat in it, at first only kissing and holding each other.

"I couldn't wait any longer to see you," he mumbled into my hair. He had driven all that way just to see me. I could hardly believe it.

After a while we decided to go to a cheap Chinese place, and there we continued chatting happily about the transformations at Oldwood, Martha and Sam, Maya and her dancing, his recent clients and a little about KY. It was so lovely to be sitting with Gavin, sipping jasmine tea, instead of spending the usual lonely evening that I had anticipated. Every now and then he took my hand across the table and stroked my fingers with his thumb. It was strange to see him in that context, and I could hardly believe that he was there.

It was only later, when we were both in my B&B room, that I mentioned Brazzaville. The bed was far too narrow for two people, but we managed. I hoped we hadn't made too much noise. As the evening light drained from the cloudy sky, we sat cross-legged and naked on the bed, facing each other, the little air that came through the window blowing faint breaths of coolness on our sweating bodies. I could hardly see his face in the twilight, but his hair was on end and the set of his shoulders was achingly familiar.

"Africa," he said. "Oh."

"Do you think I should go?"

Silence. "It would be an adventure."

"I'd be broadening my horizons."

"Yes."

I felt there was something that he wasn't saying.

"But it's such a long way from Oldwood," I said, "and I really do care what happens to the wood. It seems as if the house will be spared, with all these new plans, but what about the wood? We haven't won the battle yet. I know we've got a lot of support, but when you're up against developers and vested interests … "

"I feel as strongly as you do about the wood, you know that. We must win. I think there may be hope. Ryan dropped a hint the other day."

"Oh? What did he say?"

"Nothing much. We'll have to wait and see, but apparently there is hope."

"I don't really want to go so far away and leave it," I said in a small voice. And leave you, I thought.

Another silence.

"How committed are you to this job?" he asked.

"It's a job. I know I was lucky to get it. But not nearly as committed as I am to saving trees. The whole future of the planet depends on trees," I said, and I thought desolately of bulldozers, chainsaws and centuries-old trees toppling and crashing. My going away and broadening my horizons would solve nothing where Oldwood's very real problems were concerned. But what difference could one person make, anyway?

"In the past decade, a hundred and thirty million trees have been destroyed," he said quietly.

It was hard to get my head around such a figure.

Silence fell once more. What was he thinking about? I wanted him to hold me again, but he didn't move.

"You said that you would be going away yourself," I prompted him dully.

"Yes."

So we would both be going. We had only just come together, but we would be far apart. No doubt he had found a job, just as I had, and naturally he needed to earn a living and leave space in the house for Martha and Sam and the future baby. Where would he be going? I felt a wind blowing across endless miles between us. Phone calls and text messages were all very well, but I wanted him. I wanted him. Could a long-distance relationship possibly last?

"Jaki," he burst out, "it's probably much too soon, but I have to say this. You see, I've got a plan. I'm going to India."

"India?" We would be whole continents apart. Thousands and thousands of miles. I shut my eyes. "Oh."

"It's a reforestation project in Sikkim. Planting trees. For at least six months. Actually planting trees and doing something useful, not just trying to influence people. It will be hard work and the living conditions will probably be tough."

"I expect they will."

He talked about the NGO that had launched the project, about basic living expenses, about vaccinations and the monsoon. I was scarcely listening. All I was thinking was that he would be so far away.

"But Jaki – I hardly know how to ask you this."

"What?"

"Would you – no, it's probably too soon."

"Go on."

"Would you consider chucking all this up?"

"You mean – ?" I opened my eyes wide.

"Yes, I do. Will you come with me?"

CHAPTER TWELVE

All the workmen and helpers had gone home for the night and I was left alone with Roselily.

We had walked together through the house, inspecting the changes. Furniture had been moved around and new items introduced. It wasn't only the library that had been transformed, with books neatly arranged on all the shelves. Martha's loom stood in the centre of the billiard room and hanks of brightly coloured wool hung from a chairback. In the dining room a small platform had been erected and the heavy red curtains taken down. A trail of dusty white footprints led up the stairs to a bedroom that was being converted into three toilets, and two more sewing machines had appeared in Roselily's sewing room, where I glanced quickly at the tall mirror, but saw nothing unusual. A supply of artist's materials had been stacked in the schoolroom, and I examined them for quality, wondering who had put them there. Strangers would soon be everywhere.

Later we sat in the morning room on either side of the fireplace, as we had done many times before. The days were growing shorter and the last of a crimson sunset glowed through the tall windows, glinting on a bunch of music stands and stools that had been moved in from the music room, which was being repainted.

Roselily was sitting serenely, her hands clasped on one knee.

"Are you happy about all these alterations?" I asked after a while.

"It had to happen. Nothing stays the same," said Roselily.

"I mean, yes, it's exciting and positive. An arts centre for Oakfield! But it doesn't feel like the same place any more."

Roselily said nothing for a moment. Then: "And you, Jaki. Are you the same person that you were a few months ago?

When you came to me for a wedding dress?"

I shook my head. So much had happened. I had got involved in the anti-road campaign, I had dumped Hugh, I had left Sacs de Luxe, I had moved into Oldwood Court, I had found a job in another town – and now there was Gavin. I felt a completely different person from that naïve girl glumly expecting to become a society wife.

Roselily said, "We have to embrace change, I think. And try to ensure that it's change for the better."

"It's a bit scary."

"Of course it's scary."

"I really admire you for taking all this on. Doesn't it mean an awful lot of responsibility, being in charge of this place when it really takes off?"

Roselily looked thoughtful. "It's a trust, of course. I have asked Stella and Ryan to be trustees, and Mr. Curtis is overseeing everything."

"Ryan?" I was surprised.

"Yes. He's very conscientious. I had thought of asking you and Gavin to be trustees, but … "

"Gavin's leaving. Has he told you?"

"Yes."

We relapsed into silence. Everything was going around in my head: Gavin's question, KY Voltatronics, the trip to the Congo, Lea's flat, Kylie, Diana, heavy traffic, office life ...

"Oh, Roselily, I don't know what to do! He's asked me to go with him to India. Should I give up my job? What ought I to do?" I burst out.

"I can't tell you what to do. Everything is up in the air. You're free and you have a choice."

I gnawed my knuckles.

"Do you love him?" asked Roselily, almost in a whisper.

"Yes."

The answer came out before I had had time to think about it. It was obvious. I did love Gavin. It wasn't just sexual attraction this time, or other people's expectations. This time it was love. I knew it.

"All I can tell you, my dear friend," said Roselily, and

her voice seemed to be coming from a great way off, "is to follow your heart."

Later I stood at my open bedroom window, looking out towards the treetops, domes, fans and spires of foliage stretching away into the distance. The sky was a clear blue-green, with two or three diamond dots of stars. The trees, the trees, their leaves even now beginning to turn to gold or scarlet or russet brown. There was a subtle hint of autumn in the air, a scent of damp earth, a very faint chill in the evenings. The trees stood as they had stood for centuries, as the world turned and the seasons changed, as their leaves fell and were whirled away by the gales, as frost silvered their branches, as snow outlined their dark tracery in delicate patterns. Winter would come. What else was coming? I thought of Shelley: If winter comes, can spring be far behind? Would they survive, and would their buds open into a pale green mist in spring? Would I see them again in spring, or in their summer glory?

The question hung in the air. The future was open.

But tomorrow – and a surge of warmth flooded my veins – tomorrow I would see Gavin.

***

The Assembly Rooms were jam packed and hot. Tickets had sold out weeks ago, and I heard that a black market had started up. The council had even erected a large screen in the square outside. I knew very well that Stella had been a big name, but even I was unprepared for this huge surge of popularity. She had been interviewed on television and radio and it seemed that Oakfield was seething with journalists from music magazines.

What startled me was the number of people in the audience who were wearing T-shirts printed with a 'Trees Forever' slogan. It showed Stella holding her guitar and linking her arm around a beech tree – and that beech tree image was a sketch of mine. "You don't mind, do you?" Lucy had asked before ordering a big consignment. Of course I didn't mind.

It was just one detail that I had contributed.

And of course, we campaigners were all wearing them: Gavin, Sam, Ryan, Lucy and about twenty others, all of us sitting in the front row. Only Martha was not present. Four days ago, she had given birth without complications to her firstborn, Leo, to Sam's great joy and Gavin's relief. Behind us sat Grandad, Maya and my parents.

"Such a pity Roselily wouldn't come," I said to Gavin.

"Mmm. Not her scene. But have you seen how many young people there are here? Not just Stella's generation. It must be the vintage craze."

I turned in my seat, scanning the rows and rows of T-shirted people in the audience, most of them talking to one another and fanning themselves with programmes decorated with Martha's artwork. Suddenly there was a surge of noise and the whole audience was on its feet. Stella's three accompanists, guitar, double bass and keyboard, had arrived on the platform, followed a moment later by Stella herself, gleaming in green and gold. With a start, I recognized some material that I had seen recently in Roselily's sewing room.

Stella was my aunt, yet at the same time someone completely different. She was a star. Her public persona shone out of her as she stood there with her guitar, radiant, saying a few words of welcome into the microphone. Mobile phones were flashing all around, besides professional cameras. The stage lighting was dramatic, varying from bright to dark, from a brilliant arena to an indigo cave with just one spotlight on Stella.

Then the musicians began to play, the auditorium was hushed, and Stella launched into her first number.

What can I say about that concert? Some of the songs were old favourites from her early albums, including *Carnival Night*, *Wings* and *Phoenix*, and several were completely new, some of them, as she told me afterwards, written by her late husband, Gérard. Each was greeted with rapturous applause, especially *Rain in Another Country*, which had Sam on his feet, clapping and whistling. It was amazing – "awesome," as Maya put it. Of course I knew that Stella had been a star, but I hadn't suspected how much her fans still loved her.

The event rolled on, sometimes a sea of sound, sometimes a dramatic pause, until she was singing *The Forests are Dying*, accompanied only on her acoustic guitar, and the audience was silent except for the occasional sniff. I found tears sliding down my own cheeks. Then came her finale, a rousing song called *Trees for the World*, with a chorus, and when she sang an encore, everyone joined in, singing and stamping.

When at last she could make herself heard above the roar of applause, Stella said something into the microphone. Nobody could hear. Gradually they subsided into quiet, with an occasional shout from the back. Then she reminded everyone that this concert, the first of a series, had been organized to raise funds " – to save a unique place, Oldwood Court, that I hope many of you will soon know better." Next she asked all of us to come up on to the stage, saying that she would never have got involved in the campaign if we hadn't made her aware of the importance of trees, locally and globally.

"And, as somebody once said, 'Never doubt that a small group of thoughtful, committed citizens can change the world.'"

"Margaret Mead said it," shouted a voice from the audience. It was Grandad.

Stella gave him and us a thumbs-up, and we all took a bow.

Then the Mayor came on to the platform. He boomed, "Ladies and Gentlemen" into the microphone, but a piercing feedback whistle stopped him until Gavin stepped forward and adjusted it.

"Ladies and Gentlemen, I need scarcely say how happy I am to see so many of you here tonight, from Oakfield and from far and near, and I need scarcely add how honoured we have been that Stella has chosen this venue for the very first of her comeback concerts."

Cheers again. He went on to talk at some length, about the life of the town, with some clumsy jokes about activists, and plans for future development, etc., etc. Every now and then he removed his glasses and waved them. I couldn't see his face from where I was standing, only his bulky shoulders in his jacket and the creases in the back of his neck. Looking past him at the audience, I noticed that some people were getting restive, no doubt wondering whether they could emerge before the pubs closed or how long it would take them to get home.

Then he made an announcement.

"As you are no doubt aware, Sacs de Luxe has wound up its activity in our area, and the loss of employment has dealt a severe blow to the town." Silence. A few mutterings. "However, some of you tonight may consider that this cloud has a silver lining. You have been informed of the new community arts centre due to open shortly at Oldwood Court, which I am sure will prove to be a great asset and an inspiration to young and old." Scattered clapping in the audience. "Let me say this, without more ado. I am in a position to inform you that the road scheme, which had been intended essentially to cater for the transport of materials for Sacs de Luxe, is now no longer viewed as essential to the reduction of congestion in the town. The scheme has accordingly, in short, been abandoned."

A gasp. We all looked at one another. Loud talking broke out in the auditorium.

The mayor held up his hand. "And I have a further announcement to make. Owing at least in part to the efforts of our young friends here," he half turned and gestured towards us, "I am happy to inform you tonight that the wood on the Oldwood estate has been designated a site of outstanding environmental interest. It will be preserved, and it is to receive a Lottery funded grant from the government."

The audience erupted in shouts and cheers, and on the platform we were all high-fiving and hugging one another.

"Isn't it fantastic? I can't wait to tell Roselily!" I shouted to Stella above the general din.

She only hugged me.

***

It took us some time to get away after the show. Everyone wanted to talk to everyone else, and Stella was in great demand, signing flyers and old vinyl sleeves and posing for selfies with fans and for official photos with her musicians and with us and with the mayor. Even outside in the square, people were still milling about and journalists were asking insistent questions about her future plans. Would she be returning to France, they wanted to know? I had been wondering that myself. She told them that she hoped to divide her time between both countries, which was welcome news. I thought to myself how much happier she now seemed than when I had seen her in Paris, wistful and lacking inspiration and thinking about her lost love. Perhaps she might yet find another man, I thought, as Gavin and I walked hand in hand to his van. I was so lucky. I wanted her to be as happy as I was.

Roselily, said Stella, has invited everyone involved in the campaign to come back to Oldwood after the concert to celebrate. So she took Grandad and Mum and Dad in her car, with Maya squeezed between them in the back, while Ryan, Sam, Lucy and all the others came in a variety of different vehicles. Gavin and I were in his van. It took a while to get clear of all the cars backing out of parking spaces, and the queue of traffic was so slow that Gavin made a detour. Once again I found myself looking through the windscreen at the disused buildings of Sacs de Luxe, shuttered and lightless. The car park was padlocked, but inside I could see charred, black patches where employees who had lost their jobs had been burning tyres in protest. Could any jobs be guaranteed in the current climate?

At any rate, I had resigned mine. Someone else might be glad of it.

Dusk had fallen. We had caught up with Stella's car just ahead of us, and the van's dipped headlights lit the familiar road from the centre of Oakfield to the outskirts, the country road and the gates of Oldwood Court.

The great wrought-iron gates stood open ready for us, and Stella drove through them. Just as we were turning in, I caught a glimpse of something.

Something high up in the cedar. Something moved against the sky. Was it a wing? An arm? A branch? The moon was partly covered by a wisp of cloud.

"Wait!" I said to Gavin, "What's that, way up there?"

He braked only momentarily. "Sorry. Ryan's driving right on my tail. I can't stop."

As we continued up the lime avenue I craned round and tried to look upwards out of the window, but it was impossible. The great lime trees created a dark barrier and the gates were behind us.

We all drove up to the house in a procession, parked haphazardly and alighted, with much slamming of car doors.

I expected to see Roselily in the doorway, but although the door stood open, she was not there. One lamp was lit in the hall, but otherwise the place seemed to be in darkness.

Stella led the way, switching on lights and turning into the library where the great oak table had been set with a white cloth, a collection of glasses and several bottles of champagne. Various people exclaimed over the books, and Grandad took one from a shelf and began to discourse about it.

"I'll go and look for Roselily," I said, and hurried out. I called out to her as I passed from room to room, flicking on light switches as I went. There was nobody in the morning room, where the piano was closed; nobody in the dining room; the billiard room contained only Martha's loom. The drawing room? The great expanse of parquet stretched away like a desert to the glass conservatory. I dashed along the stone passage to the kitchen, but the only sound was a tap dripping, and she was not there.

Could she be hiding upstairs, feeling shy of so many people all at once?

Perplexed, I climbed the stairs, still calling her name. There was no reply, only a soft silence. I opened and then closed every door, including her bedroom, where the bed was neatly made and the mantelpiece bare. There was no doubt about it. Roselily was not there.

At last I returned to the library, where everyone except Stella now held a glass of champagne. She was standing at the head of the table with sheet of paper in her hand. Our eyes met, but I couldn't read her expression.

"I can't find her anywhere," I said.

"What?'" said Grandad, putting down his book. "Is Ms Green not here?"

"Have you looked in the old stables?" asked Maya. "I'll go." She headed for the door.

"Wait," said Stella. Everyone stopped talking and turned to look at her, stylish in her green and gold stage costume. "I'm sorry to say that Roselily can't be with us to celebrate this great victory tonight. She's gone."

"Gone?" We frowned at one another. Gone where? For how long? People murmured. Nobody had any answers.

"She has left detailed instructions about the Community Arts Centre – where we are all standing right now. All the legal details have been successfully settled, and Ryan and I have agreed to be trustees. Everything is in order. She asks us to celebrate the start of this new chapter in the life of Oldwood Court. She – " Her voice shook. "She has left certain requests."

"But isn't she coming back? Did you know about this?" demanded Lucy.

It was what we were all wondering.

"I … from things that she said, I expected that she wouldn't be with us tonight. No, I don't know where she has gone. I don't know whether she will be coming back. I don't know anything." An expression of pain flashed across her face and was gone immediately. "She wants us to celebrate and make a success of the Arts Centre, and – and I don't know if she has been told about the wood, but if she knows, I'm sure she is very happy."

"What are these requests?" I asked.

Stella looked down at the sheet of paper. "She asks that someone should continue to feed the birds."

"I'll do that," said Ryan decisively. "I'm going to be here a lot from now on."

"She says that, if the wood is saved, then it should be left entirely alone. No tree felling, no pruning or coppicing. No removal of fallen trees. Only the paths should be kept clear."

"Right!" said Gavin.

"And she asks," continued Stella, "that you, Jaki, accept her grey cloak." She lifted it from a chair, where I hadn't noticed it.

I held out my arms and enfolded it, feeling the softness of the grey wool. I rubbed my cheek against it.

"So the mantle falls on you," said Gavin in my ear. I glanced at him, startled. He nodded.

"A toast!" said Grandad suddenly in a resonant voice. "I propose a toast to Ms Green. Without her, none of us would be here today."

"I second that!" cried Stella.

"To Ms Green! Lily! Rose! Roselily!" we shouted variously, raised our glasses and drank.

Then conversation broke out all around, discussion of the concert, plans for the Centre, speculation about the Lottery grant, curiosity about Roselily. More champagne was poured and the noise level rose. The centre of interest was clearly the house rather than the wood.

"I hope the wood won't be full of people from now on, trampling about and causing damage," I said to Gavin, anxious nevertheless.

"I'm sure there will be strict conditions attached to the grant, and everyone here is bound to accept Roselily's wishes. And anyhow, if you want to know – I have a feeling that she simply won't allow that to happen."

"How do you mean, if she's gone?"

"It doesn't matter. Even if she's not present, she still won't allow it to happen," he said. As I shrugged mentally, I thought that perhaps I would pursue that with him later. Or perhaps not. What did he know about her? Some time I would ask him how he had first met her.

Much later, only Gavin and my family were left on the premises, washing glasses in the kitchen. "It's a nice big room, but it could do with modernizing," was Mum's remark.

Grandad was sitting on a stool. "Jaki, I must tell you my news," he said. "My old house has been sold, and I'm going to move into a little ground floor flat. I've found just the place. 'Sheltered accommodation', they call it. So I will be moving out of your room, and you can move back in with your parents whenever you like."

"Unless you move permanently nearer your work, of course," said Dad.

I took a deep breath. "Actually, I won't be needing it, Grandad. I'm glad you've found a place, but I won't be around."

"What!" Mum turned from the sink.

So Gavin and I, speaking in turn, explained what we were going to do. I told them that I would not be staying on at KY Voltatronics after the end of my contract, nor would I be looking for a more permanent place to live in town.

"Interesting," said Dad. "Sikkim. Hmm."

"Oh, Jaki, is this wise? You're always chopping and changing! I don't know what's got into you since you left university," lamented Mum.

"I say good luck to you," said Stella, and I shot her a grateful glance. "And Oldwood will still be here when you come back."

"I agree," said Grandad. "Remember what Margaret Mead said (if she really said it; I must check that). You can make a difference. And I say: follow your heart, my dear girl."

I turned to Gavin and he put his arm round me. Grandad's advice was exactly the same as Roselily's.

Suddenly there was a loud "ping".

Maya took out her phone, which pinged a second time. "Two messages," she observed offhandedly. Then, "Hey! Wow! I've got a signal!"

In my bag, my own phone pinged.

A signal. In this place where mobile phones had never worked before.

A signal, or a sign?

***

November, and Oldwood Court is ablaze with lights. All over the house, lamps are alight, and in the darkest nooks and crannies tealights are burning, and votive candles in coloured glass holders, and floating candles in great bowls of water. In the library, three very tall wax candles have been lit in the fireplace, their golden flames blue at the very heart. The flames remind me of two hands placed together, palm to palm, in the namaste. I've been reading up on India.

It was Stella's idea that we should celebrate Diwali to mark the official opening of Oldwood as the Community Arts Centre, although it has in fact been active for more than a month already. Stella has been touring, and she returned to Paris to deal with some admin, but now she's back with us. I've met some interesting, not to say weird, artists and musicians and craftworkers, most of them here tonight. My contract at KY Voltatronics came to an abrupt end, to the disapproval of Ms Jackson, the triumph of Diana, the disappointment of Kylie, the annoyance of Lea over my failure to take over the flat, and the total indifference of nearly all of my co-workers. But, as Gavin pointed out, "It will still look OK as work experience on your CV".

I have no regrets, as Edith Piaf would say.

It's the Festival of Lights, and we've all bought little gifts, confectionery and cakes for one another, and we're all in party clothes. In the billiard room, Martha has just gone to ensure that little Leo is still asleep in his carry-cot, in spite of all the noise. He is rather a sweet baby, although I have to confess that I don't go all gooey over babies. Anyway, he isn't short of people who do, or who really love him, at any rate. Sam is quite the modern father, very hands-on. Above all, Martha is happy.

There is a buffet laid on in the dining room, and music is pouring out of the drawing room, where Maya and her troupe earlier put on quite an impressive display as "wood elves". Madame Walenska is here, of course, and Mr. Curtis, and all the activists and hangers-on, and a lot of people are dancing. Grandad is looking on benevolently. Stella gave us one song, *Trees for the World*, again, accompanied by a clever improvisation on the penny whistle by Gavin. He had told me that years ago he had wanted to learn the piccolo and play in an orchestra. Now Mum and Dad are dancing together, and they do look funny, but I wouldn't dream of saying so. Gavin and I have danced until I am breathless, and I tell him that I will take a short break.

Stella comes up to us with a mock curtsy. "Will you dance with me?" she asks Gavin.

"Mais volontiers, madame," says Gavin with a courtly bow. I know he has been working on his French, but he still surprises me. I watch them whirl away in a Viennese waltz. The whole room is whirling, coloured skirts swirling out and candle flames flickering as couples sweep past on waves of music.

I step out into the hall where, high on the wall in a gold frame, hangs my finished sketch of Roselily. She is our benefactress. I'm still not entirely satisfied with my drawing of her face. I can see her so clearly in my mind's eye, but I can't capture her on paper.

I'm hot from dancing, but outside it will be chilly, and I am wearing my white silk ball gown with its exquisite green and silver embroidery. I take Roselily's grey cloak from its hook, slip it over my shoulders and fasten it at the neck. I open the front door. Nobody is lingering outside, not even the few people who still smoke nowadays. Only the trees are there, leafless now in the moonlight, apart from the conifers, which look black and sharp. I love the shapes of trees in winter. I've made so many sketches of them, and although trees of the same species look similar, each one is different. They are all individual, living beings, sheltering plants and mosses and lichens, birds and small animals and micro-organisms – and helping us to live, if we will let them.

It's as if they are calling to me, standing there so still and elegant. I walk towards them. The dance music grows fainter behind me as I step into the wood.

The path has led me to the great cedar near the stone wall. I am not cold. There is the spiral staircase, leading up into the darkness of the branches. My foot is on the lowest step. The handrail is smooth and cold under my hand.

I am climbing up towards the wintry stars, clutching the skirt of my ball gown bunched in one hand. Heights no longer bother me.

Here I am on the platform among the fringed branches, and I can look outwards, towards other horizons. It's quiet, apart from the distant hum of the dual carriageway. The sky above Oakwood has a rosy glow, but on every other side the distant view is lost in darkness. India is out there, far away, and we are only waiting for the end of the monsoon. Then we'll be going.

I have made a choice. What will the future bring? Everything is up in the air, as Mum complains. For a moment, my throat constricts. I wish so much that I could have said goodbye to Roselily.

My hand touches something. Attached by a silver cord to the rail at the edge of the platform is an immensely long feather. I have never, in my life, seen such a long feather, jet black, crimson at the tip.

I know it has been left there for me.

THE END

Books by Janet Doolaege

Novels:

A PARIS HAUNTING

CANDLEPOWER

WOMAN IN BLUE AND WHITE

Children's fiction:

THE STORY OF AN ORDINARY LION

FLORA AND THE WOLF

TOBIAS AND THE DEMON

Memoir:

EBONY AND SPICA: TWO BIRDS IN MY LIFE

Available as ebooks or in paperback from all good booksellers